Libby Sarjeant	Former actor, sometime artist, resident of 17, Allhallow's Lane, Steeple Martin. Owner of Sidney the cat.
Fran Wolfe	Formerly Fran Castle. Also former actor, occasional psychic, resident of Coastguard Cottage, Nethergate. Owner of Balzac the cat.
Ben Wilde	Libby's significant other. Owner of The Manor Farm and the Oast House Theatre.
Guy Wolfe	Fran's husband, artist and owner of a shop and gallery in Harbour Street, Nethergate.
Peter Parker	Ben's cousin. Freelance journalist, part owner of The Pink Geranium restaurant and life partner of Harry Price.
Harry Price	Chef and co-owner of The Pink Geranium and Peter Parker's life partner.
Hetty Wilde	Ben's mother. Lives at The Manor.
DCI Ian Connell	Local policeman and friend. Former suitor of Fran's.
Adam Sarjeant	Libby's youngest son. Works with garden designer Mog, mainly at Creekmarsh.
Lewis Osbourne-Walker	TV gardener and handy-man who owns Creekmarsh

Sophie Wilde	Guy's daughter.
Flo Carpenter	Hetty's oldest friend.
Lenny Fisher	Hetty's brother. Lives with Flo Carpenter.
Ali and Ahmed	Owners of the Eight-til-late in the village.
Jane Baker	Chief Reporter for the *Nethergate Mercury*. Mother of Imogen.
Terry Baker	Jane's husband and father of Imogen.
Joe, Nella and Owen	of Cattlegreen Nurseries
Reverend Patti Pearson	Vicar of St Aldeberge's Church
Anne Douglas	Librarian, friend of Reverend Patti

Chapter One

The watcher on the cliff stood hidden against the backdrop of trees, as the sea turned into a boiling, mud-coloured devastation and the wind wrenched the tiles from the roofs and flung them into the air like playing cards. Satisfied, the watcher turned away.

'You remember old Matthew DeLaxley?' Peter Parker asked Libby Sarjeant.

'Of course. He came to the opening of the theatre, didn't he?' Libby sat on the edge of the stage and began sorting costumes.

'He died.'

'Oh, no! But he was a good age, wasn't he? Must have been in his eighties.'

'Is any age a good age to die?' said Peter reprovingly. 'Anyway, Harry's received an invitation to his funeral on the Isle of Wight. And so have we.'

'We? As in Us?' Libby looked up, startled.

'Yes. Matthew's cousins had apparently heard of us and wanted us to come.'

'On the Isle of Wight? Goodness, that's a bit of a trek for a funeral.'

'Ah, but get this. They've offered us a place to stay. Matthew owns – owned, I should say – a holiday home in a place called Overcliffe. Actually, he lived there, too.'

'In his holiday home?'

'No, he had his own home. But they've offered us the

1

holiday house, and, if we'd like to stay for a week, we can.'

'How incredibly generous,' said Libby, sliding off the stage. 'Is there a catch?'

Peter frowned. 'I'm not sure. Harry's being a bit close-mouthed about it, but then, he knew Matthew better than any of us did. Did you know Matthew introduced us?'

'I think I did,' said Libby. 'So when is it?'

'Next week. Harry's already cancelled all bookings at the caff. Oh, and apparently this holiday house has three double bedrooms, so we could ask Fran and Guy too, if you like.'

'Goodness! But they didn't know Matthew.'

'They don't have to come for the funeral,' said Peter.

'It seems to be taking an awful advantage,' said Libby.

'It's Matthew's, don't forget, not the cousins'.'

'Well, it might be now, actually,' said Libby. 'If he left it to them.'

'Oh, yes – probably is.' Peter stood up from his seat by the piano and stretched. 'So what will we say? Yes?'

'I'll ask Ben – and Fran – and let you know later. Will you be coming to rehearsal?'

'Am I needed?' Peter was acting as the Music Hall-style chairman in the End Of The Pier Show the Oast Theatre Company were staging at The Alexandria theatre in nearby Nethergate in August.

'Not really. I suppose I'd better organise someone to take rehearsals for a week if we're going away.' Libby sighed, and collected an armful of Victorian-style bathing costumes to take home and launder. 'I hope these don't shrink.'

Fran Wolfe, Libby's closest friend, was delighted at the thought of a week on the Isle of Wight, although her artist husband, Guy, was dubious about closing his shop cum gallery for a week.

'Can't Sophie come and look after it?' asked Libby. Sophie, Guy's daughter, was the occasional occupant of the flat above the shop.

'I doubt it,' said Fran. 'And I'm certainly not asking my lot.'

Fran's relationship with her daughters was fragile, to say the least.

Libby called Peter before leaving for rehearsal later that day.

'Ben says we four can go in his monster vehicle, and Fran has persuaded Guy he needs a holiday, and they'll join us two days after the funeral. Do we know any more about the house or the details of the funeral?'

'Hal called the cousins, but they don't do email – or computers at all, as far as I can see – so all we've got is the address of the church and the name of the property. You can look it up. Ship House, Overcliffe.'

Libby looked it up. It was mentioned in a tourist guide, but there was no website, oddly for a holiday let, so there weren't any photographs. Overcliffe, however, had more than its fair share of photographs.

'Look,' said Libby to Ben Wilde, her significant other, turning the screen towards him. Ben peered.

'That's rather nice. Is there a pub?'

'I don't think there's room for a pub,' said Libby. 'It's just a tiny cove, see? You can't even drive to it, you have to walk down that steep path there, look, and leave the car in the car park at the top. The website of this seafood restaurant tells you that.'

'Perhaps this holiday let's at the top of the cliff,' said Ben hopefully. 'It looks a bit of a climb down that path.'

Peter did, in fact, wander into rehearsal at the theatre about half an hour before it finished, and opened up the little bar in the foyer.

'What's all this, then?' asked Libby after she'd waved off the other members of the cast. 'I thought you weren't coming.'

Fran, who was also a member of the cast, having, like Libby, once been a professional actor, had also stayed behind, and Ben appeared after making sure all the backstage lights were off.

'I'm a bit worried about Hal,' said Peter, pouring drinks. 'I told you he's being a bit close-mouthed, didn't I?'

'About Matthew or the funeral?' asked Fran.

'I'm not sure. I think he'd rather go on his own, to be honest.'

Libby looked at Ben. 'Perhaps we shouldn't go?'

'Oh, no,' said Peter. 'The cousins have particularly asked for you.'

Libby's forehead wrinkled. 'But why? They don't know me.'

'Matthew had talked about you, I suppose,' said Fran, 'but you're right, it does seem odd.'

'So you came up here because ...?' said Libby.

'I thought he might talk to you, if you felt you could ask him.'

'You know he always talks to you,' said Ben. 'You're his best friend, next to Peter.'

'His one and only dear old trout,' agreed Peter, with a grin.

'Well,' said Libby doubtfully, 'I'll try. I'll pop in tomorrow lunchtime. It would be natural to talk about the funeral, wouldn't it?'

'Yes,' said Peter, Ben and Fran.

'Thanks for the vote of confidence,' said Libby.

The following morning, Libby collected her basket and strolled down Allhallow's Lane to the high street. There was nothing unusual in her visits to Bob the butcher, the eight-til-late, and Joe and Nella's Cattlegreen Nursery shop, from where she waved across the road when she saw Harry at the table in the window of The Pink Geranium, his vegetarian restaurant. He waved back.

Two minutes later, Libby was pushing open the door. Harry stood up with a grin.

'Why am I not surprised to see you? Coffee? Or alcohol?'

'Coffee, please,' said Libby with an answering grin. 'Am I holding you up?'

Harry gestured to the empty restaurant. 'Hardly.' He fetched the coffee pot and two mugs. 'And to what do I owe the

4

pleasure, as if I didn't know?'

'Matthew's funeral,' said Libby. 'Why have I – or we – been invited? And to spend the week?'

Harry's face closed up, albeit still with the semblance of a smile pasted on. 'Matthew must have talked about you.'

'I didn't know him that well.' Libby searched Harry's face trying to pick something up. 'Do you know what's behind it?'

Harry shook his head. 'Don't look a gift horse in the mouth. We get a week in a beach-front house –'

'I didn't know it was beach-front,' interrupted Libby.

'Right down at the bottom of the path, right on the beach,' said Harry, his face opening up again. 'Pretty good, eh?'

'Yes, but I still don't know why. I mean, there must be people who knew him better than we did. Not you, of course.'

'Why me?' Harry tried to sound nonchalant.

'You knew him first, didn't you? He introduced you to Pete.'

'Oh – yes, I see what you mean.' Harry leant back in his chair. 'I wouldn't read anything into it, if I were you. Just sit back and enjoy it.'

'You can't enjoy a funeral.'

'Well, no, but you can enjoy a week's beach holiday.'

'It'll probably rain for a week,' said Libby gloomily. 'You see if it doesn't.'

There was another rehearsal that night, after which, as usual Libby, Fran, Ben, and Peter joined their friends Patti Pearson and Anne Douglas in the pub. Patti came over every Wednesday for dinner in The Pink Geranium with her friend Anne and a catch-up on gossip with Libby and Fran.

'And this Matthew knew Harry in London?' said Anne, when they finished explaining about the funeral. 'And kept in touch?'

'More than the rest of us did, anyway,' said Peter.

'How did the rest of you know him?' asked the Reverend Patti.

5

'I met him in London. He introduced me to Harry, and he knew we were all part of the Kentish Actors' Association. He used to come down to productions and to the opening night of the Oast Theatre.'

'Well, there,' said Patti comfortably. 'He probably thought of you all as his young friends and talked about you to his cousins. Only natural that they should invite you to the funeral.'

'And a week's holiday?' said Libby frowning. 'I still don't get it.'

'You're making far too much of it,' said Anne. 'I think it's a lovely gesture and you should make the most of it.'

Libby and Peter exchanged glances.

'We'll see,' said Libby.

Chapter Two

'It's such a gorgeous place,' said Libby, leaning back in her deck chair. 'Pity we had to come here for a funeral.'

'Pity old Matthew had to die,' said her friend Peter reprovingly.

'Yes, of course. What I meant was –'

'It would have been better if we'd come here for a nicer reason,' Ben replied for her.

'Thanks, Ben, I would have managed that on my own.' Libby looked over the shaded deck towards a figure standing at the edge looking out to sea. 'What's up with Harry?'

'Are you being deliberately insensitive today or what?' said Peter, standing up. 'What do you *think's* wrong with him?'

Libby looked towards Ben. 'I am being a bit stupid, aren't I?'

'Yes, darling, you are.' Ben patted her hand.

'Sorry, Pete.' Libby made a face. 'I didn't realise Matthew was a journalist at the time he introduced you two.'

'He was a fairly influential editor by that time,' said Peter.

'And he came from the Isle of Wight,' said Ben. 'I never knew that, either. Although I didn't know him as well as you did.'

'I love his cousins,' said Libby. 'Priceless, all of them.'

'And obviously very close,' said Peter, casting an anxious glance at Harry, who still stood surveying the sea. 'They're coming down here for tea, you said?'

'So they said yesterday.' Libby stood up and peered up towards the house at the top of the cliff. 'It's a bit of a climb for them.'

'They must be used to it. Didn't one of them say they had a beach house down here as well?'

'They used to.' Libby frowned. 'It seemed to be a subject to be avoided, though.'

Harry turned away from the sea.

'He loved his cousins,' he said. 'They were brought up together, apparently, in the big house.'

'The big house?' repeated Peter.

'It used to stand up there.' Harry pointed. 'It was called Overcliffe Castle. A folly, really.'

The other three looked at him in surprise.

'How do you know?' said Peter, eventually.

Harry shrugged. 'Matthew told me. Told me all about the cousins.'

'Why didn't you tell me when we were organising the trip?' Peter was frowning now.

'Well, it wasn't as if I actually knew the cousins, was it?' He turned back to his contemplation of the sea.

The other three looked at each other.

'He's been more affected by it than we have,' said Libby. 'He must have known him much better than we did.'

Peter nodded. 'He did. I think Matthew looked out for him when he was in London, and I know they kept in touch after Harry moved down to Steeple Martin with me. He was a lovely old boy.'

'So Harry's lost a sort of father figure?' said Ben.

'I think so. It's so unlike him to be this … I can't think of the word.' Peter shook his head.

'Reserved. Buttoned up. Down.' Libby sighed. 'All those things. And he got worse at the reception.'

'Wake, dear, wake,' said Peter. 'It wasn't a wedding.'

'Well, it's a shame. Poor Matthew dying, and now Harry's upset. Perhaps we shouldn't have come.'

Ben cocked his head on one side. 'Now, why do you say that? You know you were as intrigued as we all were when we got the invitation.'

'Well, that's just it,' said Libby uncomfortably. 'Why on earth did these women invite us out of the blue? We hadn't been in touch with Matthew for years. At least I hadn't.'

'Only Harry had, I think,' said Peter. 'And you couldn't wait to find out why we were invited, admit it.'

'I know,' admitted Libby reluctantly, 'but now, however beautiful the island is, and however lovely Overcliffe is, I think it might have been a mistake.'

'Well, don't say it in front of them,' said Harry, suddenly appearing beside her, as a clatter of stones on the wooden steps announced the arrival of three ladies looking remarkably like characters from an Agatha Christie novel, complete with long strings of beads hanging over their long floral frocks.

'Hoo hoo!' said the first one. 'Here we are at last! Come on Honoria, sit over there. Amelia, you can go next to Libby – Harry, dear boy, sit next to me.'

'Do stop organising us, Alicia,' said the one referred to as Honoria, in a deep, thundery rumble. 'We're not in the classroom now.'

'No, dear, I know,' said Alicia, 'but I'm sure these good people have been wondering why we asked them to Matthew's funeral in the first place. And I want to get on with it.'

'We all liked Matthew,' said Libby, unsure what she was expected to say.

'Yes, dear, we know. He used to tell us all about the plays and pantomimes you put on in Kent, and he was terribly excited about your lovely theatre. He came to the opening, didn't he?'

'Yes, he did, although that was rather overshadowed –'

'By a murder. Yes, we know.' The third member of the trio, Amelia, spoke in a soft, fluttery voice that Libby was certain contained a hint of steel.

'Um.' Harry's voice, unnaturally hesitant, broke in. 'I hope I'm not going to upset anyone, but Matthew always spoke about four of you.' He looked questioningly at the three sisters.

They all nodded.

'Go on, dear,' said Amelia.

9

'That's just it, you see,' said Alicia. 'Celia was our youngest sister. And we think she was murdered.'

There was a moment of shocked silence. Libby thought Honoria was going to burst out with something, but she changed her mind and kept quiet.

Then Alicia spoke again, 'It's hard to know where to begin.' She sighed. 'But Celia was always the one of us closest to Matthew.'

'Why is that relevant?' asked Libby softly, when Alicia seemed unable to go on.

'Because we're sure it had something to do with him,' said Amelia, the harsh note of steel now stronger in her voice.

'And she never would have gone to the Beach House otherwise,' added Honoria.

Now thoroughly confused, Libby looked from one to the other of the sisters and frowned. 'You're not making this at all clear. Why the Beach House? And why Matthew?'

Alicia sighed again.

'When we were children, Celia and Matthew were the youngest and closest in age. We know he used to confide in her, and she probably shared things with him she didn't share with us.' She glanced at her sisters. 'Some of us were disapproving.'

Amelia snorted.

'Anyway, his parents owned the Beach House –' she gestured vaguely '– and Matthew used to go there on his own. We thought it was when he was worried about something. We know he went there if he was in trouble.'

'What sort of trouble?' asked Peter.

'Boys,' said Honoria. 'Opened all the lobster pots. Tipped over a tray of crabs. That sort of thing.'

'And Celia used to go with him,' said Amelia, with a sniff. 'He never asked us.'

'Well, we were older, dear, weren't we?' said Alicia gently.

'When he came back to the island to live,' continued Honoria, 'he started going down there again. He'd built that lovely place up there,' she pointed to the cliff top, 'near our house, but he still used to go down there, even though it was practically falling down.'

'He said he ought to do it up, it would be perfect for holiday makers.' Alicia shook her head. 'But of course, it wouldn't.'

'Why was that?' asked Ben.

'Because that's where Celia was killed,' said Alicia.

'Drowned,' said Amelia.

'In the storm,' finished Honoria.

'How awful!' Libby was aghast.

'And she wouldn't have gone there if it wasn't for Matthew,' said Amelia.

'Did she tell you she was going?' Peter looked intently at Amelia, who looked away.

'No,' said Honoria. 'We were all too busy looking after Matthew. He'd collapsed, you see.'

'I'd better tell you about that day,' said Alicia. 'It's beginning to sound muddled even to me. It was a horribly windy day and there was a storm warning. Matthew had seemed very frail over the last few weeks, and when the wind began to get quite violent, I decided to go over to see that he was all right.'

'Told us not to come,' said Honoria.

'You were out in the garden anyway, and Celia … well, Celia had gone out.' Alicia shook her head. 'But when I got there, I found Matthew collapsed on the floor by the french windows.' She paused, no doubt seeing the scene all over again. 'So I dialled 999 and called the girls over on my mobile phone. Lucky I had one, really, because I had to stay on the line with the operator until the paramedics got here. Well, you know how difficult this place is to get to.'

'Thank goodness Matthew's house is at the top of the cove near the road,' said Ben.

'Yes, and it was a good job we called then rather than later, because once the storm really hit the Island the poor emergency services were overwhelmed.'

'So, was it a heart attack?' asked Peter.

'Yes – the first. Second one killed him,' said Amelia.

'I went with him in the ambulance,' said Alicia, 'and then the girls realised that Celia still hadn't come back.'

'We knew she had popped out for something,,' said Honoria, 'but the car was still there.'

'Only one between us.' Amelia shook her head. 'Stupid idea.'

'So we tried her mobile phone, we all have one of those,' continued Honoria with a grim look at Amelia, 'but she didn't answer. Couldn't have gone for a walk, not in that weather, and we didn't know what to do. Police won't look for someone who's only been missing for half an hour.'

'And then the storm broke. We battened down the hatches and watched.' Amelia's voice lost its hard edge. 'And we watched our lovely cove battered and flooded.'

'Including the Beach House?' asked Libby softly.

The three sisters nodded with tears in their eyes.

'Tea,' said Harry suddenly, and Libby jumped. It was the first they'd heard from Harry since the story began.

'God, yes! You came for tea! I'll put the kettle on. Boys, will you carry out the cakes?'

Alicia gave a trembly laugh. 'You call them boys, the same as we call each other the girls.'

Libby smiled and patted her on the shoulder. 'Well, they never grow up, do they?'

When tea had been provided and cake shared, the sisters had recovered their equilibrium.

'Can you tell us what happened after the storm?' said Libby.

Alicia put down her cup. 'Of course, the telephone lines were down, the mobile signals were lost and I was stuck in the hospital at Newport. They wanted to transfer Matthew to the mainland, but the weather was too bad. The ferries were all cancelled and the helicopter couldn't fly.'

'And we were stuck in the house,' said Honoria. 'It was one of the worst times of our lives. We tried to eat although we couldn't, the power went off, and we couldn't sleep.'

'Especially with all the noise going on,' said Amelia.

'As the night went on the storm began to die down, and we both slept a little in our armchairs,' said Honoria. 'And when we woke up it was because my mobile phone was ringing.'

'And that was me,' said Alicia. 'Matthew was hooked up to just about everything, but I couldn't get home because someone at the hospital told me our road was blocked. So I was just letting the girls know. And then they told me Celia was missing.'

'So then we reported it,' said Honoria. 'And later that day, when the clear-up of the cove started, they found her.'

They fell silent again.

'And she'd been drowned when the cottage flooded?' asked Peter.

'Because she'd been knocked unconscious and left there,' said Amelia. 'She'd have got out if she'd been conscious.'

'Was that proved?' asked Libby.

'Oh, yes.' Amelia was scathing. 'However incompetent our Island police are, they did at least prove that.'

'Amelia, they are *not* incompetent.' Alicia's voice was sharp. 'They did everything they could.'

'When did you tell Matthew about Celia?' asked Harry suddenly. They all looked at him.

'Ah – you're thinking that was what killed him?' Alicia smiled at him. 'Yes, in a way, I suppose it did, although not immediately. We couldn't tell him until he was well enough, and there was all the business of the post-mortem so he didn't miss the funeral – or at least, he wouldn't have if he'd been well enough to attend – but he just seemed to be sunk in a sort of depression. He hardly spoke, he wouldn't eat, nothing.' She shook her head.

'So we brought him home,' said Honoria, 'and put him in Celia's room. We looked after him as much as we could, but the nurses came in, too. And then, two weeks ago, he had the second attack. He had written some letters, though. He asked the nurse to post them.' She looked enquiringly at Harry, who

13

shook his head.

'How terribly sad for you all,' said Libby after a moment.

'I'm sorry to ask,' said Harry, 'but you said you thought Celia had been murdered. That sounds as though the police don't, yet you said they'd proved she'd been knocked on the head.'

'They think she slipped and hit her head trying to escape,' said Alicia.

'Rubbish,' said Amelia.

'But –' began Libby, with a glance at Harry, '– why would you think she was murdered? Had somebody threatened her?'

'And you said she wouldn't have gone down there if it hadn't been for Matthew. Don't you know why she went? Didn't he tell you?' Harry was leaning forward in his chair.

All three shook their heads.

'Does that mean nobody threatened her? Or Matthew didn't tell you? Or both?' asked Libby.

'Both,' they said together.

Libby, Peter, Ben, and Harry exchanged glances. Harry gave a slight shrug. Libby took a deep breath.

'Then I can't see why you think she was murdered, except that she had a bump on her head which caused her to lose consciousness and drown,' she said.

'It didn't seem –' began Alicia, but Amelia broke in.

'Don't beat about the bush, Alicia.' She turned to Libby. 'Matthew was becoming very frail and had seemed quite depressed in the last month before he collapsed.'

Amelia nodded. 'We all asked him if anything was wrong, and he wouldn't tell us.'

'But we're sure he *did* tell Celia,' said Alicia. 'She'd been to see him the previous evening and spent a long time over there. She was very vague about it when she got back.'

Ben frowned. 'I still don't see what she would have gone down there *for*, though.'

'To find something?' suggested Peter.

'To meet someone,' said Libby. 'That's what you think,

14

don't you?'

'Well, yes,' said Alicia. 'Not just to find something.'

'Unless,' said Harry, 'she was to find something and hand it over to someone.'

'Something Matthew had hidden there?' said Peter.

'That could be it!' Amelia sounded excited. 'Something – I don't know – damaging.'

'But damaging to who?' said Harry.

'Whom,' corrected Peter. They all glared at him.

'To the person, of course,' said Amelia. 'And then they killed Celia because she knew about it.'

'It makes sense,' said Libby, frowning. 'Who did Matthew see over the few weeks before Celia died?'

The sisters looked at each other. 'Only us.'

'You didn't know of anyone unusual who was in touch with him?'

'No.' Alicia shook her head. 'But we wouldn't know anything about who might have phoned him, or been in touch by email. We don't have a computer.'

'Did the police look at his?' asked Peter.

'His what?' Honoria frowned.

'His computer. Look at his emails.'

'No, why would they?' Alicia looked bewildered.

'His wasn't a suspicious death,' said Libby, 'so there was no reason to look at his computer.'

'We could, though,' said Ben.

They all looked at him. Peter turned to the sisters. 'Yes, we could. Would you let us?'

'Oh – I don't know –' began Alicia.

'No,' said Honoria.

'Oh, yes!' said Amelia. 'And then I think we should start using it. We could start doing the shopping on it.'

'You did ask us to look into Celia's death,' said Libby gently to Alicia. 'This could be the only clue if it really was murder.'

Alicia looked at her sisters, then nodded slowly. 'All right.

Will you come up to look at it?'

'This evening?' suggested Peter. 'After you've eaten, perhaps?'

'That's fine. Meet you at Matthew's,' said Alicia, standing up. 'You know where it is, don't you?'

'Yes,' said Libby. 'We'll see you there. Half past eight?'

The sisters gathered themselves together and with a flurry of goodbyes set off up the path to the top of the cliff.

'Well!' said Libby. 'What do you think of that?'

Chapter Three

'It explains why they asked us to the funeral,' said Ben.

Harry was once more standing at the edge of the deck staring out to sea. Libby looked at Peter and raised her eyebrows. He shook his head.

'Have you been here before, Harry?' Libby went and stood beside Harry, tucking her hand into the crook of his arm. He didn't look at her.

'Yes. Years ago. Before I met Pete.'

'Did something happen? Something – unpleasant?'

Then he did look at her. 'No. Not in the way you mean.'

Libby, who didn't know quite what she meant, nodded anyway. 'Did you meet the sisters?'

'No. I don't know if they know he was gay even now.'

'But you've been here?' Libby frowned. 'How did you avoid them? Or weren't they here then?'

'Oh, yes, they were here.'

Peter came and stood on the other side Harry and leant on the balustrade. 'Hal, love, you're not exactly telling us much, are you? What's the problem? And why didn't you tell us any of this before?'

Harry shook his head and looked down at the beach below, where a small clinker boat was drawn up next to some crabbing pots.

'I stayed at the Beach House with Matthew. He'd collect me from the ferry at Fishbourne, then we'd drive somewhere – can't remember what it's called – where he had a little boat. Then we'd come round to the cove by sea.'

Ben had joined them at the rail. 'And why was it so

important you couldn't tell us?'

'I'd never told Pete.' Harry looked up then, straight at Peter, who smiled.

'Daft bugger,' he said. 'What you did before we met is nothing to do with me. And Matthew introduced us, so he did right by us, didn't he?'

Harry nodded. Libby decided to change the course of the conversation. 'In that case, you can tell us a bit more about the beach hut.'

'House,' corrected Harry. A wistful look came over his face. 'It was lovely. It was only a painted wooden place, like that –' he pointed to the little cafe a little further along the beach, 'but it was perfect. All polished wooden walls and floor, and the windows looked out to sea, away from the cove. He had a huge telescope in there, too.'

'Did he let it out?' asked Ben.

'No, I don't think so.' Harry pushed himself upright. 'I'll take you to see where it was if you like.'

'Now?' Libby asked, startled.

'Why not?' said Peter. 'It would be a good idea before we go up and start looking through Matthew's computer.'

'Right.' Libby collected the used tea things and locked the big sliding doors from the deck, and they went down the small wooden steps to the beach. Turning left, they passed the little clinker boat, a boathouse, more crab pots and two more cottages, before clambering over rocks into what was effectively a separate little bay. In the middle, well away from the wooded cliff, stood what were obviously the ruins of the Beach House.

'You can't see it from the cove,' murmured Peter, as they approached.

'No.' Harry's eyes slid away from his partner's.

'How did he get here apart from by boat?' asked Libby. 'Did he have to come down the cliff path through the cove?'

Harry sighed. 'Yes. That was why we used to come by boat.'

'Can you see it from the top of the cliff?' Libby looked up.

'Not from the car park, but there's a path through the woodland. You can see it from there. It's part of the Coastal Path, but it isn't used much because of the landslips.'

'Landslips?' said Ben.

'All this coast is prone to them,' said Libby. 'Blackgang Chine loses a bit more every year, and sometimes even the main road has to be shut.'

'So actually, the position of the Beach House was quite good,' said Peter. 'It isn't near the cliff, so probably wouldn't suffer if there was a fall. What was it originally?'

'Matthew thought it was a fisherman's hut. Or used for smuggling. As much smuggling here as there used to be at home.'

'Could that be it?' said Libby, memories of last winter's discoveries about the smuggling fraternity in Kent springing to mind. 'Modern-day smuggling? Nowhere overlooks this side of the Island.'

Harry shook his head. 'Modern-day smuggling would mean drugs or people. You couldn't get people out of here, and Matthew would never touch drugs.' He turned away and walked down to where the wavelets bustled among the seaweed.

'There's something going on here,' said Libby to Peter in a low voice. 'Not just distress at Matthew's death.'

'Or concern about his cousin's murder,' mused Peter, his eyes on Harry's back. 'And I've never known him like this before.'

'Never?' asked Libby.

'So introspective. He won't share anything with me. Even when we first got together and there were things he was uncomfortable about sharing with me, he wasn't like this. He just used to get angry and shout a bit.' Peter shook his head. 'It can't have anything to do with – all this, can it?' He turned worried eyes to Libby.

'I don't know,' she said helplessly. 'It must be a coincidence …'

'What is?' Ben came up to them having been scouting round

19

the other side of the ruins.

'This so-called mystery and Harry's …'

'Depression?' suggested Ben. 'Although it isn't that, exactly, is it? Anyway, look what I found.'

'What is it?' Libby frowned.

'Looks like a diary or an address book,' said Peter, taking the object from Ben. 'Or was, anyway.'

'It was buried over there,' said Ben. 'It's been soaked of course, but we might be able to read some of it.'

Peter tried to open the brittle leather cover. 'Not sure we will, you know.'

'Let's wait until we're back at the house,' said Libby, 'and try and do it carefully. When Fran and Guy come tomorrow, perhaps Fran can get something from it.'

'Do we show it to Harry?' asked Ben.

'Not sure.' Peter frowned. 'I suppose we must.'

'Do we think it's Matthew's then?' asked Libby.

'Makes sense, doesn't it?' said Ben. 'Come on, sleuth. This is A Clue!'

'I can't seem to get into it, though, Ben.' Libby shook her head. 'Matthew's funeral and Harry being so upset. It doesn't seem right.'

Ben put his arm across her shoulders, while Peter walked down the beach to join Harry.

'Matthew's cousins have asked you to look into it. This could even be what Celia wanted to find, what someone killed her for.'

Libby sighed. 'I know.' She turned to Ben and put her head on his shoulder. 'How did this happen, Ben? How did I suddenly become a sort of unofficial detective? It's becoming a bit of a burden.'

'I know.' He hugged her. 'And you know how worried we all get when you put yourself in danger. But actually, you enjoy the puzzle.'

'I don't enjoy the misery,' Libby mumbled into his neck.

'Of course you don't, but don't forget you make people feel

20

better when you've ferreted out the truth.'

'Although,' Libby looked up with a watery smile, 'it's the police who usually get at the truth.'

'Not always,' said Ben. 'Now, come on, let's go back to the house and see if we can make anything of this book.'

Peter and Harry had already started walking slowly back to Ship House. So far, they had spent most of their time on the broad deck which ran the length of the house. The weather was behaving like the perfect English summer, proving Libby's prediction wrong, and, as yet, the cove was not packed with holiday-makers. Both the beach cafés were open, serving a variety of freshly made sandwiches and snacks, and in the evenings both had menus based on the day's catch by the local fishermen, including the crab the cove was famous for. Yesterday none of them had felt like going out to dinner, having consumed a fair amount of funereal delicacies at the sisters' house. Harry alone had not been seen to eat much.

Tonight, they were booked in at the nearest café.

'Had we better ask if we can change our booking?' asked Libby, as they climbed the steps to the deck. 'If we're going up to see the sisters at half past eight?'

'Yes, we'd better,' said Peter. 'Seven instead of half past?'

'That'll give us enough time,' said Ben. 'All right, Hal?'

Harry shrugged. 'Fine with me.'

Libby sighed with exasperation, but didn't say anything.

Once they were settled back in their respective positions on the deck, Peter and Libby on sun loungers, Ben at the table and Harry, as was now usual, over at the balustrade, Libby started again.

'What are we going to be looking for on the computer?'

'If there's an online diary,' said Peter.

'Emails,' said Ben.

Harry said nothing.

'We might not be able to get in without passwords,' warned Ben.

'Yes, we will,' said Harry.

21

A kind of profound silence settled over the deck. Peter was the first to break it.

'How do you know?'

'Because he told me.'

'He *told* you?' Peter sounded puzzled.

Harry sighed and came to sit at the table with Ben.

'You know we kept in touch,' he said. 'The same way old friends usually do.' He looked at Peter. 'You should know there was no more than friendship.'

Peter leant over and placed a hand on his partner's arm. 'Course I do.'

'Well, we were talking on the phone one day – oh, must have been a year ago or more – and we got on to the subject of passwords. You know how you do, sometimes, and everyone complains about having to remember so many.'

'I do,' said Libby. 'I'm not very good about them.'

'Neither was Matthew. He said it was because he was getting old. And he said he had to use things that had meant something to him in the past, it was the only way he could remember them. So my name was one of them.'

'Just Harry?' asked Ben.

'Not exactly.'

'But that's only one. We'll need one to get into the computer itself and at least one more for the email programme, probably,' said Peter.

'What meant a lot to him, Hal?' asked Libby, 'apart from you?'

'There must have been other – er –' began Ben.

'Lovers?' said Harry, with the first grin they'd seen for several days. 'Yes, of course there were, most of them before he met me. But there was the man who I think was the love of his life.'

'Really? Was he there yesterday?' asked Libby.

Harry shook his head. 'No, I think he might have died about two years ago. Matthew just stopped talking about him.'

'Did the sisters know? Did he bring him here?' asked Peter.

'No. They never actually lived together, and this man had – well, a reputation.'

'A reputation?' repeated Libby. 'What, as a bit of a lad?'

'No, a reputation to keep up. A public figure.'

'Oh, God, not that old reason again,' sighed Peter. 'Scared of losing wife and family, was he?'

'I don't know,' said Harry uncomfortably. 'Matthew never told me who he actually was. All I knew was the name he used – called him by. So that would be a good password.'

'It could also be a very good reason for blackmail,' said Ben.

They all looked at him.

'But the man's dead,' said Libby. 'And why would someone blackmail Matthew about it?'

'We don't know he's dead, and what about the man's family?' said Ben. 'They could be blackmailed.'

'Using evidence found in the little blue book?' said Peter. 'But Matthew would never give it up for that reason.'

'Which was perhaps why Celia was killed – because she'd been told to say it wasn't for sale?' said Libby.

'And the killer didn't find it anyway,' said Peter.

'It makes a sort of sense,' said Libby, 'and gives us a starting point with the computer.'

'It feels like …' said Harry, and trailed off.

'An intrusion?' said Libby. 'Of course it does. But think how good it will be if we find out who killed Celia, and by extension, Matthew. Because that's what we all think, isn't it?'

Chapter Four

At half past eight, Harry led Peter, Ben, and Libby up the path to the sisters' slightly dilapidated house, perched on a ridge overlooking the cove.

'See,' Harry pointed, 'along the path that goes into the wood. That looks down to the Beach House.'

'So the sisters must have windows on that side, because they said they could look down on the cove while they were waiting for the storm to pass,' said Libby.

'And they didn't see anything suspicious,' said Peter.

'No, because they didn't sit down to watch until after Matthew and Alicia had gone to hospital. Celia would have been dead long before that.'

The front door of the house opened and Amelia waved.

'We've left the computer in Matthew's house in case we couldn't hook it up to what ever it needs in ours. I'll fetch the key.'

Libby turned to look at Matthew's house next door. A complete contrast to the sisters' Victorian stone cottage: it was more like Ship House, a dark timber-clad building with a wide deck overlooking the cove. Behind the wall of glass stood a large, professional-looking telescope. Libby frowned.

Amelia returned followed by Alicia and Honoria.

'We have to go in at the front,' said Alicia, leading them round to the more prosaic landward side, where a small hand-carved sign announced it to be The Shelf.

'Matthew said it was because it sat on a shelf of rock,' explained Honoria. She shrugged. 'Fanciful.'

'I think it's rather nice,' said Libby, and Harry smiled at her.

Alicia led the way through the house to the large sitting room that took over the whole of the seaward side. Against the left-hand wall stood a beautiful old desk on top of which, looking rather apologetic, sat a very large computer.

'State of the art,' said Peter, raising his eyebrows.

'Was he still working?' asked Ben.

'He still got commissions,' said Amelia.

'And an occasional – oh, what did he call them?' said Alicia. 'Brain piece, was it?'

'Think piece,' said Peter. 'Basically an opinion on something topical or relevant to life as we know it.'

'Yes, well, he had opinions,' said Amelia. 'Too many of them, if you ask me.'

'Who's going to have a go at the computer?' asked Ben.

'Harry and I' said Peter. 'I'm probably the best one for the technology and Harry knew him best.'

Libby turned back to the sisters, who were waiting in a patient row in front of the long couch.

'You said you found Matthew collapsed by the French windows?'

'Yes,' said Alicia. 'I know they aren't really French windows, they're just sliding glass.'

'Where exactly?' asked Libby.

The sisters looked startled.

'Er –' said Alicia.

'That side, wasn't it?' said Honoria.

'Just there,' said Amelia.

'Right by the telescope,' said Libby.

There was a sudden silence, then Ben whistled. 'Of course!'

'Of course what?' said Alicia, still looking bewildered.

'He probably saw Celia killed,' said Libby.

Alicia's hand flew to her mouth, Amelia's to her chest, and Honoria's hit the back of the couch.

Peter nodded slowly and moved towards the telescope. 'Have you looked through this since that night?'

The sisters all shook their heads. Peter bent down and

26

looked. When he stood up, he beckoned Libby, but before she could join him Amelia rushed forward.

'I want to see.'

Peter obligingly stood aside.

'I can't see!' Amelia wailed and stood aside. 'Why can't I?'

'Because Matthew was taller than you are,' grunted Honoria. 'Let me have a look.' She strode over and bent to the eyepiece. After a moment she stood up and nodded, her expression grim. 'Beach House.'

Amelia and Alicia sat down abruptly on the couch.

'He might not have seen Celia killed,' said Honoria. 'She was inside.'

'Was she, though?' said Fran.

'He might have seen her killer,' said Libby. 'I expect he was watching to see what happened as he'd sent her down there.'

'But he would be expecting to see the killer if he'd sent her,' said Harry. 'Perhaps it was something else he saw.'

'Or didn't see,' said Ben. 'He didn't see Celia come out.'

There was another silence.

'I expect we're jumping to conclusions,' said Libby. 'We can't know if that was what happened, but it does seem to be a workable theory.'

'It's not a workable theory,' said Amelia angrily. 'You're talking about my dead sister.'

'Ssh, dear,' said Alicia, patting her sister's hand. 'We asked Libby and her friends here because we think Celia was killed. We can't complain when they do their job.'

Uncomfortable with having sheer nosiness called a job, Libby said hastily, 'We're not being thoughtless, just trying to see if there's any proof. We have to – well, the police should – look at – um, well – all angles.' She shifted her feet and looked at the floor.

'Let's look at the computer,' said Peter after a moment, and they all turned thankfully to the desk. He turned on the power, and after a short wait up came the password prompt. 'Here we go, Hal, first hurdle.'

'What do you mean, hurdle?' said Honoria.

'We can't open the computer without a password,' explained Libby. 'This could be difficult.'

'Try Lucifer,' said Harry.

'Lucifer?' echoed everyone else. Peter typed it in and the screen sprang to life.

'Why Lucifer?' asked Alicia. 'Harry, dear, you were close to Matthew. Why that word?'

Harry shot a quick look at Peter. 'He – er – knew someone of that name.'

Harry? wondered Libby, or the mysterious love of Matthew's life?

'Someone in newspapers, was it?' asked Amelia. 'One of those silly columnists who hide behind stupid names?'

'Something like that,' muttered Harry.

'Here's the email account,' said Peter. 'Seems he used a web-based provider. Another password.' He turned to the sisters diplomatically. 'Any ideas?'

They looked at each other.

'One of our names?' suggested Alicia doubtfully.

'Three – no, four – sisters,' said Libby. 'Figure four.'

'Happy days,' murmured Harry. 'All one word.'

The email page opened. The sisters gaped at Harry.

That's Harry, thought Libby. So Lucifer is the other one. But why Lucifer? The Devil?

'We discussed it,' said Harry. 'I was – well – up to date with computers and stuff.'

'And we weren't,' said Honoria with a grunt. 'Don't worry, Harry. We won't mind.'

Amelia looked as it she were about to say something, but a look from Alicia silenced her.

'Exactly.' Alicia nodded. 'We wouldn't expect him to talk about things like that with us.'

'There's an email from you here, Hal.' Peter was scanning the inbox.

'Really?' Harry was surprised. 'I haven't emailed Matthew –

hadn't – for months.'

Peter nodded. 'It's dated February.'

'And it's still showing up?' Libby went to look over Peter's shoulder. 'That must mean he'd only had a few emails since then. Isn't that odd?'

'Who are the others?' asked Ben.

Peter turned to the sisters, now sitting side by side on the couch. 'Would you come and look at some of these to see if you recognise any names?'

The sisters crowded round him and peered at the screen, three pairs of spectacles on chains being raised.

'I don't understand these.' Amelia shook her head. 'What's "Frenchie98"?'

'An email name,' said Libby. 'Open it, Pete. See if there's a signature.'

"Frenchie98" turned out to be a former associate telling Matthew about an assignment he'd been given and asking for advice. They worked back from the most recent email a few weeks before Matthew had died, but found nothing in the least odd. Some people the sisters recognised, some Harry and even Peter recognised, but there was no intimation of threats, blackmail or anything untoward.

Peter sat back, and the sisters resumed their seats on the couch.

'Another email account?' suggested Libby.

Peter turned to the bookmarks. 'Nothing I can see.'

'Do you want us to go on looking?' asked Harry, going to sit on the arm of the couch beside Alicia. 'We don't want to do anything that might upset you.'

Amelia was once more silenced by her sisters.

'Go on,' said Honoria, and stood up. 'Come on, girls. Let's leave them to it.'

Amelia was reluctantly herded out, and an almost audible sense of relief settled on the room.

'I could do with a drink,' said Libby.

'Matthew wouldn't mind,' said Harry. 'I bet there's

something around here.'

He prowled the room and discovered several bottles inside a glass cabinet.

'Here. Whisky, gin, and vodka. Vodka? He never drank vodka. Pink gin, he liked.'

'Do you think we should?' said Libby doubtfully. 'The sisters might not like it.'

'Especially Amelia,' said Ben with a grin.

Libby's objections were overruled, and Harry found glasses and served them all.

'Have a look at some of the files,' suggested Ben when they were grouped once more round the desk.

'There are loads of them,' said Peter. 'He seems to have kept every piece he'd written for the last twenty years.'

'On a computer?' said Libby surprised. 'Did they have them then?'

The three men turned and looked at her.

'Oh, OK, then. They did. But wouldn't they have been on an old computer?'

'He would have transferred all the files each time he upgraded,' said Peter. 'I suppose I could look at the earliest files, but I've got a feeling that if there's anything on here it's well hidden.'

'How would this blackmailer, if that's what it was, have got in touch, then?' said Libby.

Harry went and lay down on the couch. 'How about old-fashioned phone? Safer than email. I bet we wouldn't find anything on there. Unless we had one of those experts the police use. Pity we can't get old Ian to give us a hand.'

Detective Chief Inspector Ian Connell, a sometime friend back in Kent, frequently had to accept help from Libby in various murder cases. Not that he always accepted it willingly, though, to be fair, he had been known to save her bacon when she blundered too far into a case.

'Well, he's not here now,' said Peter, 'and I think you're right, Hal. We won't find anything incriminating on here.

Who'd keep something where anyone could find it?'

'Not anyone,' said Ben. 'We can't. And you're our resident computer expert.'

'I think the only thing we've got to give us an idea is that little book,' said Libby. 'Although if that is what the blackmailer – killer – wanted, why is it still there?'

'And frankly, if there was anything in there that *was* incriminating, why had Matthew kept it?' said Peter.

'Perhaps there wasn't.' Harry was sounding far more like himself. 'Perhaps that little book was just in the Beach House and had nothing to do with anything. Perhaps Celia just went down there to tell whoever-it-was to bugger off.'

They all looked at him in surprise.

'That's actually the most likely scenario,' said Peter. 'We've been trying to complicate matters.'

'As usual,' said Ben, with a look at Libby.

'But there still has to be something that got Celia killed and that Matthew was worried about,' said Libby obstinately.

'Or maybe – just maybe – Celia went down there to secure something because Matthew knew there was a storm coming. And it wasn't murder at all, but a simple accident as the police thought,' said Ben.

Libby sighed. 'So we're simply pandering to the old ladies?'

Peter looked round at them all. 'No, I don't think so. I think Matthew was worried about something. And why send Celia to the Beach House without telling the others. And why had he been looking through the telescope at the Beach House when he collapsed?'

'We don't know that for sure,' said Libby.

'It was you who spotted it,' said Harry.

'I suggest we wait until tomorrow when Fran arrives,' said Peter. 'Perhaps she'll get something from the little book, or the Beach House itself. And if she has the slightest inkling of trouble, then we carry on. All right?'

Chapter Five

When Fran and Guy Wolfe drove off the ferry at Fishbourne, Libby and Ben were there to meet them.

'We thought you could follow us across the island, and we'd maybe stop for a late lunch somewhere,' said Libby.

'That sounds good,' said Fran. 'Where are Peter and Harry?'

'Still at Ship House. Harry's cooking something for this evening's meal. Says he's getting withdrawal symptoms.'

Ben drove across the Island, making sure Guy could keep up. Summer vegetation was obscuring most of the road signs on the narrow roads, not conducive to the visitor's ease of travel. Somewhere in the middle, they stopped at a pub, where they settled in the large garden. While Guy and Ben went to order drinks and fetch a menu, Fran put her head on one side and gave Libby a long look.

'Well?'

Libby sighed. 'What do you think?'

'Something to do with Harry. Is that why you wanted to meet us on your own?'

'I shall never get used to you and your moments,' said Libby.

'Neither shall I,' came the surprising answer. 'But that's what I feel and there's no getting away from it. So tell me.'

Libby started the story and then had to go back over it for Guy's benefit.

'So you see, we're stuck. The sisters asked us to stay because they think Celia was murdered, and we don't want to abuse their hospitality, but so far we can't find any proof. Peter said we should wait for you to pronounce.'

'Nice of him,' said Fran wryly. Her dark bob fell forward screening her face as she leant forward to pick up her drink.

'Come on, Fran – what?' said Libby. 'You're hiding something.'

Fran sat back in her chair. 'Why did you want to tell me this while Harry wasn't here?'

'Well –' Libby looked at Ben. 'Because Harry hasn't been himself since we got here. And you know he was a bit like that at home, too. And we now know he was much closer to Matthew than we thought. Peter didn't even know he'd been over here.'

'But not after Pete and Harry met,' said Ben. 'And Matthew introduced them.'

'And Harry knew – or guessed – the computer passwords,' said Libby. 'Although, to be fair, after we'd had a look at the computer he seemed more himself, didn't he?' She looked at Ben.

'Because he knows you won't find anything on there,' said Fran.

The other three looked at her, shocked.

'You think there's something to find – about Hal?' said Libby.

'I think Harry *thinks* there is,' said Fran. 'I won't know until I've seen him.'

'In that case, let's forget about it and order food,' said Ben. 'Only remember Harry's cooking tonight – don't eat too much.'

Later, they parked at the top of Overcliffe and Libby led the way past the sisters' cottage and The Shelf.

'Along there's a path along the cliff where you can see into the other cove and the Beach House,' she said, pointing past the sisters' house. She turned the other way. 'And look, there's the telescope in the window. That's where Matthew was found.'

Fran stood looking at telescope for a long moment, then turned. 'Come on, I'm looking forward to seeing Ship House and the boys.'

Peter and Harry greeted Fran and Guy with kisses and

handshakes and offered tea or coffee.

'I want to explore the beach,' said Fran. 'It's simply gorgeous here, isn't it?'

'A cross between Cornwall and the coast of Turkey,' said Guy.

'I didn't know you'd been to Turkey,' said Libby, surprised.

Guy grinned. 'You don't what I got up to before I met you and Fran. And I know this little coastal village in Turkey that you'd love. I'll take you all there one day.'

'I thought Turkey was all resorts and high-rise hotels these days,' said Ben.

'Not this place,' said Guy. 'When you go out on a boat, all you can see from the bay is a tiny line of low buildings at the foot of green mountains.'

'Could we go?' Libby asked, turning to Ben. 'It sounds wonderful.'

'I shall remind you that we are currently on holiday on the Isle of Wight,' said Peter, 'and here to do a job. At least, you are.'

Libby pulled a face. 'I wish we weren't. I almost feel that they got us here on false pretences.'

'If that was the only way they could get you to help, that makes sense,' said Fran, ever practical. 'Now, who's going to show us the beach?'

Everyone except Harry, who was still pottering in the kitchen, opted to show Fran and Guy the extent of their limited world. The walked along the beach to their right, past the two cafés and the few houses, some of which were holiday lets. At that end of the bay, a few fishing boats were drawn up, with more lobster pots and netting spread out to dry.

'It's lovely,' said Fran. 'And now, can we see the Beach House?'

They retraced their steps along the beach, past Ship House, the little clinker boat, the boathouse, the crab pots and cottages, before clambering over rocks into the next bay. Fran stopped, looking at the ruined Beach House.

'What about the people at the funeral?'

The rest of the party looked surprised.

'What do you mean?' asked Libby.

'Was there anyone there any of you had known before?'

'There were a couple of journalists,' said Peter, 'but nobody else.'

'Harry might have known someone,' said Libby, 'but he didn't say anything.'

Fran walked forward until she was right in front of the ruins. The others stayed silent. She walked round to the other side.

'Was this where you found the diary?' she called.

'That's it,' said Ben, going to join her.

'So it was a diary?' said Libby, following.

Fran smiled at her. 'I've no idea. I'll see if I can get anything on it. I've been practising.'

'Why did you ask about people at the funeral?' Guy came round the other way.

'Just a feeling. Don't murderers turn up at the funerals of their victims?' said Fran.

'But Matthew wasn't murdered,' said Peter.

'Of course he was. Indirectly,' said Fran.

They fell silent.

'Well,' said Libby cautiously after a moment, 'we did actually say that ourselves after we guessed he'd collapsed at the telescope.'

'Did you ask Harry which of those passwords were his nickname?' asked Fran.

'I did,' said Peter, frowning. 'It was Happydays. Figures.'

'Oh, Pete,' said Libby. 'It was all before you even met Hal. And Matthew introduced you.'

'I know.' Peter sighed. 'It's bloody difficult, though. I know there's more in Hal's background that I don't know. He won't talk about his childhood, just the occasional slip. And I didn't know he'd kept as closely in touch with Matthew as he had.'

'I think Matthew was more like a father than anything else,' said Fran firmly. 'And, however this goes, I think we're all

36

going to find out more than we might want.'

Back at Ship House, Harry had made tea and Fran asked for the book.

'I don't think we'll ever be able to open it,' she said, turning it over in her hands. 'But if I keep holding it I might come up with something.'

Libby came over and peered at it. 'It's blue, isn't it? And that's a bit of gold edging on the paper. It looks like an old-fashioned address book.'

'It could still be a diary,' said Peter, bringing mugs of tea. 'They still make them like that.'

'With gold on the edges?' asked Libby.

'I don't know about that.'

'Any idea if it might have something to do with Celia's death?' asked Ben.

Fran shook her head. 'Nothing at all, yet.' She looked up at them all. 'I can tell you that I knew there was something wrong, something to do with Harry, before we even set out.'

Harry looked dubious. Fran smiled at him. 'Obviously what I was picking up on was your distress, nothing about your friend Matthew or his cousin. So whether we'll be able to get to the bottom of whatever it is, I've no idea.'

'Will you come and meet the sisters?' asked Peter. 'They're quite a triple act.'

'If they want to meet us,' said Fran. 'I don't want to intrude.'

'They asked if I – we – would look into Celia's death. I'm sure they will want to meet you.'

'Have you told them about me?'

'Er –' Libby looked round at the others. 'Did I?'

Harry finished the last of the tea in his mug and stood up. 'I'm going to go up on my own and tell them. Although I didn't meet them in the past, they've known I was a close friend of Matthew's for a long time. I told them about you and Libby getting involved with stuff, and they knew about the Oast Theatre from Matthew. I think they'll be fine with it all, but I want to be the one to tell them.'

'OK.' Peter stood up and patted his arm. 'Anything we need to do about dinner while you're gone?'

'Why did he do that?' asked Libby, watching through the plate glass doors as Harry began to climb towards the sisters' house.

Peter looked surprised. 'He told you why.'

Fran joined Libby and pushed the doors open. 'No, there's something behind that.' She squinted at Harry's disappearing back. 'There's something he wants to say to them he doesn't want us to hear.'

Peter, Guy, Ben and Libby looked incredulous.

'Fran, my love, that's ridiculous,' said Peter. 'Harry's nothing if not open.'

Fran smiled at him. 'He hasn't been very open about any of this, has he?'

Peter looked confused. 'Well –'

'It's true, Pete,' said Libby.

'What hasn't he told you about?' asked Guy.

'That he'd been here in the past – in secret,' said Ben.

'That he knew Matthew better than we thought,' said Libby.

'No,' said Peter slowly. 'I always knew about Matthew. And I did say, remember, what happened before we met didn't matter.'

'But you got a bit miffed at one point yesterday,' said Libby.

'It's just not like him.' Peter went out on to the deck and leant over the railing to look at the beach.

'No, we've already said that.' Libby went up and patted his arm. 'But I expect he'll tell you all about it eventually.'

'I just hope it's nothing connected to this business of Celia's death.' Peter turned round to face the house. 'It all seems too much of a coincidence.'

Fran came out to join them. 'I'm sorry, Peter, but I do think there's a connection. I don't mean that Harry is in any trouble, but I think whatever he's not talking about has a bearing on this whole thing.'

'If it has, why won't he say?' Ben appeared beside Libby.

'Surely nothing's so bad he can't share it with us? I mean, I'm practically family.'

'You frequently don't share stuff with your family,' said Libby. 'I don't mean just you, I mean everybody. I wouldn't tell Dom, Bel, and Ad stuff I'd tell you lot.'

'Then is he protecting someone?' Peter frowned.

'That could be it,' said Fran, 'and he's gone to tell the sisters –'

'Because it's them he's protecting!' said Libby triumphantly.

'Well, it could be,' said Fran cautiously, 'but we're clutching at straws.'

'It's something from the past,' said Guy suddenly. 'Something Harry doesn't really want to remember.'

They all looked at him in astonishment. He gave a crooked little grin above the neat goatee.

'Fran must be rubbing off on me.' He put an arm round his wife's shoulders.

'And something,' she continued, 'he wants to warn the sisters not to speak about.'

Libby looked across at Peter uneasily. 'But what? Something Harry knows but doesn't want us to know? Then it can't have a bearing on Celia's death or the sisters would want us to know about it.'

'Not if Celia or Matthew, or both together, had done something Harry knew about but mustn't get out,' said Fran.

'Then we'd be shut down quicker than a drugs ring,' said Peter. 'Much as I hate to think it might be true, I think you could be right, Fran. The question is, what do we do about it?'

Chapter Six

When Harry came back to Ship House forty minutes later he announced that the ladies had professed themselves delighted to meet Fran, so he had invited them for an after-dinner drink.

'And now I need a before-dinner drink,' he said, 'while I go and attend to the kitchen.'

'Well, whatever he said to them, we aren't going to be warned off,' said Peter, as he went to fetch bottles and glasses. 'That's something.'

Libby and Fran were loading the dishwasher and washing glasses when a flurry of activity announced the arrival of the sisters.

'So nice to meet you, dear,' said Alicia, clasping Fran's hand in both of hers. 'We know all about you!'

'You do?' Fran smiled and raised an eyebrow.

'Matthew,' said Honoria. 'Kept in touch with Harry.'

'Oh.' Fran nodded and glanced at Libby. 'You knew Harry, then?'

'Oh, no,' Amelia sat down in the middle of the couch arranging necklaces and scarves as she did so. 'Only because Matthew used to talk about him.'

Harry, looking uncomfortable, came forward with offers of drinks.

'Thank you, dear, there should be some dry sherry in the cupboard,' said Alicia, seating herself beside her sister. 'We keep a few bottles of this and that for tenants.'

Libby poured red wine for herself and Fran and sat down opposite the sisters. 'If you know about Fran,' she began, 'then you know she might be able to make some sense of what

41

happened to Celia that night.'

'We know what happened,' said Amelia fiercely. 'She was killed.'

'But you don't know why,' said Fran, gently. 'And Peter and Harry haven't been able to find anything on Matthew's computer. The only thing is the little diary.'

'Diary?' repeated the sisters with one voice. 'What diary?'

'Oh.' Fran looked at Libby, who shook her head.

'We found a little book,' explained Ben, 'at the Beach House. It looks as if it could be a diary or an address book, but it's been soaked in sea water of course, and now it's dried out it's completely stuck together. Even if we could get it open we wouldn't be able to read anything inside.'

'Why didn't you tell us?' Amelia shouted, beating her hand on the arm of the sofa. 'You had no right –'

'Ssh, dear,' said Alicia. 'I'm sure they were going to tell us.' She turned to Libby. 'Weren't you, Libby?'

Libby nodded. 'Of course. We were going to ask you if you recognised it, and Fran was going to see if she could get anything from it. Here.' She fetched the book from a bookshelf.

Honoria took it and turned it over, frowning. 'Never seen it before.' She handed it to Alicia, but Amelia snatched it. 'Nor have I,' she said and almost threw it at Alicia.

'I haven't either.' Alicia held the book close to her face and peered at the cover. 'There's something on the cover.'

'In gold, yes,' said Ben. 'We couldn't make it out.'

'Neither can I,' said Fran, 'and I haven't been able to feel anything from it, either.'

Amelia made a sound like steam escaping from a kettle.

'So, have you have you thought of anything, dear?' asked Alicia, laying a firm hand on her sister's arm.

'Nothing yet,' said Fran, 'but I'm hoping to go back to the Beach House tomorrow, and perhaps you'd let me look at Matthew's house?'

'Any time,' said Honoria. 'Anything to help.'

'Fran wondered,' said Libby hesitantly, 'about the people at

Matthew's funeral. Whether we knew any of them.'

They all saw the look exchanged between Harry and the three sisters. So Fran had been right.

'And did you?' asked Alicia with a too-bright smile.

'A couple of journalists,' said Peter, watching them carefully. 'Who is it you and Harry didn't want us to recognise?'

The silence pounded on Libby's ears. She kept her eyes fixed on Alicia, not wanting to look at Harry.

Finally, he spoke. 'I should have known bloody better,' he said bitterly. 'I tried to tell them not to get you involved, but they would have it.'

Libby sat up very straight.

'Oh, you did, did you?' Her voice would have frozen steam. 'You, of all people, have encouraged people to use us – me and Fran particularly – while keeping something from us. Why did you bother? What is it we mustn't know about you? Or Matthew, come to that?' She stood up and turned to Alicia. 'I'm very sorry for the loss of your cousin and your sister, but I'm afraid we can't help any further. We'll leave in the morning.'

Alicia leapt up and grasped Libby's hands. 'Oh, dear, please don't take it like that. Harry didn't want us to ask you in the first place. He was just going to pop over for the funeral and leave it at that. But – oh! We were so distressed.' She looked round at her sisters, still keeping hold of Libby's hands. 'I think we must tell them everything we suspect, now. We can't protect people beyond the grave.'

'We aren't,' said Honoria gruffly.

'Harry, dear, you tell them,' said Alicia, giving Libby's hands a pat and then releasing them.

Harry leant forward in his chair and put his head in his hands. Peter moved closer to him and put an arm round his shoulders.

'Come on, love. Whatever it is, it's been worrying you since before we came here. Get it off your chest.'

Harry sat up and looked across at Libby.

'I'm sorry, you old trout. I didn't want to get you involved, really.' He looked at Fran. 'Or you, Fran. But they knew about you, you see. I told you that, didn't I?'

Libby nodded and sat down again.

Harry sighed. 'You see, when Matthew found me in London, he'd actually been looking for me.'

'Looking for you?' echoed Peter. 'He knew you?'

'Not knew me, exactly. Knew of me.'

'How old were you?' asked Ben.

Harry's eyes slid away to the floor. 'Sixteen.'

'Sixteen? And where did he find you?' Guy asked in a horrified voice.

'In the gutter.' Harry's tone was full of self-loathing.

Peter stood up. 'I don't think Harry should be talking about this so publicly,' he said. 'I'm sure the ladies,' he bowed to the sisters, 'won't have heard all the details –'

'No, we haven't.' Alicia raised her chin. 'And we have no wish to distress Harry.'

'It's all right, Pete.' Harry reached up to his partner. 'I'll just give you the outline. Sit down.'

Peter sat, and Harry took his hand. 'Matthew was looking for me because I'd run away from the final home where the authorities had stuck me. And he knew who I was.'

'Who –?' Libby let the question hang.

'I was the illegitimate son of someone he knew here on the Island.'

Libby and Fran gasped.

'And you knew?' Libby turned to Alicia, who shook her head.

'We knew nothing of this until after Matthew died. Harry told us.'

'Wanted to know who. If it had anything to do with Celia.' Honoria said.

'You weren't his son?' asked Ben.

'No.' Harry half smiled. 'Matthew wasn't that way inclined.'

'And we didn't know that, either,' said Amelia fretfully.

44

'Celia did.'

'He didn't think you'd understand,' said Harry. 'Sorry.'

'So you don't know whose son you are? Or were?' said Peter.

Harry shook his head. 'Matthew was concerned about me, always had been, apparently. He was one of the few people who knew the truth, that there'd been a baby who'd been – well, he said abandoned. But he said there was no point in me making contact, I'd only be denied. He just wanted to make sure I was all right.' He shook his head. 'He felt some sort of responsibility for me, I don't know why.'

'So why did you go up to speak to the ladies before dinner? What didn't you want us to know?' Fran asked, leaning towards him.

Harry took a deep breath. 'I'm worried that if someone killed Celia, it's someone that the ladies know, and probably have known all their lives, and I'm also worried that we might find out that my mother is – well, Celia.'

Libby frowned. 'And you didn't want us knowing because–?'

'I didn't want you knowing because I didn't want the ladies to know!' Harry burst out. 'I knew if you found out …'

'Celia?' Amelia's voice rose in a squeak. 'Of course it isn't Celia! We'd have known.'

'She'd have never let you go, dear,' said Alicia, going to Harry and hugging him. 'So you were doing it to protect us?'

'Couldn't have been. Too old,' said Honoria.

'Between a rock and a hard place, weren't you, old son?' said Ben, and the atmosphere lightened.

'I still don't know why you didn't tell us everything right at the start,' said Libby, going round refreshing glasses. 'None of it's so terrible, after all.'

Harry turned haunted eyes on her. 'Some of it is.'

Peter patted his arm. 'You don't have to –'

Harry looked down. 'I want to tell you and Lib. On our own.'

'Are you sure?' Libby murmured, crouching down in front

of him.

'Yes.' Harry gave her the ghost of his old grin.

'Can I get this clear then?' said Libby, as they all returned to their seats and sipped fresh drinks. 'We're still looking for who might have killed Celia – or left her to drown, anyway – in the Beach House. And Harry thinks the reason could be the possible secret of his birth.'

'And of course,' said Fran thoughtfully, 'the reason that he himself is in danger now.'

Chapter Seven

Ben and Guy offered to see the sisters back up the path after Fran had dropped her bombshell, as no one seemed to know what to say. Harry disappeared into the bedroom he shared with Peter, who followed him.

Fran got up and topped up her wineglass.

'And I'm pretty sure,' she said to Libby, 'that we still haven't got to the bottom of it. What exactly did he say to the ladies when he went up before dinner?'

'You don't think they were telling the truth?' said Libby, reaching for the wine bottle. 'Any of them?'

'Not the entire truth,' said Fran. 'The only part that struck me as true was what I said at the end.'

'About Harry being in danger?'

Fran nodded. 'He is, of course. I was picking up on that this morning, not just his own distress.'

'So is he really the son of someone here?'

'Oh, I think that part's true,' said Fran. 'I'm not sure about him wondering if his mother was Celia.'

'No, I didn't believe that, either.' Libby stood up. 'This is a crisis moment. I'm going outside for a cigarette.'

The two women leant over the railings at the edge of the deck and looked along the little beach to where the restaurant spilled its light on to the crab and lobster pots.

'Pretty here,' said Fran. 'Sad to think it could be spoiled by murder.'

'If it is murder,' said Libby. 'The police didn't think so.'

'But we think it is, don't we?' Fran smiled into the darkness. 'And so do the sisters. And Harry definitely does.'

'In that case,' said Libby firmly, 'he must have a reason. There must be something that's convincing him, making him scared.'

'He'll probably tell you and Peter, if not the rest of us.'

'No. He'll tell us about his childhood, I think, but I don't think he'll let on about this. Pete must be going through hell.'

'Could it be a letter?' Fran said suddenly.

'A letter?' Libby looked round in surprise. 'A letter to Harry, you mean?'

'Yes. An anonymous letter.'

'A threatening letter.'

They stood in silence for a while staring out at the almost invisible sea.

'We won't know unless he chooses to tell us,' said Libby eventually. 'Come on, I can hear the boys coming back.'

'Boys!' chuckled Fran. 'And we're girls, I suppose.'

'Of course we are.' Libby grinned over her shoulder. 'I don't want to grow up, yet, do you?'

Peter reappeared after Ben and Guy had returned.

'He's not telling the truth,' he stated baldly. 'And I think everything's been made worse now.'

'Yes.' Libby nodded and went to fetch a couple more bottles from the kitchen. 'And we reckon it was a lot of baloney about Celia.'

'He won't talk about it.' Peter sat down and pushed the lock of fair hair back from his forehead. 'And I'll swear he's scared.'

'Fran thinks it might be a letter.' Libby proffered wine.

'To Hal?' said Peter in surprise. 'What makes you say that?'

'It would explain why he won't talk about it,' said Guy slowly. 'If he's being threatened, perhaps?'

'But what could he say?' Peter frowned. 'He could only be threatened if he knew something that would be damaging to someone. And he's already said, he doesn't know anyone here. He didn't even know the sisters.'

'I hate to say it, mate,' said Ben, fondly patting his cousin's arm, 'but how do we know that's true?'

Peter sat looking at Ben for a long moment, then shook his head. 'I don't know. We don't.' He buried his head in his hands. 'Oh, God, this is awful. I thought I knew him. My Hal.'

'He's still your Hal.' Libby went over and sat on the arm of his chair. 'You always said – you've said in the last couple of days – it doesn't matter what he did before you met him. And you've always known he didn't have a happy childhood.'

'I thought he'd tell me when he was ready.'

'And he probably would. What he didn't know was that Matthew's death would stir up all this – nastiness.'

'He's very distressed, Peter,' said Fran. 'And I think he wants to tell you something. Not perhaps all of it, but something.'

Libby looked across at her friend. 'He said he wanted to tell me and Pete something earlier.' She looked down at Peter. 'He didn't say anything about that just now?'

Peter shook his head. 'No. He just said he didn't want to talk any more.'

'I'm still wondering why he wanted to go and see the sisters on his own before they came down here,' said Guy. 'I know I'm not up in all this detection business, but that did seem a bit suspicious.' He smiled deprecatingly at his wife.

'You're right.' Peter sighed. 'What the sisters said – well, did you believe it?'

'It was Alicia saying they'd better tell us everything that they suspect and then saying nothing that bothered me,' said Libby.

'Would Matthew have told Harry about his parentage, do you think?' asked Ben. 'You knew Matthew better than we did.'

'Not as well as I thought.' Peter smiled wryly. 'I knew there was some sort of relationship with Harry – or had been – when he introduced us, but I knew he was keen to promote our friendship. He was a right old matchmaker.'

'He was looking after Hal,' said Lib. 'So if this story of Harry being the son of someone he knew on the Island is true,

49

that someone could want Harry kept quiet. That does make sense.'

'But what about the sisters? They said they didn't know anything about it until Harry told them,' said Ben.

'Celia knew,' said Fran. 'And I think it's entirely possible that Alicia knew, too. I don't think anyone in their right minds would confide in Amelia.'

'So they knew someone had an illegitimate baby but didn't know who? Or who the baby was?' said Guy, frowning.

'Well, if the baby had been sent away, no one would,' said Libby.

'Unless it was someone who knew the mother very well,' said Fran.

'So a close friend of Matthew's, then?' Peter looked up at Libby.

'And possibly of Celia's. They were close as children, the sisters said.'

'How old was Matthew?' asked Ben.

'About eighty,' said Peter. 'No idea about the sisters, though.'

'Did they say Celia was the youngest? I wonder how much younger than him she was,' said Fran.

'I don't think Harry's the son of someone on the Island,' said Libby, gazing thoughtfully into her glass. 'I reckon he's the grandson.'

'That makes sense,' said Peter. 'If it was someone Matthew was close to they'd be nearer to his age. Too old to be Harry's parent.'

'Not if it was a bloke,' said Ben.

Peter nodded. 'No, I suppose not. All those old actors manage to father children in their sixties, don't they?'

'So, do we think the sisters and Harry know who it was after all?' said Fran. 'If so, there must be a reason they're keeping quiet.'

'And it isn't because we know whoever it is,' said Peter, 'because we don't know anyone here.'

'Oh, I give up,' said Libby. 'I thought we were going to have a nice quiet time exploring this lovely island and now look what's happened.'

'It'll all look better in the morning,' said Ben. 'And I bet Harry tells you what's going on.'

Peter smiled. 'He usually does, Libby. He's even been known to ask your advice, after all.'

'Not always a sensible move,' said Ben, and dodged the cushion thrown at his head. 'Come on, who's for a last nightcap? Then perhaps we can all get some sleep.'

The following morning, as the sky grew lighter outside the bedroom she and Ben shared, Libby lay awake, worrying about her best friend. Harry was more to her than almost anyone except Ben and her children. Lively, funny and surprisingly sensitive, he was the best sort of friend – a man who loved her for herself with no hidden agenda. And to see him so distressed, behaving so out of character, she found immensely upsetting. And the fact that it must be distressing Peter, Ben's cousin and therefore family, made it worse. Poor Peter, who had protected Harry in London, then brought him down to Steeple Martin, where he bought a run-down café, which Harry turned into the ultimately successful Pink Geranium restaurant. And finally, they'd made the relationship permanent in a beautiful civil ceremony, one of the things Harry had sought advice about, and a ceremony at which Libby was a combination of "Best Woman" and Maid of Honour. And Harry had asked her to help when a friend of his was the victim of vicious homophobia. He had surprised her, then, with his seriousness and passion.

She heard a creak on the decking outside. Sliding carefully out of bed, she grabbed her dressing gown and went to the window. Sure enough, Harry was out there, leaning on the railings, looking out over the sea, towards where in the east the sun was appearing in a theatrical blaze of colour. She slid open the window and stepped outside.

'Sleep well, you old trout?' Harry didn't turn round.

'It might not be me,' said Libby.

'Course it is.' He turned his head to look at her over his shoulder. 'Come to give me the third degree?'

Libby shook her head and went to stand beside him, leaning on the railings and staring at the sea, which had now turned into rumpled satin shot with blue, red, green, and gold.

'I made tea.' Harry gestured behind him. 'Want a cup?'

'I'll get it.' Libby went into the sitting room and found a pot of tea and two mugs set on a little table. She poured tea, added milk, and took them outside.

'Were you expecting me?'

Harry shrugged. 'You or Pete. We won't wait for Pete. He was spark out.'

'Wait …?'

'You want me to come clean.'

'I've been worrying about you half the night.'

Harry flung an arm round her shoulders. 'I know you have, petal. You love me really.'

'You're more yourself this morning.'

'Well, I was worrying about me half the night, too. And I decided I was making things worse. So you're going to get the full saga, now, unabridged.'

Libby looked down to where the sea was frothing in milky wavelets over the rocks.

'I shall need to sit down then.'

Harry pulled two loungers over to the railings. 'There. Now we can look at the view when it gets too much to look at each other.' He turned towards the sunrise. 'That sea looks like an orange fondant, doesn't it?'

Libby sat down. 'Come on, then. Tell Mother.'

Harry gave her a quick look. 'That's part of the problem. I never could.'

'Oh.' Libby made a face. 'Sorry.'

'I'll have to tell you what I know from my point of view first. Then what Matthew told me.' Harry swung his feet up onto his lounger and cradled his mug in both hands. 'I was

52

brought up in a children's home. The first one was closed down – for mismanagement, I guess, although I was too young to know. The second one was bigger. They tried to place me with foster parents, but I didn't know how to behave in a normal family situation. So it was back to the home.' He paused and sipped his tea. 'And then this boy arrived who had been out in the big wide world. He hated the home – well, none of us liked it, exactly – and he was determined to get away. So I went with him.'

'How?'

Harry shrugged. 'It was actually easy. We were bussed to school, but once we were there there was no one to keep track of us. We just walked out. Johnno had money, we walked to the station and got on a train into central London.'

'Where was the home?'

'On the outskirts of London – Surrey somewhere.'

'And you were how old?'

'Fifteen.'

'So what happened next?'

Harry's face darkened. 'We were living on the streets. I don't know what I'd expected, but somehow … anyway, you can imagine what happened.'

'Not drugs?' Libby looked horrified.

Harry smiled. 'No, although I don't know how I avoided it. No, worse.'

'What's worse than drugs?'

'Prostitution?'

'Oh – I see. Peter thought …'

'Yes, he knew – or guessed – that much. That was how Matthew found me.'

Libby's nose wrinkled in distaste. 'You mean Matthew –?'

'No.' Harry shook his head. 'I approached him. He didn't actually find me – I found him. It was pure – impure – coincidence.'

'How did he find out who you were?'

'He carted me off to an all-night cafe and gave me eggs and

53

bacon and a huge mug of tea and started asking questions. It turned out he knew the home I'd got away from and asked if I knew anyone called Harry Price.'

'No!'

'I nearly choked on my tea.' Harry grinned. 'I didn't immediately say it was me, I just wanted to know why. I got a bit belligerent, so he sort of gave up. But then he told me I was wasting my life and if I wanted he thought he could get me a job and somewhere to live.'

'Blimey! So did he?'

'Oh, I farted about a bit, and finally said yes. So he took me back to his place – no,' Harry wagged a finger at the expression on Libby's face, 'he didn't want my body. He just parked me in a spare room – he had this great mansion flat by Battersea Park – and in the morning I told him who I was.'

'How did he take it?'

'He just smiled and said he'd guessed. I reminded him of someone. But he wouldn't say who. So off we go to this club he knows where he goes straight through to the kitchen and the next thing I know I'm employed as a kitchen boy. Living in.'

'Bloody hell, you fell on your feet.'

'Don't I know it. Now you know why I was so grateful to Matthew.'

'So now tell me the story from Matthew's point of view.' Libby settled herself more comfortably on the lounger. The sun was higher now, the sky pale blue, the sea pearl grey.

Harry turned to look towards the sea. 'Now it gets difficult,' he said.

Chapter Eight

'Matthew said he knew my grandmother.'

'Not your mother?' said Libby.

'No. I got a bit annoyed and said if he knew my grandmother, why didn't he know my real parents and why I'd been farmed out. All he would say was that it wasn't his story, but he'd promised my granny to look out for me.' Harry shook his head. 'God knows what would have happened to me if he hadn't found me.'

'Was it really a coincidence that you bumped into each other?'

Harry looked surprised. 'I approached him, remember? How could it have been otherwise?'

'He could have been prowling around that spot for days – weeks, even – just waiting for you to turn up.'

'I'd never been there before. It wasn't my patch. I was strictly a West End bloke, this was Fleet Street.'

'Oh. Just a thought. What happened next?'

'I carried on working at the club. Matthew and I met from time to time, I learnt the business and hung around the gay bars in the meantime. When I was about nineteen, Matthew told me my grandmother had come from the Isle of Wight, where he himself lived. That was when he brought me here for the first time.' Harry nodded towards the next cove. 'Did you know that was actually called Candle Cove?'

'Candle …?'

'They lit candles for the ships. I'm not sure if it was to lure them in or warn them of the rocks.'

'Smugglers, then.'

'Oh, yes. And, when the tide's in, you can't get out of the cove because the rocks are under water and it's too dangerous.'

'So when you stayed there you really were marooned?'

'Yes. But he sailed me all round the island to show me where everything was. And told me about his family.'

'But didn't introduce you to anyone?'

'No. I gathered it was because no one else knew about me.' Harry shook his head. 'And I guessed there must be some kind of scandal. Although what it could have to do with Granny I've no idea. I would have thought any scandal would be attached to my parents, whoever they were.'

'OK, so coming up to date, what is it you didn't want the sisters to tell us? What made you so scared?'

'After Matthew died, Alicia sent me a letter that had arrived at The Shelf. It said that the writer knew I existed and told the sisters to tell me.'

'Bloody hell. Did it say the writer knew your name?'

'No.'

'Then how did Alicia know he – or she – meant you?'

'It said something like "your cousin wouldn't tell me the name of his young friend". And that he knew all about the scandal.'

'Why did Alicia assume it was you?'

'Because I've spoken to the sisters on the phone over the last few years, and they've known Matthew and I were close. I was the only "young" friend he had.'

'So there *was* a letter.'

Harry looked startled. 'What do you mean?'

'We wondered if you'd received a letter. A threatening letter. Fran did.'

'Well, it wasn't exactly sent to me, but yes, I suppose she was right. She often is.'

'I don't understand why this person would send a letter to the sisters – was it to all of the sisters? – virtually announcing his or her intentions. If it did, of course.'

'It didn't exactly, it sounded more like a warning. And it was

56

addressed to Miss DeLaxley, so it looks as though the writer didn't know much about the family.'

'Why?'

'DeLaxley was Matthew's surname, the sisters were cousins on his mother's side, and anyway, they all married, so have different names now.'

'I still don't get it.' Libby was frowning. 'If the writer didn't know much about the family, how did he know about you? And why didn't you want them to know? They'd already read the letter.'

Harry sighed. 'Because the morning after the funeral – bloody hell, that was only the day before yesterday – I got up early and went for a walk on the beach. When I got back there was a note pinned to the railings – here.' He gestured. 'It said –' he took a deep breath ' – "I know you now." That was all.'

'Someone had been watching?' Libby's eyes were round with shock.

'Must have been. And that *was* a threat.'

'And you didn't want any of us to know you'd been threatened? Why?'

'Because you'd all go round protecting me and we'd probably leave the Island.'

'And that would be bad – why?'

'Because, actually, I want to find the bastard who killed Celia and then Matthew. Because he did kill Matthew.'

'So you let the sisters think it was their idea to call us in?'

'Let's say I put the idea into their heads. Well, Alicia's head, anyway.' He smiled. 'I did tell them it wasn't a good idea because you'd cause mayhem.'

'Gee thanks. You said last night you didn't want them to call us in.'

Harry cleared his throat and looked away. 'For their benefit.'

Libby slapped his legs. 'I shall never believe a word you say again, Harry Price.'

Harry sat up and swept her into a bear hug. 'You love me really.'

'Yes.' Libby's voice was muffled against Harry's towelling robe. 'Let me sit up.'

Harry let her go and peered into his empty mug. 'More tea?'

'In a minute. Tell me first why you've been so pre-occupied. Is it just the threat? You weren't yourself even before we came to the Island.'

'I'd read the first letter. It was anonymous, and it seemed sinister. I thought someone was looking for me.'

'So were you a bit scared about coming here?'

'A bit. But I agreed with Alicia that Celia could have been murdered and that letter seemed to confirm it. And then the note. It shook me.'

'We could tell,' said Libby. She stood up. 'Come on, let's make some more tea and you can go and give Pete a cup.'

'And tell him everything,' said Harry, following her into the kitchen.

'Will he mind you've told me first?'

'No. I think he expects it. I must say, you old trout, I feel better.'

'But still a bit scared?'

Harry nodded. 'I just hope Pete doesn't try and drag me off the Island when he hears.'

'He might want to.' Libby poured boiling water into four mugs. 'And you can hardly blame him. I do see why you were keeping quiet – I think.'

'Will you tell Ben?' Harry paused with two mugs in his hands.

'If you want me to. And Fran?'

'Better everyone knows. But I don't want to do it.'

Libby sighed. 'I'll see if I can't get them all on to the deck.'

'You were up early.' Ben was sitting up in bed when she went in with his tea.

'Yes. Do you think you could bring your tea outside? I'm going to make tea for Fran and Guy – oh bother, Guy likes coffee – and see if they'll come out there, too.'

'Why?' Ben's eyes narrowed suspiciously.

58

'To tell you Harry's story.'

Twenty minutes later, Libby finished the story and looked at each of her listeners in turn.

'Well? What do you think? Do you understand why he was nervous? Why he lied?'

'Not really.' Guy frowned. 'Well, yes, I do, about being threatened, but one thing – the note he found pinned to the deck. How did he know it was for him?'

'Oh!' said Libby. 'I hadn't thought of that.'

'Whoever it was had pinned it there after seeing Harry go out on his own. They were watching.' Fran was staring towards Candle Cove.

Libby involuntarily looked over her shoulder.

'That makes sense,' said Ben. 'What do we do now? What does Hal want us to do?'

'I don't know, apart from finding out who killed Celia. And Matthew by default. He's telling Pete now.'

'Pete may well want to cart him off home,' said Ben. 'And I don't blame him.'

'But if that someone is after Harry, they know who he is and could come after him anywhere,' said Fran.

'But why *are* they after Harry?' Libby scowled at her mug.

'It isn't Harry personally, is it?' said Fran. 'It was Matthew's "young friend". Whoever this person is, they knew that there was someone connected to the old scandal, but they didn't know who.'

'How did they know it was Matthew's "young friend"?' asked Libby.

'I don't know.'

'How do we find out?'

'Just what I was asking.' Peter's voice issued from behind them. He strolled over and pulled up a chair. 'It's someone who knows about the old scandal. So shouldn't we look into that, first?'

The other four looked at him in surprise.

'You want to go on with this?' asked Libby. 'We thought

you'd want to drag him off the Island.'

'I do, but the place to start, surely, is this old scandal, and we can't look into that from Kent. We need to talk to people.'

'But who?' said Guy.

'The sisters, first. Together or separately?' said Fran.

'They always seem to be together,' said Libby. 'I don't know how we would separate them without turning it into an inquisition.'

Fran turned to Peter. 'Who was Lucifer?'

They all looked at her.

'Who?' said Peter.

'Oh, I know!' said Libby. 'The love of Matthew's life, Hal said. What made you think of that?'

'Because he's the only one Matthew might have told.'

'But he died, Hal said.'

'No, he said he might have died. Matthew just stopped talking about him.'

'Sounds like the end of the affair, to me,' said Guy. 'If this man had died, Matthew would have told Harry, surely. Everyone wants a shoulder to cry on.'

Peter nodded. 'So do we look for him or the scandal?'

'I don't see how we can possibly find anything out about Lucifer,' said Libby, 'so we'll have to start with the scandal. Do you think any of the people at the funeral knew about it?'

'Well, one did,' said Harry, joining them on the deck. 'Because that's where he saw me, obviously.' He sat down on the edge of one of the loungers and looked round at them all. 'Now you know about my sordid past, what do you all think?'

'I think you need to know about your parents,' said Fran. 'Matthew should have told you the whole story.'

'But he was protecting someone from this scandal,' said Libby. 'And trying to protect Harry, too.'

'So how do we find out about the scandal, which was obviously about my parents?' Harry leant back on the lounger and swung his feet up. 'Ask the sisters? Because they must know, surely.'

'It doesn't seem as though they do,' said Fran. 'If Matthew wouldn't introduce you to them, there was a reason. Perhaps they would have seen a family resemblance, or something?'

'They haven't noticed it now,' Libby pointed out.

'And someone is still concealing that scandal,' said Peter. 'Although why you should be a threat when you don't even know what it is, I have no idea.'

'Perhaps they're watching me to make sure I don't know.' Harry sighed. 'Perhaps when we leave the Island, they'll heave a sigh of relief and forget all about it.' He swung his legs off the lounger and stood up. 'And if you believe that, you'll believe anything. Eggs Benedict for breakfast, anyone?'

Chapter Nine

'Is there any way we could get to meet the funeral guests?' Libby wiped her plate to get at the last remnants of breakfast.

'I don't see how. We don't know any of them,' said Harry, pouring coffee.

'The sisters do,' said Peter. He seemed happier this morning, Libby thought. Probably because Harry had now told him the whole – rather garbled and improbable – story.

'We talked about that earlier,' said Fran. 'I wish we could talk to them separately, but we can't really.'

'Why don't you two go up on spec and just talk to whoever you find? They can't be together all the time. Someone will have to go shopping, or do the gardening. Or something.' Guy looked from Fran to Libby to see how his suggestion had gone down.

Fran looked at Libby. 'I suppose we could.'

'Of course we could. And they asked us into all this – they can't object.'

'Amelia can,' said Harry.

'Oh, it seems to me Amelia can object to anything,' laughed Peter.

'Let's go up now,' said Libby, standing up.

'And avoid the washing-up?' said Ben.

'Loading the dishwasher you mean,' grinned Fran, pushing her chair back. 'I'll just go and clean my teeth.'

'You don't think we're too early?' said Libby ten minutes later as they climbed towards the top of the cliff.

'It's nine thirty. I suppose it is a bit early.' Fran stopped.

'But don't old people get up very early?'

'I think that's a myth. My mother didn't.'

'But I often see our old ladies in Nethergate off to do their shopping at nine. I'm not usually dressed by then.'

'Well, it's no use speculating. We're on our way now.' Libby started off up the path again. 'And we've been seen, anyway.'

Amelia was waving from outside the little house.

'Hello! Did you want to see us?'

'Yes, please,' puffed Libby. 'No wonder you're fit, if you have to keep going up and down that path!'

'Oh, we hardly ever go down. When Ship House is let we have a cleaner who goes in – she'll be with you today or tomorrow, I think – and there's no reason for us to go down otherwise. We're not beach people.'

'What *do* you do with yourselves?' Libby asked.

'Oh, this and that.' Amelia turned towards the house and Libby noticed her faintly discontented expression. Not enough, she thought.

'I think Alicia's already gone shopping.' Amelia peered into the room on the right of the front door as she led them inside. Fran and Libby exchanged triumphant glances. 'But Honoria's here. In the garden, probably.'

Libby was grinning broadly at the accuracy of Guy's prediction.

'Well, perhaps we could just have a quick word with you, Amelia,' said Fran quickly, before Libby disgraced them both.

'Me? Why?' Amelia raised perfectly pencilled eyebrows.

'We were wondering about the people at the funeral, and if any of them had – well – known about whatever might have happened in the past.'

'I don't suppose so. They're an uninteresting bunch.' The discontented expression intensified. 'There's nothing to do on the Island any more.' She took them into a comfortable but slightly shabby sitting room and indicated chairs. 'It used to be such fun when we were younger.'

'Have you always lived here?' asked Libby, as she sank into a large chintz-covered armchair.

'Oh, no, dear.' Amelia preened slightly. 'I've lived all over the world. My late husband was in the Diplomatic.'

'Goodness!' said Fran, in appropriately admiring tones. 'You must have led such an interesting life.'

'Oh, it was. That's why ...' Amelia stopped and shrugged. 'Oh, well, that's not what you came about, is it?'

'No, you're right,' said Libby. 'You were going to tell us about some of your old friends who were at the funeral.'

'Was I?' Amelia frowned. 'Oh. I suppose ... Let me see. The Dougans, they were there. We've known them since we were children. Lady Bligh, of course, and that strange son of hers. Oh – Amanda Clipping was there, with some man in tow.' She paused. 'There were a lot of people I didn't know. I expect Alicia will remember more. She never left the Island.'

'What about Honoria?' asked Fran. 'Would she remember?'

'I've no idea. You'll have to ask her.' Amelia turned a sulky face away from them.

'And the people you mentioned,' Libby pressed on. 'They were all here during your childhood?'

'Amanda wasn't, but her parents were. They live in Surrey now, I believe. She lives in the family home – when she's here.'

'Oh? Not a permanent resident then?'

Amelia sniffed. 'Too busy, apparently. She's something to do with television, they say.'

'Ah.' Libby nodded wisely. 'But the others, the Dougans, wasn't it? And Lady Bligh? They were here?'

'Look,' said Amelia, turning back to face them. 'I don't know what you're expecting to find, but you can rest assured none of these people had illegitimate babies or anything like that. We'd have known.'

'We're simply trying to find a reason for Celia's murder,' said Fran gently, 'and if you want us to do that, we have to look at all the background.'

'We'll go and find Honoria, shall we?' asked Libby,

standing up. 'Just point us the way to the garden.'

Amelia stood up and pulled back a heavy velvet curtain, revealing a French door. 'Go round the side of the house. That's where the kitchen garden is.' She pulled the door closed behind them and drew the curtain across.

'As if she's blotting us out,' said Libby, staring at the closed door. 'What *is* up with her?'

'Partly, reduced circumstances, I should think,' said Fran. 'She's also a bit of a snob and thinks herself a cut above her sisters. We must find out what Celia did with her life, too, don't forget. If she was murdered, it might have nothing to do with Matthew.'

Libby led the way round the house to where they found Honoria digging in a raised bed amid a forest of bean sticks.

'So this is where you can see down into Candle Cove,' said Fran, peering down through a screen of scrubby trees.

Honoria straightened up, a hand in the small of her back. 'Where we sat during the storm.' She nodded at the house, where two tall windows stood open. 'Help you?'

'If you don't mind,' said Libby. 'We've just been talking to Amelia.'

'We wondered if any of the people at Matthew's funeral could have known about – well – Harry's family,' added Fran.

Honoria grunted. 'Shouldn't think so. Not many of 'em around.'

'Around years ago, do you mean?' said Libby.

'Dead, most of 'em,' said Honoria. 'Old Lady Bligh and the Dougans about the only people.'

'So most of the people at the funeral wouldn't have known anything about a scandal back – well, whenever it was?'

Honoria shook her head. 'Ask Alicia.'

'We shall,' said Fran. 'You'd know everyone, though? You've lived here all your life?'

Honoria shrugged. 'Most of it.' She returned to her digging.

'You lived on the mainland?' persisted Libby, making a face at Fran. 'So you could have missed something that happened during that period?'

'Would have been told,' said Honoria, without looking up.

Libby opened her mouth and shut it again at a look from Fran.

'Thank you, we'll let you carry on gardening,' said Fran. 'Perhaps we'll see Alicia another time.' She turned and shooed Libby in front of her.

'I wanted to know –' began Libby.

'I know – when she was away. But it was beginning to sound like an interrogation, and she obviously wasn't as proud of her time off the Island as Amelia.'

'So what's she hiding?' said Libby as they came out in front of the house and The Shelf.

'Probably nothing,' sighed Fran.

'What do we do now?'

'Wait for Alicia?'

'We don't know how long that'll be.'

'Oh, not long,' said Fran with a grin. 'I can hear a car.'

Alicia appeared from the direction of the car park at the top of the cliff laden with shopping bags. Libby and Fran hurried forward to relieve her of some of them.

'Thank you, dears.' Alicia pushed a wisp of hair off her forehead. 'Were you waiting for me?'

'We've seen Amelia and Honoria,' said Libby as they followed her into the house, 'so we were actually just leaving.'

'Well, now I'm here you can have a cup of coffee and tell me what you talked to them about.' Alicia led the way into the large kitchen and filled a kettle before beginning to unpack her bags.

'We were asking if either of them thought any of the funeral guests would know of anything in the past,' began Libby, as Fran took tins out of a canvas bag.

'Do you mean connected to Harry?'

'Well – to his – um – relatives.'

Alicia took instant coffee out of a cupboard. 'Let me see … when would it have been?'

'We don't really know,' said Fran. 'Going by Matthew's age, which was – what? Mid-eighties?'

'Eighty-one,' said Alicia. 'We're all in our eighties. Except poor Celia, of course. She was the baby, only seventy-eight.'

'So if someone had a baby, they were either your sort of age now, or at least in their sixties, given how old Harry is.' Fran was emptying another bag.

'Thank you, dear.' Alicia poured water into a tall coffee pot. 'Just leave them on the table and I'll put them away later. Now, let's think.' She pulled out a chair and sat at the table, resting her chin on her hands. 'Who did the girls say might remember?'

'Only a couple of people,' said Libby, sitting on the other side of the table. 'The Dougans and Lady Bligh.'

'Yes, they're all our generation. Most of the others are younger, so it could have been anyone. I didn't know everybody there, you know.'

'People who've left the Island?' asked Fran tentatively. 'Amelia said she lived away for some time, and so did Honoria.'

'Did she?' Alicia looked surprised. 'She doesn't usually talk about it.'

'She didn't actually talk about it, just said she had,' said Libby. 'Was it at the same time Amelia was away?'

'Amelia was away for a long time.' Alicia went to fetch milk from the fridge. 'She came back between her husband's postings.'

Libby and Fran exchanged glances. This was difficult.

'So what about other people who left the Island?' asked Fran.

'Well, we wouldn't know any of them any more, unless they came back to visit. The only people who do that are the Clippings.'

'Oh, yes,' said Libby. 'Amelia mentioned Amanda Clipping. Her parents live in Surrey?'

'Yes.' Alicia sighed. 'They moved when John got his promotion. We all thought they'd come back when he retired as

68

they kept the house here, but they stayed there. I suppose they'd made friends.'

'So Amanda uses the house. Does anyone else?' asked Fran. Both Alicia and Libby looked surprised at this question.

'I don't think so. Amanda comes for the odd weekend and at other times. She sometimes brings guests.' Alicia began to pour coffee.

'Amelia said she had a guest with her at the funeral,' said Libby.

Alicia laughed. 'I don't suppose she put it like that. Yes, she had a young man with her, although they were both with another man in a wheelchair. I didn't know him.'

'So she had two men in tow,' said Fran with a smile.

Alicia twinkled. 'That's how she put it, isn't it? Amelia can be a terrible prude, but it's mainly because she hates getting old, and was considered a beauty in her day, and very daring. We were all surprised when she married her rather dull Roy.'

'Security?' suggested Libby.

'I suppose so. So tell me what Honoria said.'

'She just confirmed that the only people at the funeral who would have known you all when you were young were the Dougans and Lady Bligh.' said Fran.

'And that she'd moved away?'

'We asked,' said Libby. 'She just said she had and that was that. We didn't like to ask any more.'

'But you're dying to know.' Alicia smiled at them both. 'Actually, we were all off the Island at more or less the same time, although I was only away very briefly.'

'When was that?' asked Libby.

'In the fifties. Is it important?'

'If you were all away together, that would be why you don't know what happened,' said Fran.

Chapter Ten

'Celia wasn't away then,' said Alicia slowly, breaking a long silence.

'When was it?' asked Libby, practically on the edge of her chair.

'In the fifties,' said Alicia with a sigh. 'I married and went to the mainland, but I was back by fifty-five.'

'And Honoria?' Fran asked quietly.

'She was away until – until about fifty-eight.' Alicia was looking out of the window.

Libby looked at Fran and grimaced.

'If you want to talk to the Dougans or Lady Bligh,' said Alicia briskly, turning back to face them, 'I'll give you an introduction, if you think it'll help Harry.'

Libby's eyebrows shot up.

'I don't think we could just turn up and ask questions,' said Fran. 'We haven't got the right.'

'We're actually trying to find out about Celia, anyway,' said Libby. 'You said she was here during the fifties.'

'Yes.' Alicia seemed to crumple. 'I don't seem to be able to keep up with all this. I've got rather muddled. How did we get to Harry and the nineteen-fifties from my poor sister?'

'I'm beginning to wonder myself,' muttered Libby.

Alicia sat looking at her for a moment.

'So what you're saying is that someone we knew became pregnant while at least Honoria, Amelia, and I were away, and Matthew knew about it? But he'd already gone, too. University first and then he went to London.'

'Didn't he ever come back?' asked Libby.

'Yes, for weekends and sometimes longer. More than we did. And I suppose Celia was here some of that time.'

'What did Celia do? We haven't heard much about her,' said Fran.

'She wasn't twenty-one until – when was it? – nineteen fifty-six. So she was here most of that time. She used to go and stay with Matthew sometimes – not until she was eighteen, though.'

'Nineteen fifty-three,' said Fran. 'So did she go over for the coronation?'

Alicia smiled. 'Do you know, I believe she did!'

'Were you on the mainland then?' asked Libby.

'I was in … France.' Alicia's eyes went to the window again.

'Oh?' Libby caught Fran's eye and said nothing else.

'Well, unless we can talk to someone who might have known what Matthew and Celia knew, I'm afraid we won't get any further,' said Fran. 'Unless you know anything about the letter?'

Alicia's eyes shot back to meet Fran's. 'Letter?'

'Yes. The letter you received and sent to Harry before the funeral.'

'I – we –'

'Didn't it occur to you that you might be putting Harry in danger by allowing him to come here?' said Libby.

'And us?' put in Fran.

Alicia's mouth was hanging open.

'So if you'd like us to stop now, we'd be quite happy to,' said Libby untruthfully.

'After all,' continued Fran, 'you've hardly been straight with us, have you? And none of you have told us the exact truth. You've all been keeping back what happened to you in the fifties. How did you think we could find out what had happened to Celia if you didn't tell us the truth?'

Alicia's face was now chalk white, except for each cheek sporting a flaming spot of colour.

'We'll leave you to think it over,' said Libby, standing up. 'Thanks for the coffee.'

'They're watching us,' she muttered, as she and Fran walked past The Shelf on their way to the path and the wooden steps.

'I know. Honoria's peering round the side and Amelia's curtain was twitching. I wonder what they'll do next?'

'Council of war, I should hope,' said Libby, grabbing the rickety handrail. 'And deciding to tell us the truth, the whole truth and nothing but the truth.'

'I suppose it's their generation,' said Fran. 'It wasn't done to show emotions, or wash your dirty linen in public, pregnant girls were hidden away and their babies removed from them –'

'And if that's what happened to Harry's granny, somewhere along the line, that baby found out who he was. Or who his mother was,' said Libby.

'And somehow, granny found out about Harry, so she must have known where her baby went in order to keep an eye on Harry.'

'But we know Harry was in care for most of his childhood. All of it, as far as he can remember.' Libby stepped with relief on to the beach and made for Ship House. 'So do we have a council of war now, too?'

'I think we should.' Fran climbed the steps to the deck. 'Shall we have another cup of coffee? I didn't drink mine at Alicia's.'

'It wasn't very nice,' said Libby. 'Shall I make us a nice cup of tea?'

'Good idea. And we ought to see where the men are.'

The men, it turned out, were nowhere to be seen, so Fran and Libby took their tea out on to the deck and picked the most comfortable loungers.

'I can't believe how lovely this place is,' said Libby. 'I want to go and look at some of the other bays.'

'I bet that's what the men have done,' said Fran. 'Guy looked as though he'd been sitting still for too long.'

'He sits still most of the time, doesn't he? Either painting or in the shop?'

'He goes for long rambles on his own in the evenings,' said Fran. 'Didn't you know?'

'No.' Libby was surprised. 'And I knew him before you did.'

Fran grinned. 'I know. And thank you again for introducing us.'

Libby laughed. 'I suppose I did, didn't I? And I was so jealous of you and Ben.'

'Just because we'd worked together before.' Fran leant back and crossed her ankles. 'Well, we sorted it all out, didn't we? And now we'd better try and sort out these old ladies.'

'And Harry. Do you really think he's in danger?'

'Someone wants him to think he is,' said Fran. 'Otherwise, why the note?'

'But they may just be warning him off the Island.'

'But he has no idea who this person is, or why they're warning him. If he knew, at least he could take precautions. But I think he's a threat simply by being here. Or being alive.'

Libby gasped. 'Oh, Fran, no!'

'I don't know for sure, but that's logical, isn't it? His presence is a threat to something or someone.'

Libby shook her head. 'I can't see our Hal being a threat to anyone.'

'It's what he is, not who he is,' said Fran. 'If we go back to the granny, she had an illegitimate child who was sent away, then the child of that child appears also to have been sent away, we don't know why.'

'So, an inheritance, do you think?' said Libby. 'Hal's standing in the way of someone inheriting?'

Fran frowned in concentration. 'If the parent who gave away Harry went on to have other children, maybe.'

'We don't even know whether the parent was mother or father,' said Libby.

'Yes, but the law of primogeniture doesn't hold good any more, unless you're royal.'

'So it doesn't matter? In that case it wouldn't matter if Harry was born first. The inheritance could be left wherever the – um – will-writer wanted.'

'Unless there was a will already in existence that named Harry.'

'Blimey!' Libby's eyes were round. 'Do you think that's it?'

Fran shrugged. 'I don't know, but it's one idea. Now we've just got to find out what was going on here in the early fifties.'

'Supposing it isn't, though,' said Libby after a minute. 'There's still Lucifer.'

Fran looked thoughtful. 'And he could have been at the funeral without anyone knowing, if he's still alive.'

'That's the trouble with funerals,' said Libby. 'You don't have a useful guest list. Anyone can turn up.'

'But not everyone gets invited back to the wake,' said Fran.

'When have you ever known a private wake? It's usually just "and afterwards at so-and-so" isn't it?'

'And if it's a public venue anyone could be there,' agreed Fran. 'Yes, it's a thought. So we needn't be looking for someone connected with the past of the Island after all.'

'And that's a problem,' said Libby. 'We have absolutely no way of knowing who or why. It's a brick wall.'

'What would make Harry a threat to Lucifer?'

'Simply the fact that Harry was close to Matthew. Perhaps he thinks Harry must know who he is and he's still worried about his cover being blown.' Libby frowned. 'And in this day and age, it could bring worries about more than just being gay.'

Fran looked startled. 'You mean …?'

'Paedophilia. If that man was high-profile – well, you know what's happened to people over the last couple of years.'

'That would certainly be worth keeping quiet, but it's mere speculation. Far more than the illegitimate child theory. We know that's fact, at least.'

'Except we've no way of finding out any more about it.'

'Unless whoever threatened Harry shows his or her hand.'

'So we need to make sure Harry's never alone?' Libby

looked worried. 'And if this is the person who killed Celia, he might not care about killing other people, too.'

'I think I know what you mean,' said Fran, with a wry grin. 'But I also think the blue book is the best clue we've got.'

'But we can't open it.'

'I think we could try.' Fran stood up. 'I'll go and get it. It must be completely dry by now.'

'Even if it is, and we do manage to open it, the writing would be unreadable.'

'It's worth a try, isn't it?' Fran went inside and returned with the little blue book.

'I'll get a knife,' said Libby. 'We could possibly slide a knife between the pages, unless they're stuck into a solid wodge.'

'Good idea,' said Fran absently, turning the book over in her hands. Libby watched her for a moment, then went to fetch the thinnest knife she could find from the kitchen.

'There's something here after all,' said Fran, as Libby handed her the knife. 'Perhaps the damp was masking it.'

'And perhaps you just didn't know enough background.'

'No, because I get flashes without background sometimes, don't I? I don't know what it is, though.'

Libby frowned. 'Then how do you know there's something in there?'

'It's a sort of series of pictures. Flashes – a bit like lightning, or one of those annoying TV documentaries where they swing the camera all over the place.'

'Can you make out anything at all?'

'No, it's more like – well, colours really. But there's definitely something there.' Fran laid the book on the table. 'Come on, let's see what we can do.'

She inserted the tip of the knife carefully under the cover and began to work it gently back and forth. Suddenly, the knife slid all the way in and the cover was loose. Fran removed the knife and looked at Libby.

'Now what?'

'Open it, of course. See if there's anything there.'

Fran opened the cover, and they both peered down at the first page.

'Nothing,' said Libby, 'not even faded nothing.'

Fran picked up the book and ran her thumb over the edge of the pages. 'We might be able to get some of these open. Feel.' She handed the book to Libby.

Libby frowned as she investigated the edges, cover and back. 'Why would we be able to open it now? Why not the other day?'

'It's completely dried out now,' said Fran.

'But usually when that happens, the pages stay stuck together for ever,' said Libby.

'Not necessarily. This has now become "air-dried", although we didn't do it as a conservator might. Try and fan the pages.'

'How do you know so much about it?' Libby handed the book back.

'I had a friend who worked in the British Library.' Fran gently ran her thumb across the pages again and, sure enough, they began to fan. Slowly, and not individually, but the book, it appeared, was open.

Chapter Eleven

Libby gasped.

'I think you're magic.'

Fran looked up and grinned. 'I just picked up a lot of trivial information in my wicked past.'

'You've never been wicked,' said Libby. 'Can we open it properly?'

Fran carefully opened the first page that came away freely. 'Barely readable.'

'But can you tell what it is?'

'Address book,' said Fran, 'as far as I can tell.'

Libby moved her chair closer. 'The print's OK, it's the writing that's faded.'

Fran opened another page. 'This one's worse.'

'Can you find the "L" section?' asked Libby.

'I don't know, why?'

'See if Lucifer's there.'

'He wouldn't be listed under a nickname,' said Fran, opening a couple more pages. 'I think this is a waste of time after all.'

'Can you read *any* of the names?'

'Just.' Fran peered closely at the book. 'Here: "Andrew Foster". The address is – Wycliffe – Terrace, is that?'

'No post code,' said Libby.

'Probably before the new system came in,' said Fran. 'No phone number, either. There was, by the look of things, but washed away.'

Libby sighed. 'I thought we'd got somewhere, then. You're still not getting anything from it?'

Fran shook her head. 'I think we should give it to the boys. Guy's really good with this sort of thing, and if he can make any sense of any of the names, Harry – or even Peter – might recognise them.'

'And meanwhile, we do what?'

'Have a look at the Island?'

'Just us two?'

'Why not? The boys have gone off on their own.'

'We'll wait until they come back, though, won't we?' Libby stood up. 'Then we can tell them about our visit up top.'

It was almost twelve o'clock before Harry, Peter, Ben, and Guy appeared from the direction of Candle Cove.

'Did you miss us?' Ben grinned up at Libby as he made for the steps.

'We wondered where you'd got to. We've been back ages.'

'No joy with the girls, then?' said Harry.

'Not really, although we did learn that they'd all been off the Island in the fifties, so something could have happened then that they don't know about.' Fran handed the blue book to her husband. 'I've managed to get this open, but we can't decipher much. Would you have a go? Then Harry might recognise some names.'

Harry looked dubious, but Guy took the book eagerly. 'Book restoration! Years since I did this.'

'Told you,' Fran said to Libby.

'Where have you been?' Libby asked as Peter and Harry made for the sitting room.

'We walked right through Candle Cove into the next little bay and up to the cliff top,' said Ben. 'There's a footpath that leads across a field to a lovely little pub.'

'Oh, right!' Libby grinned. 'So you just had to stop and have a pint?'

'We actually had coffee,' laughed Guy, coming to sit at the table with an assortment of items he appeared to have assembled from the contents of the kitchen cupboards.

Harry came back to the deck and peered at Guy's

assemblage. 'Can I watch?'

'I think that's the idea,' said Guy.

'We'll leave you to it, then,' said Libby.

'Why? Where are you going?' Ben strolled over and slung an arm round Libby's shoulders.

'Out to explore, like you did. Only in the car.'

'It's lunchtime,' said Peter, reappearing from the direction of the kitchen.

'We'll have a pub lunch,' said Fran. 'We'll see you later. Come on, Lib.'

Leaving the four men clustered round the table while Guy worked on the blue book, Fran and Libby climbed once more to the top of the cliff, past the sisters' house and The Shelf.

'Which way, then?' said Fran, 'and whose car shall we take?'

'Yours?' suggested Libby. 'Although you've brought Guy's. Yours would have been great for navigating these little roads.'

They climbed into the car and drove out of the car park.

'Turn left when we get to the main road,' said Libby. 'We can drive right along the coast road towards Freshwater.'

'So where are we going?' asked Fran when they were out on Military Road, the sea on their left, as sparkling and blue as any holiday brochure, and the gentle landscape on their right. Ahead, they could see the promontory of Freshwater.

'I don't know. Ahead is Freshwater and Tennyson Down. And there's the Needles. I haven't been here since I was a child.'

'Can we go across to the other side? I'd like to see the forest and see if we can't see a red squirrel.'

'OK. Look there's a turning coming up – try that.'

Fran took the lane on the right, which proved to be as narrow as some of those they had discovered in Kent the previous November and December.

'Now which way?' Fran peered around for a signpost.

'We want one which says Newport and nothing does,' said Libby. 'Oh, this way – right. And then we'll find a turning on the left, I suppose.'

Eventually, by way of Brighstone Forest, Calbourne, and Carisbrooke, they found their way to Parkhurst Forest.

'But nowhere to eat,' said Libby.

'Let's go back to Carisbrooke. There was a pub there,' said Fran.

However, as they attempted to take a short cut back to Carisbrooke they came across a tiny pub set back from the road, with a blackboard outside announcing "Fresh Food – 12 till 2".

The inside was typical of seventeenth-century inns, dark, but lightened with fresh cream paint and a cheerful-looking barmaid reading a newspaper.

When they'd both ordered sandwiches and drinks, they were directed to the garden, where they found a table under a spreading beech tree.

'Hello.'

Libby squinted up into the face of a tall, well-built woman some ten years younger than she was.

'You were at Matthew DeLaxley's funeral on Tuesday, weren't you?' The woman held out her hand. 'Amanda Clipping.'

'Oh, yes.' Libby stood up and took the outstretched hand. 'I'm Libby Sarjeant. You were pointed out to us as being the daughter of the DeLaxleys' oldest friends.'

'Fran Wolfe,' said Fran, also standing and shaking hands.

'Yes, I was there as a deputy for my parents. I'm afraid they're a bit frail to travel these days.' She looked at them quizzically. 'Were you friends of Matthew's from his London days?'

'Yes, although we live in Kent,' said Libby. Did you know him well?'

'No, I'm afraid I didn't, although I wish I had. He sounded a lovely old boy.'

'He was. Fran didn't know him either, but the rest of us did.'

'I thought I didn't see you at the funeral,' said Amanda, with a slight frown at Fran. 'Yet you said …'

'The sisters came to us for drinks yesterday and were telling us all about some of their old friends – and Matthew's, of course,' said Libby.

A waitress came up behind them and unloaded plates of sandwiches and two frosted glasses.

'I'm sorry, I'm disturbing your lunch.' Amanda began to turn away.

'No, it's perfectly all right,' said Libby, wondering how she could prolong the conversation and perhaps winkle some information out of the woman.

'I ought to get back to my friends anyway.' Amanda gestured to a table on the other side of the garden where one man sat on a bench and another, his back to the garden, sat in a wheelchair.

'Oh, yes – you were all at the funeral, weren't you?' said Libby.

'Don't tell me the sisters pointed my friends out to you, too? They don't know them.'

'Oh, no,' said Libby hastily. 'I just remember seeing you all. They were friends of Matthew's too, were they?'

Amanda raised a quizzical eyebrow. 'In a way,' she said. 'I'll leave you to your lunch. Nice to have seen you.'

Before Libby could think of anything to say, Amanda had turned and walked back to her table.

'She's telling them all about us,' muttered Fran into her glass.

'Are they looking at us?' asked Libby. 'Not that she could have told them much about us – just that we were London friends of Matthew's.'

'You did say we came from Kent.'

'So?'

'They know where to find us – and therefore Harry.'

'What *are* you talking about?' said Libby, sitting up straight and directing a minatory look at her friend.

'Someone's on Harry's case, aren't they? All they know so far is what Harry looks like.'

'And you're suggesting …? Don't be daft. Amanda wasn't around in the fifties if we're still looking at the illegitimate baby theory.'

'What about the old boy in the wheelchair?'

'We can't see how old he is, and to be honest, although I said I did, I don't remember them from the funeral. Wait, though –' Libby frowned. 'He could be Lucifer, I suppose?'

'Now we've got our two stories muddled,' said Fran. 'And we're getting stupidly suspicious.'

'You started it,' accused Libby, 'saying they were after Harry.' She picked up her sandwich.

Fran sighed. 'I know. But that was what came across.'

Libby stopped in mid-bite. 'What? You mean …?'

Fran nodded. 'It was just a flash.'

'Why didn't you say?'

'I thought you'd realise.'

'I'm not bloody psychic,' said Libby, and laughed. 'Sorry. No pun – if that *was* a pun – intended.'

'No.' Fran sighed. 'I wish I wasn't, either. It's infuriating. I feel as though I absolutely *know* something for certain, yet have no way of validating the knowledge.'

'What exactly was it you knew?'

'As she came over, I knew they – all of them – were looking for Harry. That's why I stood up, even though I hadn't even been at the funeral. I knew.'

'I wondered why you did that,' said Libby. 'But is it a "good" looking, or a "bad" looking?'

'I would have thought it could only be bad.'

'So we've solved the mystery? Already? They killed Celia, too?'

'I can't feel any link to that,' said Fran, 'but maybe I wouldn't. I'm not connected to that.'

'You haven't been connected to other things you've known about.'

'I have in a vague way, if you think about it. I've no connection to Celia at all, I didn't even know Matthew.'

'I suppose so,' said Libby grudgingly. 'So we still don't know. We're going to have to investigate the Clipping.'

'Or her parents.'

'Maybe that's her dad!' Libby brightened up.

'No.' Fran shook her head. 'The sisters knew the parents, didn't they? They'd have recognised him. After all, they spotted both men, Alicia confirmed it. And Amelia had certainly taken notice of the younger man.'

'Well, we're going to have to do some investigating, whatever,' said Libby. 'If they're after Harry, we need to know.'

'So does Harry.'

'How do we go about it?' Libby finished her sandwich and pushed the plate away. 'And do we start now, or go and see the red squirrels?'

'Finish our drinks first, go and see the squirrels, if possible, and then go back to Overcliffe. We can be thinking about what to do on the way.'

'Look – they're going,' said Libby and buried her face in her glass.

As she passed, Amanda Clipping paused by their table. The younger man continued pushing the elder towards the tiny car park.

'It was nice to meet you. Are you staying on the Island?'

'Yes, just for a few more days. We're off to the forest now, to see what we can see,' said Libby.

'You must be sure to see all our attractions. We've got more per square mile than anywhere in the country.' Amanda bestowed on them a benign smile, and passed on.

'Did you get a good look at the men?' whispered Libby.

'The younger one. About forty, dark hair, checked scarf, quite slight. The older one was wearing a cap and a scarf and was very bundled up.'

'I wonder why? It's not exactly cold.'

'He's old and in a wheelchair,' said Fran.

'He might not be,' said Libby darkly. 'He could be in

disguise.'

Fran looked at her in amusement. 'You've been reading too many detective novels,' she said.

Chapter Twelve

Parkhurst Forest provided a glimpse of a red squirrel and far too much evidence of small winged biting things. After half an hour, Libby decided it was time to go back to Overcliffe.

'We'll die of blood poisoning, otherwise,' she said, as they made their way back to the car. 'And besides, we need to talk about the Clipping.'

'I don't see what we can do,' said Fran. 'Except, I suppose, look up census records if they're available. Nineteen fifty-one would be nearest. There wasn't one during the war, was there?'

'Who would we look up? Her parents? She wouldn't have been born then.'

'No.'

'Those men. They could just have been friends of hers, but it's very odd to take friends to a funeral. Pity the three Graces didn't ask to be introduced.'

'Perhaps they could now,' said Fran, unlocking the car. 'Write notes to all the attendees, thanking them for coming.'

'But they said they didn't know a lot of them.' Libby climbed in and buckled the seat belt. 'So they couldn't.'

'They know the Clippings' address. It's the old family house,' said Fran.

'Let's go and ask Alicia, then.'

'If she'll write?'

'No, I was just going to ask her where the house is.' Libby grinned. 'Then we can go and snoop at it.'

Conveniently, when they got back to Overcliffe and parked the car, Alicia was coming out of The Shelf's front door.

'Just collecting post,' she said waving what looked like a

batch of junk mail. 'All rubbish, of course, but they will keep sending it.'

'What are you going to do with The Shelf?' asked Libby. 'Sell it? Or let it like Ship House?'

'We haven't decided yet,' said Alicia, looking uncomfortable.

'We saw Amanda Clipping while we were out,' said Fran. 'With her two friends. Did you say you didn't know them?'

'I can't say, I did, dear.' Alicia frowned. 'But they must have known Matthew, I suppose. Perhaps Matthew was a mutual friend? After all, Amanda does work in London, and Matthew did for years, so …'

'The older man in the wheelchair we thought must have been Amanda's father,' lied Libby, 'but you said he wasn't?'

'Oh, no, dear. Not a bit like. Although I haven't seen John for years, of course. Or Christine. We keep in touch at Christmas, of course.'

'Where did they live on the Island?' asked Fran. 'You said Amanda lives there now?'

'Only when she comes over for a visit, which isn't very often. She sometimes brings friends for a long weekend, as far as we know. She doesn't visit us, of course.'

'But she does see some people?' said Libby.

'Oh, we only know because she goes into the little shop near the house. We use it, too.'

'Oh?' Libby tried to contain her impatience. 'Is it close, then?'

'Yes, dear. Just along the road towards Blackgang, then you turn right and go through a few houses. Just there. Not far at all if you run out of milk. The Clippings' house is just past it. Lovely place.' Alicia smiled wistfully. 'Big, greystone manor. Did you know we've got more manor houses here than anywhere else in the country?'

'And more attractions, Amanda told us today,' said Fran.

'It's because the Island's so small, everything has to be crammed in.' Alicia smiled gently and turned to go into her own house.

'Shall we go?' said Libby, as they watched Alicia shut her front door.

'I suppose we could.' Fran turned to go back to the car. 'But Amanda will probably be back there by now. She might spot us.'

'We could be going to the shop,' suggested Libby. 'We could actually buy something. Chocolate, perhaps.'

'Oh, yes, that's essential.'

'Don't be sarky. Or wine? We probably need more wine.'

Fran laughed. 'Undoubtedly. Come on then.'

Once again, they set out towards Blackgang Chine, keeping an eye out for a turning on their right.

'There,' said Libby. 'The signpost says "Beech".'

Fran turned right down a lane little wider than the one they'd followed earlier that day. On either side open farmland stretched into the distance, and ahead the spire of a church sailed above a small copse. Rounding a bend, they came to a row of terraced cottages and a black and white sign announcing itself as "Beech". The last cottage boasted a shop front adorned with all manner of items hanging beside its door and in front of the window.

'Beech Stores and Post Office,' Libby read. 'They're lucky they haven't been closed down.'

Fran pulled into the side of the road between two large SUVs. 'This can't be their only catchment area. But you'd think the people here could just as easily go into Niton or Chale, wouldn't you?'

'Well, I don't care, I'm just glad it's here,' said Libby, climbing out of the car. 'We can just go in and be nosy tourists. Come on.'

The shop was crammed with everything from tinned beans to buckets and spades. Wellingtons in a variety of colours stood on the floor below a shelf full of wine, a crate of earthy potatoes rubbed shoulders with bags of cat litter.

Libby selected a bottle of red wine, more by price than

because she knew the label, and took it to the man who was watching them with interest from behind the post office counter.

'Hang on,' he said. 'I'll come out.'

He emerged behind a counter piled high with newspapers. 'Can't take anything but post office money behind there,' he said with a friendly smile.

'We were surprised to find not only a village shop but a post office tucked away here,' said Libby. 'Weren't we, Fran?'

'Bit off the beaten track, aren't we?' The man wrapped the bottle in blue tissue paper.

'Is this all there is to the village? Just this row of houses?' said Fran.

'No, bless you! Just up the road behind the trees is our church, and the rest of the houses, and then there's our two manor houses.'

'Two?' said Libby. 'We knew there was one – the Clippings' house?'

'Oh, yes, that's Beech Manor. Mandy's staying there at the moment with a couple of friends, I think.'

'Yes, she came over like we did, for a friend's funeral,' said Libby.

'Oh, ah? That'll be old Matthew, then?'

'Yes. We're staying at Ship House.'

'You'll know the sisters, then?'

'Oh, yes,' said Libby, with an answering grin. 'In fact it was Alicia who directed us here.'

'She's the best of them now Celia's gone,' said the shopkeeper with a sigh. 'She were a smasher.'

'Really?' said Fran. 'We didn't know her. Terrible how she died.'

'Always seemed a bit funny to us.' The shopkeeper took Libby's money and turned to put it in the till.

'What? How she died?' Libby looked at Fran and raised an eyebrow.

'Yes.' Libby's change was handed over. 'Didn't seem quite

90

right, somehow. Celia was – oh, I dunno – like a woman twenty years younger. Really on the ball, you know?'

'But Alicia told us she got caught in the flood,' said Fran.

'Well, yeah – but why? She'd have seen what was happening. She'd have had time to get up them steps out of Candle Cove even if she couldn't get back into Overcliffe.'

'Steps? We didn't think there were any,' said Fran.

'Oh, you have to know where they are.' He smiled ruefully. 'And old Celia, she knew everything about this Island, she did. She knew where the bodies were buried.'

'Bo – oh!' Libby laughed. 'She knew more than the others?'

'Her and Matthew. Thick as thieves, there were. Knew all about all the old Island families.'

'I wish he'd told us more about the Island,' said Libby. 'We knew him on the mainland, you see.'

'Oh, I knew you was overners.' He grinned. 'Now, did you want to know where Mandy's house is?'

'Yes, please. Although I'd never dare to call her anything but Amanda.'

'Oh, I've known her all me life. Same age, see? Not the same schools, obvious, but same Sunday School. Now, you go out of here, turn left up the road past the church and you'll come to the gates on your left. Big old gates, they are, with lions on.'

'Well, thank you for all your information,' said Libby, holding out her hand. 'Sorry, don't know your name?'

'Bernie Small, pleased to meet you.' Bernie shook hands with both of them. 'And give my best to Alicia.'

'We will,' said Fran. 'Thank you.'

'Well,' said Libby when they were outside. 'That was interesting.'

'Wasn't it.' Fran unlocked the car and put the wine inside. 'And now we're going to have a look at Beech Manor.'

The church, shielded by the little copse of – naturally, beech trees – was only a hundred yards further on from the shop, standing amid a sprinkling of modern bungalows and older cottages. Further on still, they came to the gateposts with the lions Bernie had told them about.

'I wonder why everyone had lions on their gateposts?' said Libby. 'Was it after Landseer did his Trafalgar Square lions, do you suppose?'

'These look a bit older than that.' Fran peered up the drive. 'It is a nice house, isn't it?'

Built in grey stone, as Alicia had said, Beech Manor was a symmetrical building with a welcoming look. It wasn't large, but had the look of a building happy in itself and its surroundings.

'It doesn't match Amanda, somehow,' said Libby.

'She doesn't match it,' said Fran. 'That's what it is.'

'Well, she's not here now,' said Libby. 'No cars.'

'There'll probably be a converted stable round the back,' said Fran, 'and no, we aren't going to look.'

'Oh, all right.' Libby grinned. 'I suppose now we've seen it, we might as well go back home.'

'Today?' said Fran, startled.

'Oh, sorry, I mean back to Overcliffe, not *home* home. We could have a look at the church, I suppose?'

'It'll be locked, I expect.' Fran turned back to the lane. 'Look, do you think that's the other manor house?'

Across the road, another pair of gates stood open to a drive which curved away to the left behind dense shrubbery.

'Let's go and look.' Libby darted across the road and stepped cautiously round the right-hand gate post.

'You'll get done for trespassing if you're not careful,' said Fran, catching up with her.

'I don't see any security cameras, and the gates don't look as if they've been closed for years,' said Libby. 'And there's no one about.' She edged forward. 'Look! There's the house.'

This house was far more imposing than little Beech Manor across the road. It sprawled from its obviously Tudor central block to two irregular wings built, said Libby, rather after the style of Osborne House.

'Somebody had pretentions of grandeur,' she concluded.

'I don't know,' said Fran. 'Just trying to curry favour with the Queen, perhaps.'

'Or keep up with fashion. Does it look well kept to you?'

'Not that well. The grounds look good though.'

'Beech Manor was better kept. I wonder who does that if Amanda isn't here most of the time?'

'I don't think we can ask Bernie Small about that. He thinks we're mates of Amanda's and would know,' said Fran.

'Do we suppose this is owned by one of those old Island families he mentioned?' said Libby, as they turned to retrace their steps towards the car.

'Now, that we *could* ask him,' said Fran. 'That would be natural curiosity.'

As they approached the shop, Bernie Small was outside collecting vegetables to take back inside.

'Find it?' he asked.

'Yes, thanks, Bernie, but no one was there,' said Fran.

'We think we saw the other manor house across the road,' said Libby. 'Would that be right?'

'Oh, yeah. Etherington Manor,' said Bernie. 'Old Lady Bligh's place.'

Chapter Thirteen

'Is that significant?' Libby asked, when they were in the car heading back to Overcliffe.

'What, that Lady Bligh lives opposite the Clippings?' Fran swung into Niton and followed the one-way system towards the Undercliff.

'I suppose it isn't really.' Libby sighed. 'They all live this side of the Island. Obviously they all know each other. And the DeLaxleys lived at Overcliffe Castle, didn't they? All of them in posh houses.'

'I wonder which was the senior branch of the DeLaxley family?' Fran frowned. 'Matthew's or the sisters'?'

'What difference does that make?' asked Libby.

'Who inherited the main bulk of the DeLaxley estate? If Matthew was the son of the eldest son it would be him, which would mean that everything belonged to him. On the other hand, if the sisters were daughters of the eldest son ...'

'But you said there's no rule of primo-whatsit any more,' said Libby.

'But there was. Unless their grandfather divided everything equally between his children.'

'We're assuming it was sons not daughters,' said Libby.

Fran gave her a quick surprised look. 'But they're all DeLaxleys.'

'What –' Libby began, then thought for a moment. 'Oh, of course. If it was their mothers who had been DeLaxleys, they wouldn't be DeLaxleys, would they?'

Fran sighed. 'No, Libby.'

'Shame their castle isn't there any longer. I wonder what

happened to it?'

'I'm more interested in what our new friend said about Celia,' said Fran.

'Her knowing where the bodies are buried? I took him literally at first.'

Fran laughed. 'I know. Sometimes, Libby, you're priceless!'

'I know,' said Libby smugly.

Fran parked in the car park at the top of Overcliffe and Libby wandered over to where a green metal notice informed the public that this had been the site of Overcliffe Castle.

'Demolished in the sixties,' she told Fran. 'I wonder why?'

'We'll ask the ladies,' said Fran. 'I can think of several questions we need to ask them in view of what we've learnt today.'

'How did Celia know so much more than they all did about the Island families?'

'And how well the Clippings and Lady Bligh knew – know – each other.'

'Really? Why?'

Fran was frowning again. 'I don't know. It seems important, somehow.'

'Her son,' said Libby suddenly. 'Amelia said Lady Bligh was there with her awful son. Or something like that.'

'Ye-es,' said Fran slowly. 'I wonder if that means anything?'

'It means Amelia doesn't approve of him.'

'She doesn't approve of most things,' said Fran. 'And the other thing I wanted to ask was about the steps.'

'The steps? Oh, from Candle Cove. No – no one's mentioned them. In fact, hasn't somebody said you can't get up to the top?'

'Harry did, didn't he?' Fran wandered down to the sisters' house and peered along the path that led along the cliff. 'You can see down into it from here, can't you?' She started along it.

'Fran! You can't! The sisters will see you!'

Fran looked over her shoulder. 'I doubt it. Look.' She gestured. The path descended below the level of the sisters' house, and the bank above was thick with vegetation. 'They'd look straight over the top of this.'

'OK,' said Libby nervously, following her friend into the tunnel-like pathway.

'And that's it.' Fran stopped. 'You can't get any further.'

Sure enough, the bracken and brambles closed over the path which had fallen away into rubble.

'So where are the steps?' asked Libby, trying to peer down to the bay below.

'They must be the other side,' said Fran, standing on tip-toe to try and see over the brambles. 'That makes sense, because if they were this side, they'd come up straight into the sisters' back garden.'

'Come on, let's go back,' said Libby. 'I'm dying for a cup of tea, and the men will be wondering where on earth we've got to.'

As they emerged at the top of the pathway, they found Amelia waiting for them with a puzzled look on her face.

'What were you doing down there? It doesn't go anywhere.'

'No,' said Fran ruefully. 'We discovered that. We were hoping there might be a way down into Candle Cove.'

'Of course not *there*' Amelia was scornful. 'If there had been, Celia would have come –' she broke off, looking stricken.

'Would have come up when she heard the storm coming?' Libby finished for her.

Amelia nodded, her eyes wide.

'Come on,' said Fran, taking her arm. 'Let's go inside. I think we need to talk to all of you again.'

Alicia and Honoria were in the kitchen and looked surprised at the sudden entry of their sister in the firm charge of Fran and Libby.

'A few more questions,' said Fran, sitting down at the kitchen table. 'We've just established that you all thought Celia would have tried to get out of Candle Cove when she heard the storm coming.'

Alicia and Honoria looked at one another.

97

'You have?' said Alicia cautiously.

'Amelia confirmed it,' said Libby. 'What we don't know is why this alarmed Amelia so much. Also, why has no one told us about the steps from Candle Cove?'

Alicia and Honoria both sat down on the other side of the table. Alicia put her head in her hands.

'The steps have crumbled,' said Honoria gruffly. 'Not safe.'

'And they're the other side,' said Amelia.

'We guessed that. Now, why is Amelia alarmed?' Fran looked at each of them in turn.

Alicia raised her head. 'I don't know.'

'Oh, come on!' said Libby. 'This is getting silly. You asked us over here to look in to Celia's death, which you say is murder. We've investigated as much as we can while you've consistently sidestepped the truth all along the way. What is it you haven't told us this time?'

'Was it,' said Fran shrewdly, 'that you really *did* know that Celia was going down to the Beach House that day after all?'

There was a shocked silence, while all three sisters avoided looking at one another.

'We knew she'd gone out,' said Amelia. 'We told you that.'

'I think you've hit the nail on the head, Fran,' said Libby. 'Useless conspirators they'd make, wouldn't they?'

Alicia took a deep breath. But no words came out.

'You told us,' said Fran gently, 'that it was only after Alicia went to the hospital you realised Celia hadn't come back. That doesn't sound quite right.'

Honoria and Amelia exchanged glances.

'Look, if you know that Celia went to the Beach House after all, and if you know what it was about, why are you asking us to find out?' Libby wasn't gentle. 'Honestly! You are three very twisted old women. We had all this the other night when poor Harry got put on the spot. I'm really getting very angry with you, and apart from now having to find out who or what is after Harry, I'm not going to help you any more. Come on, Fran. We've got other people to talk to.'

Suddenly there was a wall of sisters between Libby and the door.

'No.' Honoria looked more than ever like a bulldog. 'Didn't know what Celia was going for. Didn't know anything. You need to tell us everything.'

'I'm sorry?' said Libby coldly. 'I think that should be my line. Now, get out of my way. I have no scruples about man-handling old ladies.'

Honoria looked ready to take anyone on in unarmed combat, but Amelia and Alicia subsided and moved away from the door.

'Thank you,' said Libby, and swept past Honoria, who glowered after her.

'Why did you do that?' Fran asked quietly as she followed her friend down the cliff.

'What do you mean?' Libby looked back, surprised. 'I did it for exactly the reason I told them. I'm fed up with them.'

'There's more to it than that,' said Fran. 'There's a reason they're hiding something.'

'Well, of course there is! They want to know who killed Celia in case it's someone who knows this big secret they're keeping.'

Fran stopped at the bottom of the steps and looked at her friend in astonishment. 'How did you know?'

'It's obvious,' said Libby, climbing up to the deck of Ship House. 'Don't tell me you hadn't worked it out?'

'No, actually I hadn't, although now you've said it, it *is* obvious. How much does Harry know?'

'Only what he's told us, I imagine. Come on, let's tell the boys and see what they say.'

The men were all in the sitting room watching football.

'You were a long time,' said Ben.

'Sorry, but we've been finding things out,' said Fran. 'Libby has, anyway.'

Harry stood up and stretched. 'Come and tell me about it in the kitchen, then, petal. I'm fed up with football.'

'I'm not interested anyway,' said Guy. 'I'll come with you.'

Ben grinned. 'We'll all stay here and have a cup of tea. I don't want to watch the football, either, and I think Pete was nearly asleep.'

Tea was made and room made for Libby and Fran on the couch, after which they recounted the day's adventures between them.

'You have had a busy day,' said Ben.

'So you think whatever it is they're hiding has nothing to do with Harry?' said Peter.

'If you think back to their behaviour right from the start, Harry's always been a sort of by-product,' said Libby.

'Thank you, sweetie,' said Harry.

'You know what I mean. They gave you the letter because they didn't want to be bothered with it. All they wanted to know was who'd written it, because that person might know their big secret.'

'I don't get it.' Guy was frowning. 'That letter said Matthew wouldn't tell the writer about the young friend. They must have thought – well, they did, didn't they? – that meant the writer was the killer.'

'Yes, which was how their devious old minds worked. Get Harry to find out who it was, then they would find out if he or she knew their secret,' said Libby.

'I think I see,' said Ben, 'but it's very convoluted.'

'So it's nothing to do with me after all?' Harry looked round at the circle of faces.

'Yes, it is. We still know you were your grandmother's grandson, whoever she was,' said Fran, 'and somebody is watching you. We know that.'

'How are the two tied together?' said Guy.

Libby shrugged. 'We don't know that they are.'

Fran turned to her husband. 'How did you get on with the book?'

'Not brilliantly.' Guy stood up and fetched the book from the table behind the couch. 'Here. Most of the pages will open, but the ink's become virtually invisible. And some of it's turned to papier-mâché.'

'It *is* an address book,' said Libby, as Fran turned the brittle pages. 'I wonder how far back it goes?'

'It's not a new book,' said Fran. 'I mean, not a recent one. It could go back a long way.'

'I wonder if it is what the murderer was looking for?' said Ben.

'If there was a murder,' said Peter.

'Would the killer murder Celia because he couldn't find what he wanted, or because she knew something about him – or her?' said Libby.

'Or simply she knew who he was and he couldn't risk her telling anybody,' said Fran.

'That's the most likely,' said Harry. 'And we still don't know if what he or she wanted is anything to do with me.'

'We've been assuming it is because of what Matthew told you, putting it together with the letter the sisters received and the note you found here,' said Peter. 'But that could be something completely different.'

'And I think the sisters believe that it is. None of them are being helpful about finding out who Harry's gran was.' Libby sighed.

'And they've almost been avoiding the subject of the Island in the fifties,' said Fran.

'So what we need to do,' said Harry, 'is find out what *was* happening on the Island in the fifties. Stands to reason.'

Chapter Fourteen

The laptops and tablets all came out.

'Fu ... blow me,' said Harry. 'There was a rocket-testing site at the Needles.'

'Late fifties,' said Libby. 'Too late. Your parent needs to have been born in the early fifties. Wish we knew which sex we were looking for.'

'There are a lot of videos,' said Peter. 'But it's all nostalgia stuff.'

'Everything keeps referring back to the derestriction of the Island in 1948,' said Ben. 'Could that have something to do with it?'

'It's because of the proximity to France,' said Fran. 'The beaches were restricted areas.'

'They were in Kent, too,' said Libby, 'and all along the south coast.'

'Most of the sites are referring to the freedom from rationing, the fashions, and the holiday-makers,' said Guy. 'No different from Nethergate, really.'

'Hmm.' Libby shut her laptop and stood up. 'I don't think we're going to find anything out here.'

'No.' Fran followed suit. 'There was obviously no big news story around that time.'

'But we don't want a big news story,' said Peter. 'Don't you think it could be the opening up of the Island? More people coming in?'

'Could be,' said Harry, looking interested. 'When did rock'n'roll start?'

'Not until the late fifties,' said Ben. 'It wouldn't have been that.'

Libby was staring out at the sea. 'I've had an idea,' she said.

The other five looked at each other with foreboding.

Libby turned round. 'Don't you want to know what it is?'

'Go on,' said Ben.

'What?' said Harry.

'Why don't we have a memorial service for Matthew?'

There was a stunned silence.

'Libby,' said Peter eventually, 'we've just been to his funeral.'

'I know,' said Libby, 'but not everybody knew about it. You said yourself there were only a few people from London there.'

'I don't see how this would help find Celia's murder or Harry's stalker,' said Ben.

'I think I do,' said Fran. 'If it could be a public notice of some sort …'

'If you're thinking of doing it in London …' began Peter.

'Not that many people from the Island would go,' finished Guy.

'Exactly,' said Libby triumphantly.

They all looked at each other in bewilderment.

'But then we wouldn't know,' said Harry.

'Oh, think about it,' crowed Libby. 'You're all so thick!'

'Come on, you old trout, don't be a cow, and tell us what you mean,' Peter aimed a kick at her.

Libby sat down again. 'If we suggest to the sisters that we hold a memorial service in – yes, London – for all the people who might not have learnt about his death and who couldn't come to the funeral, and anyone who did come, of course, who would be bound to come?'

'Er – us?' suggested Ben.

'No, Harry's stalker! Who we think is also the murderer.'

'Why would he?' Guy asked.

'Look – remember the letter? It said that Matthew wouldn't tell the writer who Matthew's young friend was, and then Harry found that note, suggesting that someone is actually looking for

104

him.'

'And found me,' said Harry.

'Yes, but nothing can happen to you here,' said Libby reasonably. 'There's always someone with you, and usually several people. Also, this place is so difficult to get to, anybody would be spotted.'

'Thanks,' said Harry. 'I feel really safe.'

'We don't know that anyone's actually *after* Harry,' said Guy.

'Well, he is the illegitimate grandson of – of – of somebody,' said Libby.

'Do you realise how melodramatic all this sounds?' asked Peter.

Fran smiled and put her laptop on the coffee table. 'It does.' She turned to Libby. 'Despite everything, all we've got is these three women deciding their sister was murdered, keeping some sort of secret from us, and the fact that Harry appears to be the target of some sort of attention. Nothing else.'

Libby looked round at her friends. 'Is that what you all think?'

One by one they all nodded.

'So no memorial service, then?'

'No, petal.' Peter came to stand next to Libby and gave her a kiss on the cheek. 'An enormous challenge to organise, not to mention money spent as well, and for what?'

Libby sighed. 'Just an intellectual exercise, then?'

'Not for me,' said Harry. 'I'd still quite like to know who I am.'

Libby smiled at him gratefully. 'Perhaps we could see if we can't just do that?'

'And ignore the three harpies?' said Ben.

'I don't see why not,' said Fran. 'They asked us to help and then kept things back. They haven't helped at all. I vote we just have the rest of our holiday here, and see if there's any way we can track down Harry's relations. That's all we can do.'

'Well, if that's what you all think ...' Libby looked round

the group and sighed again. 'OK. In which case, surely it's time for a drink before dinner, isn't it? And what are we doing for dinner?'

They walked into Ventnor for dinner, and strolled down The Esplanade to watch the sunset.

'It's not unlike Nethergate, is it?' said Guy. 'It's still an old-fashioned seaside town.'

'It's my favourite on the Island,' said Libby. 'But there are lovely places everywhere.' She turned to Harry. 'And some really exciting new restaurants and chefs, Harry. Shall we try them?'

'How do you know all this?' asked Ben, amused. 'You haven't been here for years.'

'The internet, of course. I went on a bit of an Isle of Wight binge after we heard about Matthew.'

'I'd like to see the other side of the Island,' said Harry suddenly. 'You know, where it looks like it's all trees and no buildings.'

'We were over there this morning,' said Fran. 'Perhaps we could have a proper look at that side of the Island tomorrow?'

'Starting with Seaview,' said Libby, 'and work our way along.'

'We should have brought a bloody minibus,' said Peter.

'We can get all six of us into mine,' said Ben. 'No one minds squashing up, do they?'

'Lovely,' said Libby happily. 'A proper family outing.'

The next morning, when they all piled into the car, Libby said, 'Shall we point out Amanda's house on the way?'

'Won't it take us out of our way?' said Fran, squashed between Harry and the off-side rear door.

'We can double back,' said Libby. 'I worked out the route on the laptop this morning.'

'Directions, then, please,' said Ben from the driving seat. 'Left or right?'

As they drove towards Beech Manor, Libby remembered

106

Fran's odd feeling about Amanda Clipping and her friends.

'We didn't tell you that, did we?' she concluded after recounting the preceding day's encounter.

'This is it,' said Fran, and Ben pulled in as close to side of the lane as possible.

'And that one belongs to Lady Bligh,' said Libby.

'I suppose she couldn't be my grandmother?' said Harry, following Fran out of the car and strolling across the road to peer up the drive.

'No, you said Matthew told you your grandmother died,' said Peter, joining him at the gates. 'But I bet she knew her.'

'They all did,' said Fran. 'Lady Bligh, Amanda Clipping's parents, the three – four – sisters, and that other couple we don't know about. What was their name?'

'The Dougans,' said Libby. 'And they were all at the funeral.'

'The senior Clippings weren't,' said Guy.

'No, but Amanda was, as their representative,' said Libby.

'And she and her mates were looking for me,' said Harry thoughtfully. 'Why don't we pop over and see if they're in?'

'Look, it was only a feeling, Harry,' said Fran. 'You can't just ring the bell and say "Here I am", can you?'

'Be very interesting, though, wouldn't it?' said Harry, as he crossed the road towards Beech Manor.

'Was it one of them that wrote the letter?' asked Guy.

'Or wrote the note?' said Libby.

'How do I know?' said Fran. 'I only get flashes, not life histories.'

'I wish we could find out who the bloke in the wheelchair is,' said Libby. 'I'm sure he's got something to do with it.'

'We're not investigating any more, Lib, remember?' warned Fran.

'We are – just into Harry's threats.' Libby beamed up at him. 'Aren't we, Hal?'

He grinned down at her. 'Yes, old trout. Perhaps the invalid is my dad – what do you reckon?'

'And the other one is his legitimate son who wants to get Harry out of the way?' Ben laughed.

'You never know,' said Libby. 'The trouble is, we've absolutely no way of knowing or finding out. We normally have some sort of way in but this time we've nothing.' She paused. 'Unless … have you got your birth certificate, Hal?'

'Yes, of course. I had to apply for a copy when I got my passport.'

'Oh, yes, the home would have had your original, wouldn't they?'

'That was only a short form, anyway,' said Harry. 'You have to have the long form to apply for a passport.'

'So you know your mother's name?' said Peter. 'I never thought of that. Have you looked her up?'

'By the time I was applying for a passport I was with you.' Harry smiled fondly at his partner. 'It just never occurred to me.'

Peter slung an arm around Harry's shoulders and squeezed. 'Course.'

'Well, if we're not going to knock on any doors,' said Ben, 'can we get going? Time's getting on.'

They all piled back into the car, and Harry, now up against the rear passenger door, waved a valedictory hand out of the window at Beech Manor. 'Just in case they were looking,' he said.

'Well, if they were,' said Fran, 'and they actually were looking for you, it won't hurt for them to know we might be on to them.'

'All very cloak and dagger,' said Ben. 'Let's just go and enjoy our day.'

It wasn't until much later in the day, having left the car in a car park, they were walking through woodland on the north side of the Island at the top of the cliffs overlooking the drowned prehistoric Bouldnor Battery, when Libby said, 'I can't just leave it alone, you know.'

Beside her, Ben groaned. Ahead, Peter looked over his

shoulder. 'What?'

'I said, I can't just leave it alone,' repeated Libby.

Peter and Harry dropped back and Fran and Guy hurried up behind.

'Why am I not surprised?' said Peter, his head on one side.

'We did agree we should try and see if we can't find out about Harry's parentage,' said Libby defensively, 'and it all does seem to link up.'

'You mean Celia's murder?' said Harry.

'Alleged murder,' corrected Ben.

'Well, doesn't it?'

'I'm not sure if we and the sisters haven't linked it ourselves,' said Fran.

'It was the letter that did that,' said Guy. 'The one they received that they sent on to Harry.'

'And before that there was nothing to link them.' Ben shook his head.

'I don't suppose the sisters had thought of me much,' said Harry. 'Matthew and I weren't always in contact. That email you saw on his computer was about the last time we were in touch.'

'Yes, I wanted to ask you about that letter, Hal,' said Libby. 'You remember when the sisters came down to tea the day after the funeral?'

'Yes.' Harry gazed longingly over the view of the Solent towards the mainland. Libby dug him in the ribs.

'That was a set-up, wasn't it?'

Chapter Fifteen

Peter, Ben, Fran, and Guy were studies in shock.

Peter found his voice first. 'What *are* you talking about?'

'Harry knows.' Libby was watching Harry triumphantly. 'And if you all think about it, so will you.'

'Can we go back to the car?' said Harry. 'I think I've had enough sight-seeing.'

Without a word, they all turned back towards the car park. It wasn't until they reached the car that Harry spoke again.

'Libby's right. It was a set-up.'

They all looked at Libby.

'Go on, then,' said Fran. 'Explain.'

'Harry actually asked them if there weren't four of them. Remember? He said he thought Matthew had spoken about four cousins.'

'And that was when Alicia told you about Celia, of course,' said Fran turning her gaze on Harry.

'And ...?' said Peter.

'Why did Harry ask? He already knew.' Libby looked up at him. 'Didn't you, Hal?'

He nodded.

'I'm not following this at all,' said Guy. 'Someone start at the beginning.'

'Hal explained to us that the sisters had forwarded the letter to him, and that they had been in communication after that. He even said he tried to stop them involving us. That right, Hal?'

He nodded again.

'So please tell us, darling boy, why all the secrecy? Why didn't you tell us about the letter when you first received it?

111

And the sisters' suspicions about Celia's death?' Peter was looking like a thundercloud.

Harry sighed. 'Because I didn't want to get involved. I didn't want you to get involved. By the time they sent me the letter we all knew about Matthew's death and I wanted to go to the funeral. When the sisters said they were inviting you as well I just went along with it, hoping to wriggle out of it somehow. When you said Fran and Guy were coming to join us for a few days, I guessed we'd be in trouble.'

'So you don't think Celia was murdered?' said Ben.

'Oh, I don't know. I did wonder – well, you know I did – if somehow it could be linked to my parents, but ...' He trailed to a stop.

'You know,' said Peter, stuffing his hands in his pockets and scowling at his best beloved, 'if you'd told me as soon as you got this letter, and then we'd told Libby straight away about the sisters' mad ideas, this would have been far less complicated.'

'I know that now,' said Harry grumpily.

'But the further you got in, the worse it got,' said Ben. 'I know.' He unlocked the car. 'Pile in, people. Let's get back to the Ship.'

'So what are you going to do now?' asked Fran, when she and Libby were squeezed in the back seat between Peter and Harry.

'Nothing we can do, really,' said Libby. 'I don't want to give up, but I don't know how we can possibly trace Harry's granny, and we really have no way of finding anything out about Celia's death, which we'd already decided, hadn't we? We can try with Hal's birth certificate and see if it takes us anywhere, but that will have to wait until we get home tomorrow.'

'We could try looking it up online,' said Fran.

'That will only give us members of the household, and suppose there are more than one?'

'I'll dig it out tomorrow night and let you know then,' said Harry, 'although I don't know what good it will do.'

'Didn't you ever wonder about your family before?' asked Fran.

'Well. of course I did, but only in a – I don't know – a sort of vague way. Matthew wouldn't tell me anything, and by the time I met Pete it didn't seem to matter.'

'Well, if nothing else happens, I don't see why we should bother,' said Peter.

'What do you mean?' asked Libby. 'If nothing else happens?'

'Like that note. If no one appears to be "after" Hal, as you put it, why should we bother?'

'I'd quite like to know, now,' said Harry.

'Course you would,' said Libby, patting him on the knee. 'So would I.'

'I thought you were going to show me one of these famous chefs tonight, by the way,' said Harry. 'Bit late now, isn't it?'

'Oh, bugger, I forgot. Oh, well, we'll have to come over again some time.'

'Not sure I'm keen on that idea,' said Peter.

'Don't be daft,' said Harry. 'It's a lovely place.'

'But a bit spoilt now,' said Peter, 'you must admit.'

Instead of Libby's designer chef, they ate that night at the cafe on the beach again.

'Do we go in to say goodbye to the ladies tomorrow?' Ben asked as they shared the last of the wine between them.

'Oh, we have to. Apart from anything else, we have to give the key back,' said Libby. 'However annoying they've been, they've given us a free week's holiday.'

The candles on the tables flickered in the slight breeze and light wavered over their faces, showing varying degrees of thoughtfulness.

'If you can call it that,' said Peter. 'Not sure I would.'

'It's been interesting,' said Guy. 'I've never really been involved in one of your cases before.'

'Yes you have,' said Fran. 'You always are.'

'Only on the sidelines,' said Guy.

'Providing support,' agreed Ben.

'Well, we'll go back to normal tomorrow,' said Libby. 'Just Fran and me putting the world to rights.'

When they finished dinner, they strolled back to Candle Cove and had a last look round the Beach House.

'I wonder what really happened here,' said Libby.

'You are *not* going to find out,' said Harry, linking his arm through hers. 'I shall let you research my old ancestors just to keep you busy when we get home, but to be honest, I feel a bit like Pete, only don't tell him.'

'What?' asked Libby, amused.

'I want to get away from the Island,' said Harry in a theatrical whisper.

'Look, here are the steps,' called Guy from the other end of the cove.

'You'd never know they were there, would you?' said Peter, as they all came over to inspect the crumbling steps hidden behind a wall of vegetation.

'Could you actually get up them, though?' said Ben. 'They don't look very safe.'

Harry tried to push through the bushes, but Peter pulled him back.

'Oh, no you don't, we've had enough trouble without you ending up with a broken leg.'

Harry brushed pieces of wood off his sleeve. 'Tell you what, I don't reckon Celia could have got up there, anyway.'

'Not our problem any more, ducky, you said so,' said Libby. 'Come on, let's go and have a nightcap on our lovely deck.'

The following morning was a bustle of packing and cleaning. Blessed with four men who were adept at looking after houses, Fran and Libby didn't find themselves with the bulk of the cleaning, although they both ended up doing most of the packing.

'That's it,' said Libby looking round. 'We've finished. Let's start carrying things up to the cars.'

'Are we all going in to see the sisters?' asked Harry, looking nervous.

'I think we ought to,' said Fran. 'Libby and I can go in first, and perhaps they'll come out to say goodbye to the rest of you.'

But in fact when they reached the top of the steps, Alicia, Amelia, and Honoria were waiting for them.

'I saw you,' said Honoria. 'I was weeding.'

'Ah,' said Libby, with a weak smile. 'Well, here's the key, and we wanted to say thank you for letting us stay in the house.'

'It was a pleasure,' said Alicia. 'I'm only sorry …'

'You wouldn't find out who murdered Celia,' snapped Amelia.

Before Libby could make an angry retort, Fran stepped smoothly into the breach.

'We had no access to any of the facts,' she said. 'If you don't think the police did a good enough job, speak to them about it.' She turned to Alicia. 'Thank you for allowing Guy and me to stay, too.'

Each of the men bade a polite goodbye and Harry surprised them all by going up to give Alicia a hug. She kissed his cheek and stepped back, wiping her eyes.

'Sorry,' she said. 'It isn't …'

'Important,' Honoria finished for her, glaring at Amelia. 'Doesn't matter. Safe journey.'

Fran and Guy got into one car and Ben, Libby, Peter and Harry got into the other. As they pulled away, Libby turned and saw the three sisters still standing watching them.

'I wonder what that was all about it?' she said.

'I think they've been arguing among themselves,' said Ben.

'Yeah, I reckon so.' Harry wriggled into a comfortable position in the back seat and stretched his legs as far as they would go. 'That Amelia was the problem.'

'Mad because we wouldn't find out about her sister, yet unwilling to tell us the truth. In fact, it almost seemed as if she was the one hiding something,' said Libby.

'More than the others?' asked Peter.

'I think so, although Honoria was less than forthcoming, and we never found out what they were all doing on the mainland in the fifties.'

'Except for Amelia,' said Ben. 'Her husband was a diplomat.'

'Oh, well.' Libby shrugged. 'I don't suppose we'll ever see them again, so we might as well forget about them.'

The journey home was uneventful, and to round off the week, when they arrived in Steeple Martin, Fran and Guy broke their own journey to join the others for dinner in the pub.

'Nice to be back,' said Harry. 'I've quite missed the old caff.'

'At least you haven't got to open up tomorrow,' said Peter.

'No, but I'll have to go in to sort out ordering and make sure everything's OK. You got to work, Ben?'

'I'll go up to the office. I don't suppose there's much for me to do, but I ought to let the tenants know I'm back.'

'I've got to open the shop,' said Guy. 'We're almost into high season, now. You saw how many families were on the Island. That'll be the same in Nethergate.'

'Yes, all the ones with pre-school children,' said Libby. 'Which reminds me, I haven't seen Jane and Imogen for ages. How are they?'

'Fine as far as I know. Jane occasionally walks Imogen down to the ice cream shop, so I see them then,' said Fran. 'I haven't see Terry, though.'

Jane was assistant editor on the local paper, the *Nethergate Mercury*, and lived with her husband Terry and their daughter in a beautiful Georgian terraced house left to Jane by her aunt.

'We'll go and see her this week, shall we?' suggested Libby. 'I'll give her a ring in the morning and find out when she'll be free.'

'And I suppose I'd better check with the children and see how they are,' sighed Fran.

'Don't let them bully you,' laughed Libby. Fran's daughters were notorious for trying to take advantage of her.

The party broke up.

'I'll ring you to see if you've found that birth certificate in the morning,' said Libby to Harry, as they parted outside the pub.

'OK,' said Harry. 'Anything to keep you out of mischief.'

Ben and Libby walked back to Allhallow's Lane.

'Don't let the search for Harry's parentage take you over, Lib,' said Ben. 'Best leave all Isle of Wight business on the Isle of Wight.'

'I know,' sighed Libby, 'but I've still got this niggling feeling.'

'Well, stamp on it,' said Ben. 'It was all a bit emotional over there, feelings swirling round like black ink.'

Libby looked at him in surprise. 'How poetic, Ben!'

'That's what it felt like, however beautiful the place was.' Ben took out his key to open the door of number seventeen. 'And this is our little oasis of calm.'

Libby giggled. 'Is that what it is?' She looked round at the cluttered interior.

'Complete with alcoholic refreshments,' said Ben with a grin. 'Nightcap?'

'Why not?' Libby sat down on the sofa and stretched her legs. 'Funny without Sidney, though, isn't it?'

'We'll pick him up from Mum tomorrow,' said Ben, pouring whisky. 'He'll be even more of a walking stomach after a week at the Manor with her.'

Sidney, a cat known for his appetite and sulky disposition, was a silver tabby with attitude.

'And I'll pick up Harry's birth certificate,' said Libby, accepting her glass.

'Oh, dear,' said Ben.

Chapter Sixteen

Libby went with Ben to the Manor the following morning, to see his mother Hetty and collect Sidney. Leaving Ben in the estate office, she heaved the cat basket out into the car and drove home, where Sidney put his tail between his legs and crawled under the sofa.

'Be like that, then,' said Libby. 'I'm going to see Harry.'

When she tapped on the window of The Pink Geranium five minutes later, Harry had papers and laptop spread all over the big pine table in the window. He looked up and beckoned.

'Having trouble?' Libby asked sitting down opposite him.

'Not really,' sighed Harry. 'I just hate paperwork.'

'I thought Donna took care of all that at home these days?'

Donna, Harry's erstwhile right-hand woman, had had the temerity to produce a child, not something compatible with working six nights a week in a restaurant, especially when married to a registrar at the local hospital.

'She can't order the food, though. Only the regular orders, and I'd run everything down because we were away for the week. Coffee?'

'Please. Did you find the certificate?'

Harry got up to fetch the coffee pot from its retro seventies housing. 'Yes. Wasn't hard. It was in with the passports.' He put the pot down and handed Libby an envelope.

'So you were born Harry Price,' said Libby, spreading the document on the table. 'Your mother named you.'

'Father's not there, though.'

'No. So at least we know you're the son of a man.'

Harry looked at her oddly. 'Yes, dear. And a woman.'

'You know what I meant. Granny's illegitimate baby was a boy.'

'Funny, innit?' said Harry. 'Illegitimate. Never used now, is it? I know as many unmarried couples with children as married ones. More if anything.'

'Much easier just to live together. Look at Ben and me.'

'But Pete and I are married – partnershipped or whatever – and Guy and Fran are, too. Doesn't that tell you something?'

'What?' said Libby warily. 'Has Ben been talking to you?'

'Not about that, no. But we all know he'd like to get married.'

'Once bitten and all that,' said Libby. 'And he also wanted us to go and live at Steeple Farm.' She shuddered. 'I'm so glad we didn't.'

Harry leaned back in his chair and regarded her critically. 'I still don't know what you had against that house.'

'It's creepy.'

'None of the people who've stayed there have thought that.'

'No, I know. It's just me. And we're not talking about me. Jeanette Price – that's who we're talking about.'

Harry shrugged. 'I don't know why. She had me put into care, she didn't want me. And if my father's name isn't recorded we can't go back any further, can we?'

Libby frowned. 'Hang on – you weren't adopted.'

'No.' Harry sighed again. 'I *told* you. I was in children's homes.'

'How far back do you remember?'

'Why? I was always in them. I went to a couple of foster homes, but that didn't take.'

'So what's your earliest memory?'

Harry frowned. 'What is all this? What are you getting at?' Then a look of enlightenment passed over his face. 'Oh, I see! You think she might have kept me for a while?'

'Well, if you'd been given up for adoption as a baby, you wouldn't have this sort of birth certificate. You'd have an adopted one.'

'You think I was taken into care by social services?'

'Doesn't that seem likely?'

Harry nodded slowly. 'So what now?'

Libby put a hand over his. 'Would you like to see if she's still alive?'

'If I'd wanted to I would have done it before now.'

'No, you wouldn't. You weren't even bothered enough to look at this properly when you got it.'

Harry topped up his coffee mug, a stubborn look on his face. Libby took the pot from him and topped up her own.

'OK. You don't want to find her. But you said you'd let me look into your ancestors to keep me out of mischief, didn't you? I could just try and see if she's around, still. I wouldn't get in touch with her unless you said so, of course.'

Harry shrugged. 'All right. But you'll tell me if you do find her, won't you?'

'Of course. And you never know, it might be one of those stories where you were taken against her will.'

Harry closed his eyes. 'Lib, you can be bleedin' tactful. Now I'm going to worry about that.'

'Oh!' Libby's hand flew to her mouth. 'Oh, Hal, I'm sorry. I didn't think.'

'No. You often don't.' Harry pushed his mug aside. 'Sod it. I need more than coffee now. Want a drink?'

Libby looked at her watch. 'Isn't it a bit early?'

'Ten past twelve. No, it isn't. I'm going to have a beer. What about you?'

'Red wine, please,' said Libby guiltily. 'And I hope no one sees me.'

Harry threw back his head and laughed. 'If you had a reputation to ruin I'd understand that.'

After a glass of wine and a sandwich with Harry, Libby returned to Allhallow's Lane and rang Fran to report.

'So I'm going to look Jeanette up. You can do it free on a couple of those ancestry sites, can't you?

'What exactly are you going to look up?'

121

'Oh. I don't know. Death certificate?'

'She won't be that old. Her age is on the certificate, isn't it?'

Libby looked. 'No. Just her name – oh, and address. I could look that up on the census form, couldn't I?'

'You can try. I expect you'll try anything you can.'

'Well, of course. All I really want to know is why anyone would want to know anything about Harry. Why it looked as though he was being threatened.'

But before Libby could settle down with her laptop, there was washing to take out of the machine and hang up, and another load to put on. Sidney, recovered from the ignominy of travel in the cat basket, watched helpfully.

'That's the trouble with holidays,' Libby told him. 'There's so much washing at the end of them.'

With a cup of tea as a reward when she'd finished, Libby went back in to the sitting room and opened the laptop. However, looking for Jeanette Price wasn't going to be as easy as she'd hoped.

When she tried checking the census records she found that the earliest available was for 1911, which didn't seem likely to be of much use. So all Libby had was a name. And even that could have been false. No age, and the occupation section was given as unemployed.

'Now where do I go?' Libby asked aloud.

She realised she didn't even know where Harry had been taken, or, indeed, any of the names of the homes. He might tell her the name of the last one, but that, if it still existed, wouldn't give her any details. She rang his mobile.

'I'm stuck, Hal, so it looks as though I won't be able to find out anything after all. You might be able to get some info from the home you ran away from, but that's about it.'

There was a short silence. 'It was the Aviemore Home in Surrey. Well, outskirts of London, really.'

'So you do know. You gave me the impression you didn't. They wouldn't tell me anything, anyway, even if it's still there.'

There was another silence.

'Hal? What's the matter?'

Harry sighed. 'It's still there, all right. I donate to them every year.'

'Harry!' Libby screeched into the phone. 'Why on earth …?'

'Look, I've never got too close, and as far as they know, I'm just another benefactor. I felt I ought to try and help others who were like me.'

'Well, they know you. You could ask them.'

'They only know my cheques,' said Harry. 'I've never been there.'

'They must have your address, though? Don't they send you – oh, I don't know – an acknowledgement? Newsletters?'

'Yes,' said Harry, sounding amused. 'They know who and where I am.'

'But you don't want to know, do you?'

'Well, I must admit to being curious now, but only mildly.'

'Will you ask, then?'

'I'll think about it.'

'And you'll let me know?'

'Yes, Lib, I'll let you know.'

And with that, she had to be content.

The whole puzzle still intrigued her, though. And although the sisters had definitely been holding something back, Libby still wanted to know what had been going on in the late forties and early fifties on the Isle of Wight. She poured herself another cup of tea and tapped the Island into the search engine.

This time she went right through as much of the history as she could, including the fact that Charles the First had been imprisoned at Carisbrooke Castle, a fact she thought she already knew, up to the laying of PLUTO, the underground pipeline laid to take fuel to the troops after the D Day invasion, which she also vaguely knew about. Also during the war, she was surprised to find that Operation Sea Lion, the German plan to invade Britain, had plans to land at Ventnor from Le Havre. This, of course, had never happened, but it seemed quite logical to Libby. After all, the Island was right between England and

123

France, and, if captured, would have been an excellent base for a marauding army.

None of these interesting facts, however, would appear to have anything to do with Matthew, Celia, or Harry's grandmother, who, despite what the sisters said, Libby was still inclined to believe were the same person.

Ben came home with the news that they had been invited to dinner at the Manor.

'I think Mum was a bit lonely while we were away,' he said.

'She saw Flo and Lenny, though, surely?' Lenny was Hetty's brother and Flo her oldest friend.

'I expect so, but she's got used to having me around in the estate office almost every day, even though we hardly ever bump into each other. She just brings me the odd cup of coffee.'

Libby eyed him uneasily. 'You don't want us to move in there, do you?'

Ben laughed. 'No. You and Mum together in a kitchen I don't think I could take.'

'We've been together in a kitchen before now,' said Libby, somewhat huffily. 'We were together loads when we held that writers' thing.'

'And look how that turned out,' said Ben.

'That wasn't anything to do with Hetty and me, though,' said Libby.

After Ben's father's death, they had added en-suites to all the bedrooms and turned the Manor into a mini conference centre, which was just beginning to work when they held a writers' reunion weekend that unfortunately spawned an unpleasant murder. Since then they'd done very little with the Manor, although they occasionally put up visiting performers appearing at the theatre.

They took the back way to the Manor, to the end of Allhallow's Lane where it petered out into a track across Manor fields, past the restored hop-pickers' huts, down to the theatre, a converted Oast House, and finally to the Manor. Hetty was, as usual, in the kitchen.

'Pour yerself a drink, gal,' she told Libby. 'Ben, go and get a bottle of the good claret.'

Libby poured a gin and tonic for herself, and topped up the one standing at Hetty's elbow. 'Smells lovely.'

'Steak and kidney pud,' said Hetty. 'Now tell me all about this Island business.'

'Ben didn't tell you?'

Hetty looked at her scornfully. 'What do you think? Just said you got yerself mixed up in something.'

'Well, it wasn't quite like that,' said Libby, and explained. By the time she'd finished, the three of them were sitting at the kitchen table with the pudding in the middle.

'Well,' said Hetty. 'It do seem to me to be a lot like our little business.'

Libby shot an uncomfortable look at Ben.

Hetty began serving the pudding. 'After all, I fell fer our Susan in the war, didn't I? Could it be something like that?'

'Oh!' said Libby, surprised. 'I hadn't thought of that. For some reason we were all fixated on the fifties.'

'It's a possibility,' said Ben. 'That sort of thing happened in wartime.'

'But I kept our Susan,' said Hetty. 'Looks like this 'ere woman didn't.'

'I don't think she was allowed to,' said Ben.

'Different class,' sniffed Hetty. 'Like yer father's.'

Libby determined to put this theory to Fran in the morning, and possibly Harry too, but in this she was pre-empted by a call from the man himself, sounding, she had to admit, a little strange.

'Lib, it's me.' He cleared his throat.

'Yes, Hal? I was just going to call you.'

'Can you pop round instead? I've got something to show you.'

'OK – what is it?'

'I've had a letter from Matthew's solicitor.'

Chapter Seventeen

Libby made it to The Pink Geranium in record time, to find Harry in the same position as he had been yesterday, but this time with only a letter and his smart phone in front of him.

'Did it come here?' asked Libby, a trifle breathless after her dash down the high street.

'No, it went home. Pete left early to go up to town, but I texted him. He said – well, look.' Harry turned his phone round to show Libby a text.

"Do what you always do – call the old trout."

'Charming,' said Libby. 'So what's in this letter?'

'Matthew's left me some money.'

'That's brilliant, Hal! So why the long face?'

He handed over a sheet of paper. 'Letter from Matthew himself.'

Libby's mouth fell open and she picked up the letter.

"Dear Harry," it began, "I'm sorry you'll be reading this after I'm gone, and even sorrier I wasn't able to tell you anything before, but now my cousin Celia has died, I don't feel quite the same about keeping quiet.

"Your grandmother was raped, and it was, in those days, incredibly shaming for the girl and her family. I'm not sure things have changed much these days. However, she was sent away to the mainland to one of those ghastly mother and baby homes, and the baby, a boy, was adopted. It wasn't normal for the natural mother to be informed of the name of the adoptive family, but I managed it. We'd always been close, you see, and she managed to smuggle a letter out to me.

"So, between us, we kept track of the boy, who led a staid

127

and boring existence for years, until he met a young woman called Jeanette Price in the seventies."

'There she is,' said Libby, looking up. Harry was leaning back in his chair, his chin slumped onto his chest. He didn't react, so she went on reading.

"The outcome of this relationship was you, Harry. Your father was, quite frankly, horrified when Jeanette announced she was keeping the baby and wanted to get married. He reverted to his usual priggish, snobbish self and walked away. Jeanette had the baby and tried desperately to keep you, but she was alone and without money, although, because I knew about her (I was the most enterprising detective you've ever known) I gave her a little money when I could, but anonymously. Then one day, she caught me with the envelope just as I was going to put it through her letter box. She was in floods of tears because social services, or whatever they were called in nineteen eighty-three, had taken you into care."

Libby looked up again at Harry and decided not to say "I told you so".

"So I was able to keep track of you, you see. I suppose I should have stepped in and tried to adopt you myself, but they didn't like single males to adopt in those days, and particularly gay single males. If I had, you would naturally have learnt about your relations, and your grandmother was still, even after all those years, so haunted by shame she couldn't bear to meet you.

"She did, however, make provision for you in her will. She left this in my care, and I now pass it on to you. I have since learnt that your father has come back to the Island, I believe because he has found out about his parentage. He would have no reason to be here otherwise. I haven't seen him because since my illness and my cousin Celia's death I've been confined to bed. He has written to me, but the letter is gone, like Celia. I shall not tell you his name as it would serve no purpose, if he didn't want you when you were born, he is not fit to have such a son now. Your mother, however, would probably like to know that you are well, and, with this in mind, I have left her current name and address with my solicitor, who will act as an intermediary if you so wish.

"I wish I could have done more for you, Harry, but at least I've kept an eye on you, and lived to see you and Peter together. Do pay my respects to your friends at that lovely theatre, Peter, of course, and finally, to you, my boy, my love."

Libby felt her throat tighten and tears prickle under her eyelids. The silence around them lengthened until it was broken by a chirp from Harry's phone. He sat up and picked it up. Libby sat back in her chair and surreptitiously wiped her eyes.

'Text from Pete,' said Harry. 'Asking if I've told you and what have you said. What have you said?'

Libby shook her head. 'I don't know what to say. It doesn't actually tell you much more than you already knew, does it? Except that you can, if you like, get in touch with your mother. She might tell you more about your nasty father.'

'What it doesn't say is if Celia was my grandmother, despite what the old girls said.'

'It doesn't say she wasn't,' said Libby. 'And that letter. "Gone" he says, "like Celia". Is that why Celia went to the Beach House? In response to that letter? Was she meeting your father?'

Harry went white. 'My father killed Celia?'

'I'm sorry,' said Libby, feeling wretched.

Harry heaved a great sigh. 'Well, I suppose my grandfather raped my grandmother, whoever he was. Not specially good blood in the genes.'

'Oh, don't talk like that,' said Libby, standing up. 'Is the coffee on?'

Harry nodded, picked up Matthew's letter and folded it carefully. Libby came back to the table with the coffee mugs.

'So what are you going to do?' she asked. 'Are you going to accept the money?'

Harry looked up in surprise. 'Of course I bloody am! That family owe me.'

Libby looked doubtful. 'Well, your father does, but none of it's your gran's fault, whoever she was. And what about Jeanette?'

Harry's mouth twisted. 'You were right, weren't you, you old cow? She didn't want to give me up.'

'So will you ask to meet her?'

'I don't know. I think I'll write a letter to her and send it to the solicitor. He can either ask her if she wants it, or just send it to her straight away.'

'I wonder if she knows any more? Did she know your father's real name?'

'She might have done, but not who his real parents were. Matthew says he didn't know that himself until later.'

'Why would he kill Celia, though?' Libby said. 'If he wrote to Matthew asking if he had information and Celia went to meet him ...'

'To tell him Matthew didn't have any information? He could have bopped her in a temper.'

'What about the address book? Now we know Matthew kept tabs on everybody, perhaps ...' Libby frowned. 'No, I don't know where I was going with that.'

'What about the letter that the old girls sent to me? It could be my father – he said he wanted to know about the "young friend". Was he actually looking for me – his son?'

'If so, why write that note you found?'

'How do we know it was the same person?' Harry was looking more cheerful. 'That could have been kids.'

'I'd still like to know what it was those women were hiding,' said Libby. 'Was it that Celia was your grandmother?'

'But why would they hide that?'

'Because of the shame of the rape?'

'In this day and age?'

'They aren't of this age, though, Hal. They're pre-war vintage.'

Harry sighed. 'Spose so.' He picked up his phone. 'Better text Pete back.'

'And tell him the old cow is as bemused as you are.'

Shortly after this, Libby went home with Harry's permission to tell Fran all about it.

'Come down here,' Fran suggested. 'We can have tea at the Blue Anchor.'

'If I come now,' said Libby, looking at her watch, 'we can have lunch.'

After calling Ben to let him know where she was going, Libby managed to galvanise her old Romeo the Renault into action and drove down to Nethergate on the coast.

'We'll have lunch with Mavis at the Blue Anchor,' Fran told her as they strolled along Harbour Street, 'then one of Lizzie's ice creams on the way back.'

'Just like being back on holiday,' said Libby.

'Only I really prefer being here,' said Fran.

Outside the Blue Anchor, Bert, captain of the *Sparkler*, and George, captain of the *Dolphin*, sat under Mavis's cheap canvas gazebo, comfortably smoking and drinking tea, waiting for the tourists to finish their lunches and decide to take a boat trip round the bay. They waved to acknowledge Fran and Libby, as Mavis came out to take their order.

'Nice 'ere, innit?' said Libby, after Mavis had retreated to the fastness of her kitchen. In front of them, the *Sparkler* and the *Dolphin* bobbed quietly at anchor, with a few small sailing dinghies clustered round them. The sun on the wavelets made sequins on the sea, and, at the waterline, small children squealed and bounced. It was all very tranquil.

'So tell me all about this letter,' said Fran. 'What was in it?'

Libby recounted the contents of Matthew's letter and Harry's reactions.

'Any conclusions?' asked Fran, when she'd finished.

'Only that Jeanette Price is the only one with any answers.'

'And Alicia, Amelia, and Honoria,' amended Fran.

'Well, yes, them, but they aren't talking.'

'And Amanda Clipping,' said Fran.

'Really?' Libby's eyes opened wide.

131

'She was at Matthew's funeral with two unexplained guests. Her parents were around at the time of the grandmother's rape, and I sensed something when we met them in that pub garden, remember?'

Libby thought for a moment, then looked up to thank Mavis for the tuna salad she had plonked in front of her.

'You know Matthew says he's heard Harry's father has come back to the Island because he's discovered about his parentage and has written to him? Suppose he was the old boy in the wheelchair?'

Fran nodded. 'That occurred to me, too. We couldn't see much of him, and he could have been younger than he appeared.'

'How old would Harry's dad have been in the late seventies?'

'Late twenties, thirty? Depends when he was born, and we don't know that.'

'So around sixty now. The impression given by that wheelchair bloke was of someone at least eighty, but ...'

'Yes,' agreed Fran, 'impossible to tell.'

'So who was the younger one? And what were they doing with Amanda?'

'She could have been their guide to the Island. Perhaps it was just chance that he knew her and there was a link to Matthew and Granny. And the younger man could just have been Amanda's toy boy. That was certainly what Amelia thought!'

Libby sat bolt upright and choked on a piece of tuna.

'I've thought of something!' she gasped, wiping streaming eyes. 'Suppose it was Amanda's parents who adopted Harry's dad!'

'Good lord!' Fran stared at her. 'That makes sense. And would be how Matthew was able to keep an eye on everybody. They left the Island, and Alicia said they never came back.'

'And they live in Surrey!' said Libby.

'What does that have to do with anything?'

'That's where Harry's last home was. Coulsdon, I think.'

'I don't think that's relevant,' said Fran, 'except that it's all on the outskirts of London.'

'Do you think that's what the sisters were hiding?' asked Libby.

'If it was, I really don't see why,' said Fran, frowning.

Libby sighed. 'No, neither do I. Perishing women. I suppose we'll just have to wait until Harry finds out if his mother wants to meet him.'

'You do realise that you *are* still investigating, whatever you said on the Island.' Fran grinned across at her friend.

'We,' corrected Libby. '*We* are still investigating. Now come on, I want one of Lizzie's strawberry ice creams.'

Chapter Eighteen

Libby was frustrated. There was nothing she could possibly do to help with the search for Harry's parentage or to discover whether Celia had been murdered, and if so, by whom. In the past when mysteries had dropped into her lap or tripped her up, she had been able to keep following lines of enquiry, but this time she had nothing. Harry told her he had written a very difficult letter to Jeanette Price, with Peter's help, and sent it to Matthew's solicitor, who would forward it if he felt it was the right thing to do. So all he, and Libby, could do was wait.

Meanwhile, life went on. Libby painted a couple more small pictures for Guy's Nethergate shop, and attended rehearsals for The End Of The Pier Show. The first time they had done this it coincided with a murder investigation, and even involved a member of the company, but it hadn't put anyone off. It had been such a success the management company had asked them to repeat it. Libby and Peter had sourced more music hall and variety material, called in favours from everyone they knew, including their musical director, Susannah, and her drummer, David Fletcher, who, despite his memories of the previous year, decided he was happy enough to come back. He was, however, going to stay in Peel House with Jane and Terry Baker rather than the cottage he had hired last time. 'That really *does* have bad memories,' he told Libby on the phone.

Rehearsals were held at their own theatre, and Libby spent as much time as possible there, planning and drawing vague pictures of the sets she wanted. She was rummaging in the wardrobe store the following Friday when she heard her mobile ringing in the dressing room.

'Bother.' She disentangled herself from a pile of Victorian bathing costumes and made for the door, but of course the phone stopped ringing. Reaching it, she found a missed call from Harry and her heart missed a beat.

'What?' she said breathlessly when he answered.

'What *have* you been doing?' Harry asked, sounding amused.

'Sorting out costumes. What's happened? Have you heard from Jeanette?'

'No, sorry to disappoint you, but I have heard from the solicitor.'

'Really? What about?'

'You remember your mad idea to hold a memorial service?'

'Yes? Oh – no! Really?'

'Yes. A proper Fleet Street one. Or what was Fleet Street.'

'Not St Bride's!'

'St Bride's. Pete can't believe it. And we've been invited.'

Libby sat down at the dressing table. 'But who by? Who's organising it?'

'I don't know. I was so surprised I forgot to ask.'

'If it's St Bride's, it must be some of his newspaper pals, mustn't it? It's the Fleet Street church, after all. I didn't realise he was that well known.'

'Not by the general public,' said Harry, 'but in his world he was. And he still did what the old girls called "brain pieces".'

Libby laughed. 'I suppose they'll come, too? Might be awkward.'

'We only have to say hello, then you can avoid them.'

'Is it just you and Pete and Ben and me?'

'Yes, I'm afraid so, but Fran didn't know him, did she?'

'No, she won't mind.' Libby thought for a moment. 'You don't suppose Lucifer's behind it, do you?'

'Could be. In which case you'd better keep your eyes open.'

'I always do, but it would be pretty useless in this case,' said Libby. 'A St Bride's memorial service attracts plenty of well-known people – he could be anybody. And what about the person who wrote to the sisters? And left you the note?'

'He or she or they will probably be there too,' said Harry, 'but again, we don't know –'

'Unless it's someone we recognise from the Island,' Libby cut in.

'Well, that's not many, is it?'

'There's Amanda Clipping. Fran and I met her. Fran thought her parents might be your father's adoptive parents.'

'Lib, you can't expect everything to fit neatly into slots like a jigsaw.'

'They're more likely to go to this than the funeral, don't you think? London's nearer to Surrey – or do I mean the other way round?'

'Surrey practically is London,' said Harry. 'London postcodes and everything.'

'There you are then,' said Libby. 'So when is this service?'

'Next Thursday. How will you contain yourself?'

'Oh, you! Aren't you interested?'

'I've got over it a bit now. Pete and I have talked the whole situation into the ground, and yes, it might be nice to know a bit more, but it doesn't actually matter. I'm happy and settled, and now I've got a bit of money coming so I can upgrade the caff a bit.'

'Don't change it too much, Hal! It's perfect as it is.'

'Can't do much, can I? It's a terraced shop, after all. There isn't even room to extend the kitchen.'

'What about the flat? You could turn that into another dining room.'

Harry let out a whoop. 'The woman's a genius! Great idea. I'll tell Pete.'

'I aim to please. So we're going up Lunnon on Thursday, then. What time?'

'Service is at half past two. We'll sort out details nearer the time. OK?'

Libby locked up the theatre and went over to the Manor, where she found Ben in the estate office.

'So you'll be able to peer through your spyglass at the whole congregation and pick out the murderer,' said Ben.

'Oh, ha ha. Look if you don't want to go, I'll go with Harry and Pete. You didn't know him that well, did you?'

'I didn't think you did!'

'Better than you, anyhow.'

'No, I'll come, if only to keep an eye on you.' Ben got up from behind the desk. 'Come and get a coffee with Mum.'

Later, Libby called Fran.

'Sorry you aren't invited,' she finished.

'I'm not,' said Fran. 'It would be frankly ridiculous for me to go when I'd never met the man. But watch your back.'

'Eh?'

'I'm sure that it will have got out, on the Island at least, that you were snooping round –'

'We hardly snooped at all!' Libby broke in, indignantly.

'That nice man in Beech –'

'Bernie Small.'

'– will probably have told Amanda that her "friends" were looking for her. And what's the betting she went and asked the sisters about us?'

'Hmm,' said Libby. 'And no doubt told anyone else who might have been interested, like her parents.'

'Or old Lady – what was her name? Bligh. And the other people.'

'Duncans? Something like that. They were at the funeral, too. But why would she tell them all? And why would they be interested?'

'Dougans. Because they were all the same generation as Matthew and probably know whatever it is the sisters are hiding.'

'And you think a bunch of geriatrics are going to try and shut me up?' Libby laughed. 'I'd like to see it.'

'Libby,' said Fran, exasperated, 'just remember how many times you – and I, come to that – have been in quite – er – *dangerous* situations. It's not funny. And we are talking about suspected murder here, not just illegitimate children.'

'I know, I know. But it looks as though it's Harry whoever-it-is would like to find, not me. The service will give them another chance.'

'Then both of you will have to take special care.' Fran was sounding worried now. 'It'll be crowded. Don't be in the middle, and don't stay with the sisters, if they're there.'

'Well, of course they will be. And why not? Not that they're likely to want anything to do with us ... Oh. I see. That could be what identifies us.'

'Exactly. Will you talk to Harry about it?'

'Yes, Mum, I will. Promise.'

Harry was inclined to pooh-pooh the idea much as Libby had, but Peter took it seriously.

'Perhaps we shouldn't go after all,' he said after rehearsal that evening.

'The bloke's left me money,' said Harry. 'I can't not go.'

'It was your grandmother's money,' said Libby.

'He looked out for me all my life,' said Harry. 'Well, since I was sixteen, anyway. I don't know where I'd have ended up if it hadn't been for him.'

Susannah called across from the auditorium doors. 'I've got special leave as it's Friday. Coming to the pub?'

'Yes,' called Libby. 'Won't be long.' She turned to Harry. 'By the way, what are you doing here? Why aren't you in the caff?'

'We had an early party booking, and they'd all gone by nine, so I shut up shop. Come on, let's go and get drunk.'

Peter sighed and grinned at Libby. 'What shall we do with him?'

'Your problem,' said Libby, grinning back. 'I'm going to find mine.' She went up on to the stage and called for Ben, who appeared from the workshop wearing a fetching shade of blue paint. Libby sighed.

* * *

Libby, not known for her patience, spent the next few days in a

139

fever of anticipation.

'You'd think you were going to a special treat, not a memorial,' said Ben one evening.

'I know, I'm sorry. I'm the only one who seems to be – to be – well, I don't know, actually.'

'Is Fran still worried?'

'She warns me every time I speak to her. Has Pete said anything to you?'

'No, not much. I think he still doesn't want us to go.'

Libby frowned. 'Do you honestly think Hal could be in danger from someone?'

'Honestly – no. I mean, why? We've been through all this.'

'Suppose Lucifer's still alive and is jealous?'

'Oh, come on, Lib!' Ben laughed. 'Lucifer's probably Matthew's age! And Matthew's dead. Why would he be jealous?'

'Oh, OK, clasping at straws there.' Libby sighed. 'I insist that we stand right at the back of the church, though. Preferably with our backs to the wall.'

On Thursday, the four of them travelled up to London in the morning in time to have lunch before arriving at St Bride's church in Fleet Street.

'Let's wait,' said Libby, as they looked down towards the church door, crowded with people. 'Wait until they've all gone in.'

The other three looked at her, but although eyebrows were raised, no comment was made, although Harry made a great show of sighing and shuffling his feet. Finally, just as someone in vestments appeared at the door and looked round, Libby rushed them all forwards. They were smiled in and handed service sheets, and Libby, as she had wished, was able to stand right at the back.

'I'm sorry there are no seats left,' whispered the verger. 'Full house.'

The organ swelled and the choir processed in.

'Do you usually have a choir at these things?' whispered

140

Harry.

'I think you can have what you want,' whispered back Libby, just as the door creaked open behind them and another latecomer was ushered in.

They all looked. The woman looked at them and paled.

'Jeanette Price,' whispered Libby.

Chapter Nineteen

Harry, after one look, swallowed hard and faced the front. Throughout the service he didn't look at his mother once. Libby had been almost certain the woman would turn tail and flee, but she stayed exactly where she was. Libby wondered if her feet hurt. Hers certainly did, but at least she could lean against Ben.

Many people spoke about Matthew, some of them well known, some only known in their own industry. Libby stared at them all hard, trying to decide which one was Lucifer, if indeed any of them were. Or was he hiding in plain sight in the body of the congregation? Or, she reflected with resignation, he could be dead.

At the end of the service, Jeanette Price, if it was her, shot out of the doors before anyone else and Libby muttered under her breath. But, to her surprise, as they left the church, there she was, waiting. As Harry came level with her, she spoke.

'I knew you were coming. I got your letter. If you don't want to do this now, I'll go.' Her voice held a faint undertone of an accent, which Libby guessed had been ruthlessly expunged over the years.

Peter went to take Harry's arm, and Ben and Libby moved back out of the way of the rest of the congregation who were now surging out of the church, chatting and hugging.

'Several well-known faces,' murmured Ben. 'Look, there's Fay Scott.'

Libby craned to see the theatrical dame on the arm of a theatrical knight.

'Isn't that Andrew McColl?' she whispered.

'Yes – and there's George Fredericks.'

'Who?'

'The author, you ignoramus. The Inspector Carney series.'

'Oh, yes. I loved the TV series.'

Ben shook his head at her.

'There's the Clipping woman,' Libby whispered. 'I don't see either of the people who were with her on the Island.'

'The sisters have just come out,' said Ben, who at half a head taller than Libby could see further. 'Amelia's talking to two couples, their sort of generation I would say.'

Libby stood on tiptoe and craned her neck. 'The elder Clippings and the Dougans, perhaps,' she murmured. 'I wish we could ask.'

As they watched, Amanda Clipping went up to the group of older people and slipped her arm through that of one of the women.

'I was right,' muttered Libby, nudging Ben.

As they watched, the press of people between them cleared and Alicia and Amanda looked straight at Ben and Libby. Libby, about to wave, saw the horror that passed over Alicia's face and the speed with which Amanda marshalled the whole party down the path into Fleet Street.

'Well!' she said to Ben. 'What was that all about?'

'At least they didn't see Harry, or who he was talking to,' said Ben, turning back to where Harry and Peter were still talking to Jeanette. 'Perhaps we ought to go back there, now.'

As they approached another man appeared at Jeanette's side.

'Mr Price, I'm very pleased to meet you. I'm Ronald Deakin, Matthew's solicitor. I see you've met Mrs Landor.'

Ben and Libby stopped short of the group as Harry shook hands and introduced Peter. Then he turned and grinned at Libby.

'And these are our friends, Libby Sarjeant and Ben Wilde. They were friends of Matthew's, too.'

Libby and Ben shook hands all round, Libby in a fever of curiosity and impatience.

'I believe the people who organised this event are holding

144

some kind of reception back at their offices,' said Ronald Deakin. 'Will you be going?'

'No,' said Harry. 'I didn't know any of his work associates.'

Libby opened her mouth, then shut it again when the other two men agreed with Harry. Jeanette Landor also shook her head.

'I thought – we thought – that perhaps Jeanette would like to come and have a drink with us before we go and catch our train,' said Harry. 'Will you join us, Mr Deakin?'

'I'm afraid I can't,' said Deakin with a smile. 'Although I do need to talk to you fairly soon, Mr Price. About the will.'

'Of course,' said Harry. 'I'll ring you in the next couple of days and make an appointment.'

Libby marvelled at how composed and mature Harry sounded. Quite unlike his normal self.

Ronald Deakin took his leave and the other five looked at each other.

'This is my mum, Lib,' said Harry. 'Doesn't look old enough, does she?'

Libby saw Jeanette's face soften and saw him take a deep breath. 'Indeed you don't,' she said aloud. 'I suppose I expected you to be about my age, but you're so much younger.'

Jeanette gave a wobbly smile. 'It's very nice to meet you all.'

'I expect,' said Ben practically, 'you would prefer to talk to Harry alone, so why don't you two go and have a drink together, and Pete, Libby and I will meet you back at Victoria.'

Libby dug him in the ribs, but Ben took no notice.

'Actually, I'd like Pete to stay, if – er – Jeanette doesn't mind.'

She shook her head and smiled at Ben. 'Thank you,' she said.

Ben pulled Libby down into Fleet Street and marched her firmly towards the Strand.

'What did you do that for?' she complained. 'He won't know what questions to ask her.'

'Libby.' Ben stopped and turned her to face him, oblivious to the other pedestrians who muttered and surged around them. 'Hal has just come face to face with the mother who gave him up thirty-odd years ago. What he wants to know is personal to him, and to her. It is not part of an investigation.'

Libby blinked at him and felt her throat go tight. Without a word, she took his arm and began walking again. They didn't stop until they reached a favourite pub of Ben's off Drury Lane.

'I'm sorry,' said Libby, after Ben had ordered drinks. 'I wasn't thinking.'

He gave her a crooked smile. 'No, love, you weren't.'

Libby sighed. 'I've got so used to being important in Hal's life …'

'You still are,' said Ben. 'I doubt he's going to make Jeanette his favourite woman at this stage of his life. But they need to get to know a bit about each other to see if they want to get any closer. And I'm sure he'll remember to ask about his father.' He smiled and patted her hand. 'Don't worry about it.'

An exchange of text messages saw Peter and Harry meeting Ben and Libby in The Iron Duke at Victoria Station half an hour before the train back to Canterbury. Tucked into a corner table, Harry raised his glass to his friends.

'Thanks for being here,' he said. 'Couldn't have done it without you.'

'We didn't do anything,' said Libby.

'You came up to the service,' said Harry. 'And you were there on the Island.'

Libby looked at Ben and nodded. 'We were.'

'And now you want to know about Jeanette,' said Peter. 'It was thoughtful of you to leave us alone with her, Ben.'

Libby nudged Ben's leg with her own and saw him smile out of the corner of her eye.

'Well,' said Harry, 'there isn't much. She met my dad when he was working in London. She said he was very buttoned-up at first, but gradually he seemed to change into a different person, as though he was trying to make up for not having much fun in

146

his early life.'

'Were they working together?' asked Libby.

'In a way. She was a trainee in the company, only sixteen. When he began to take notice of her, she was – in her own words – dazzled. And after a works do of some sort – well …'

'So how old was he at that time?' asked Ben.

'She didn't know exactly, but quite a bit older than she was. She was still living with her mum and dad.'

'Difficult,' said Libby.

'Not really. He had a flat in London. He'd been commuting at first, but when he began to "break out" as she put it, he found this flat. Off Vauxhall Bridge Road, in fact,' said Harry, nodding in the direction of that road.

'One of the mansion blocks,' put in Peter, 'so not squalid.'

'And then, after a few months, she discovered she was pregnant,' continued Harry. 'He was horrified and kept saying it had only been a bit of fun. She told her parents, who supported her decision to keep the baby –'

'That was quite unusual thirty years ago,' said Libby.

'I suppose so. Anyway, she wanted to keep the baby and bring it up herself, but after a while it was too much for her and social services came and took it – me – away.'

'And where did Matthew come in?' asked Ben.

'He turned up out of the blue on her doorstep one day. She says she has no idea how he found her, because she'd moved from her parents' house, and from the company where she met my father. He said he knew the baby's – my – grandparents and they wanted to make some sort of contribution to my upkeep.'

'If that was so, why couldn't she keep you?' asked Libby.

'I'd already been taken away.'

'Couldn't she have got you back?' said Ben.

'Apparently it was very difficult, and maintaining she had an income from an anonymous donor would be highly suspicious.' Harry sighed. 'So that was that.'

'Well, at least you know his name now,' said Peter. He nodded at Libby.

'Really? So …?'

'Doesn't help. Keith Franklin.'

'So, he wasn't brought up by the Clippings when they went to live in Surrey,' said Libby.

'No. And Jeanette has no idea if he was formally adopted or not. In fact, she didn't know he was adopted until Matthew found her.'

'What about you, though? How did Matthew track you down?'

'She doesn't know. She told him where you'd gone – or at least the Social Services department who'd taken you, but that was all she knew.'

'So no nearer, then.' Peter drank the last of his wine.

'But Matthew kept in touch with her?' said Libby.

'Intermittently. And in the early days he helped her out with money. She says he was her fairy godfather, but she knew nothing about him.'

'We could try Keith Franklin on the birth certificate site,' said Peter. 'If we took an educated guess as to his birth year.'

'There's an application for access to birth records on the government site,' said Libby. 'If you were adopted. Harry wasn't, so it doesn't apply to him.'

'I could have done, though,' said Harry. 'Just didn't see the point. But I don't think you can do it for someone else.'

'Anyway, you'd have to know the adoption dates before you could look for the birth date,' said Peter, 'and we don't know either.'

'So frustrating,' said Libby, scowling into her drink.

'Look,' said Harry, 'I've met my mother, and I know now she didn't abandon me. I don't think I really want to know any more about my background. I've done my best to forget where I was when Matthew found me, and I'm happy. So shall we forget it?'

Everyone looked at Libby.

'Of course,' she said sensing relief all round. 'As long as you're allowed to forget it.'

'What?' Harry frowned.

'As long as whoever was watching you on the Island doesn't come after you again.'

'I can't see why they should,' said Peter.

'Did anyone see the expression on the sisters' faces back there?' asked Libby. 'Or the way the Clipping woman got everyone out of the way?'

'There's something still hidden,' said Ben, 'and it's worrying those people. But it really is their problem, not Harry's, or ours.'

Libby sighed. 'I know, and I'd just as soon not have to think about it. We've got an End Of The Pier show to work on.'

Harry leaned across the table and gave her a kiss.

'And if anyone does come after me, who's the first person I'd turn to?' he said.

Libby grinned. 'Chief Inspector Ian Connell, I expect!'

'Oh, yes, the dishy Inspector,' said Harry with an answering grin. 'But don't worry. This is the end of the matter as far as we're concerned.' He raised his glass. 'Cheers!'

As Libby raised her glass to respond, she couldn't help feeling a twinge of apprehension. Was it the end?

Chapter Twenty

Life once more settled back into its normal pattern in Steeple Martin and Nethergate. Harry went to see the solicitor, Ronald Deakin, about Matthew's will, and discovered that he had not only inherited some money, he was also now the proud owner of Ship House and the Beach House. The sisters, Matthew's cousins, had inherited The Shelf and the remainder of his estate.

'So what is Harry proposing to do about that?' asked Fran, as they lay in deck chairs on the beach at Nethergate, where they were supposed to be finalising details of the End Of The Pier Show.

'He says he'll settle some of the money on Jeanette, but he doesn't know what to do about the properties,' said Libby, squinting against the sparkle of the sun on the wavelets.

'Doesn't he think Matthew left them to him for a reason?'

'They used to stay at the Beach House together,' said Libby. 'Perhaps it was a sentimental reason.'

'In that letter, Matthew said he wouldn't tell Harry the name of his father, but we know it now. Would it be worth asking the sisters if they know him, now he's back on the Island?'

'I don't think Harry would like that,' said Libby. 'And for all we know he's left the Island again. He'd know by now there was nothing there for him. Harry's gran left money for him in her will, not her own son.'

'Does he know that, though? Might he not want to find out?'

Libby bent a searching look on her friend. 'What are you thinking? Are you having moments of insight again?'

'I just wondered if Keith Franklin might think the money should have come to him.'

Libby looked doubtful. 'Why would he? He was properly adopted, we've been told. No claim on his real parents at all. Granny only left Harry money because she knew through Matthew that Keith had abandoned him and his mother.'

Fran stared out at the sea. 'Hmm. There's still something odd, though.'

'Probably, but Hal wants to leave it, so we should, too.' Libby returned to the sheets of paper on her clipboard. 'Now, did we ask the Alexandria to have the glitter curtain up by Friday?'

'This isn't like you,' said Fran. 'You're usually only too happy to be nosing about.'

'But I don't want to upset my friend,' said Libby firmly. 'And he's been upset enough already.'

Fran shrugged, and struggled to her feet. 'Come on, then. Let's go back and have a cup of tea before we take all this to the theatre.'

Balzac, Fran's black and white long-haired cat, leapt straight into Libby's lap as she sat down in the window, butting her chin with his head and purring loudly.

'I wish Sidney was as friendly as Balzac,' said Libby.

'He wouldn't be Sidney if he was friendly,' said Fran, bringing mugs in from the kitchen. 'And I still can't believe Balzac is as friendly as he is, given how long he was left on his own.'

'Oh, don't,' said Libby with a shudder.

Fran spread the papers from their clipboards out over the table. 'What have we got to take up there, then?'

'The proofs of the programme, the publicity shots and the lighting plot,' said Libby.

'And the music,' said Fran. 'For the rest of the orchestra.'

'I can't believe they're paying musicians for us,' said Libby. 'Bass, trumpet, and saxophone. Going to sound brilliant.'

'Are they paying Susannah and David?' asked Fran.

Libby shook her head. 'No, we are. I had to, as the others are being paid, but they're part of our company, not The

Alexandria's.'

'Well, drink up, and let's get this stuff down to them. I promised Guy I'd go and help him change the stock around after closing today.'

Libby discharged Balzac onto the window seat beside her, finished her tea, and began to collect up the documents.

Her mobile rang.

'Lib.'

'Harry? What's up?' Libby's eyes met Fran's.

'I – er –' she heard him clear his throat. 'I've had a letter.'

'A letter? Yes?'

'An anonymous letter.'

'Oh, Harry! Have you called the police?'

'Sounds so pathetic.'

'Remember what we said the other day in London? You'd call Ian?'

'I didn't – you did.'

'Well, do it. Now. Or shall I do it for you?'

'Um.'

'Or Fran? She'll do it, if you like?'

Harry sighed. 'No, I'll do it. Has he got a private line at the station?'

'Yes – hang on, I'll give it to you.' Libby looked at her phone wondering how to find a number while she was still on a call, but Fran silently held out her own, showing both Ian's private numbers. Libby read them out.

'OK,' said Harry. 'I'll try now. Where are you?'

'Nethergate. Just going to the Alexandria. I'll call as soon as I get back.'

'OK.' Harry sounded gloomy as he ended the call.

'Why didn't you ask him what it said?' asked Fran as they left Coastguard Cottage.

'It was obviously not a good letter, and he'll tell me when I get home. I'll ring you, of course.'

'He might not want you to.'

'Of course he will. It's got to be about this whole Island

153

business, and you've been involved with most of it. We'll find out soon enough.'

In fact, they found out sooner than Libby had hoped, as her mobile rang again while they were in the manager's office at the Alexandria.

'I'm so sorry,' she said to the manager, after glancing down to see who was calling, 'but I'd better take this.' She moved away from the desk. 'Chief Inspector Connell. How can help you?'

Ignoring the manager's surprise and Fran's frustration, she moved out of the office.

'Where are you?' asked Ian. Libby explained. 'Your friend Harry's just called me. He said you knew all about this situation. He sounded a bit confused to me.'

'I don't know what's in this letter,' said Libby, 'but I do think, whatever it is, you should take it seriously if it's a threat.'

Ian sighed. 'How the bloody hell do you keep getting yourself mixed up in these situations?'

Libby was indignant. 'It's not my fault! I don't go looking for these situations. They just land on me.'

Ian sighed again. 'I want to talk to Harry, and I'd like you to be there.'

'Do you want us to come in to the station?'

'No. It's Wednesday today, isn't it? Do you still go to the pub after rehearsal?'

'Yes,' said Libby in surprise, 'but you can't do a formal interview in the pub.'

'This won't be formal. I've got to assess the seriousness of the situation before I do anything else. Harry said this started when you were all on the Isle of Wight. Does that mean all your little clan?'

'Yes.'

'And will they all be there tonight?'

'All except Guy. He's not involved with the show.'

'What about your lady vicar?'

'I expect she'll be there.'

'Does she know all about this?'

'Only a bit. We told her about going to the memorial service last Wednesday, and she knew we'd been to the funeral on the Island.'

'Will Harry talk about it in front of her?'

'I don't know. I'll ask when I get home.'

'All right. Ring me.' And Ian ended the call.

Going back into the office, Libby apologised to the curious manager, answered a few more questions and left, a simmering Fran behind her.

'What did he want?' she burst out, as soon as they were outside. Libby told her.

'Guy will come with me whether he's finished his stock or not,' said Fran when Libby had finished. 'He actually had some ideas while we were over there, didn't he?'

'And there's the notebook,' agreed Libby. 'He knew more than we did about getting that rescued.'

'Go on, then. Get back to the village and talk to Hal, then I'll see you at rehearsal. If you need to talk to me first, ring me.'

'Of course.' Libby leant forward and kissed her friend's cheek. 'Couldn't do it without you.'

Libby pulled in to the side of Steeple Martin high street outside The Pink Geranium. Peering inside she could just make out Harry at the back of the restaurant. She switched off the engine and got out of the car. Harry was at the door before she reached it.

'Do you want tea?' he asked, leading her to a back table.

'Just had some at Fran's,' said Libby. 'Ian called me, by the way.'

'Why?' Harry frowned. 'Didn't he believe me?'

'Oh, yes,' soothed Libby. 'He's coming to the pub tonight to talk to us all about what we remember on the Island. He wants to assess the situation before deciding on a course of action.'

Harry's eyebrows rose in surprise. 'Taking it seriously, then?'

'Seems to be. What does the letter say?'

155

Harry pushed a piece of paper towards her using the edge of a knife. 'Ian said don't handle it any more than you have to.'

Libby tucked her hands under her thighs and began to read.

"Harry Price, you must keep quiet. Do not interfere where you are not welcome or there will be serious reprisals."

'Is that it?' Libby looked up. Harry nodded. 'What did it come in? When?'

'A brown envelope. I kept it.'

'Postmarked?'

'By hand.'

'Oh – golly!' Libby's hand flew to her mouth. 'So he's here?'

'Or she.' Harry nodded.

'And what do they mean? Keep quiet?'

'I guess that anything we found out while we were over there we mustn't talk about. Not that we found out much.'

'No.

Libby sounded thoughtful. 'What we didn't find out was who, if anyone, had murdered Celia.'

Harry heaved a sigh. 'Honestly, they *are* batty. How did they think you could do that?'

'I've no idea. But there's something in their – or Celia's – past that they don't want to come out. And when you think about it, that's the most likely reason she was left to drown. If she was.'

'And is it connected to Granny and her rape?'

'Well, don't forget your father came back to the Island and wanted to meet Matthew. Are we assuming now that it was him Celia went to meet?'

'In which case he's a murderer.' Harry shuddered. 'Oh, bugger. I really didn't want to have to think about this again.'

'I know.' Libby patted his hand. 'But I'll tell you something – I'm much happier now Ian's involved.'

'Will he be able to stay involved? Won't the Island force take over?'

'You've received that letter here. His stamping ground, not

theirs. I expect they'll work together, don't you?'

'If they work at it at all, and don't say it's all some gay bloke's imagination.'

Libby gave him a reproving glare. 'You know Ian better than that.'

Harry gave her a wobbly smile. 'I hope so. Thanks, Lib. I'm glad we'll all be together tonight.'

'By the way, Ian asked if Patti and Anne would be there. We can adjourn to my place if you don't want to talk in front of them.'

'Actually, how about you lot and Ian come to the restaurant. I'll explain to Anne and Patti none of us are going to the pub. You can tell 'em afterwards if you like. I expect they'll go straight back to Anne's.'

'Good idea,' said Libby. 'Will you call Ian, or shall I?'

'I'll do it,' said Harry bravely. 'And I'll see you here just after ten.'

Chapter Twenty-one

It was a solemn-faced group of people who met at The Pink Geranium at a quarter past ten that evening. Patti and Anne had accepted the change to routine and, as predicted, gone back to Anne's house, and Harry had made sure all the other diners had been out of the building before ten. By the time the theatre group arrived, Detective Chief Inspector Ian Connell was already at the big table in the window, and Harry was setting out glasses.

'I've got the coffee on,' he said as they came in. 'Who wants what to drink?'

When they were settled with their choice of beverages, Ian asked Harry to begin.

'Where, though?' asked Harry, looking round at the others. 'Back when I was a child?'

Ian looked startled.

'No,' said Libby. 'We can fill in the background as and when. Just start with the letter from the old ladies.'

So Harry began his tale. Between them, they told Ian about events on the Island in chronological order, backtracking into explanatory side-notes if required. Ian took notes and looked thoughtful.

'So,' he said finally, when Harry had shown him the note and the envelope. 'Someone thinks you have information that is damaging at best, or dangerous at worst.'

The rest of the group looked at each other.

'That's about what it comes down to,' said Peter.

'And given the reaction to your – investigations – on the Island by the Misses DeLaxley –' he glanced at his notes, 'they would seem to have the best motive.'

'I know.' Fran frowned. 'Their whole attitude was completely irrational. One minute wanting to know who killed their sister, the next refusing to tell us anything about the background.'

'And they were scared,' said Libby, and went on to describe the moment she and Alicia had locked eyes at the memorial service. 'Oh, and they aren't DeLaxleys any more. They all married.'

'What are their surnames?' asked Ian, pen poised.

'I don't know.' Libby looked at Harry. 'Do you?'

'No.' He looked surprised. 'When they forwarded the first letter, it was signed "Alicia, Amelia, and Honoria, Matthew's cousins". Nothing else.'

'They were DeLaxleys by birth, though?'

'I suppose so,' said Harry.

'I'll look up the report of the other sister's death,' said Ian. 'It'll be a starting point. And Matthew's obituary in the local paper.' He looked round at them all and poured more coffee. 'It has occurred to you that the reason they wanted to find out who killed Celia – if she *was* killed – is probably because of whatever they're scared of.'

'Because it might have got out, you mean?' said Ben.

'Yes, it had,' said Libby. 'And I think all the people we've come into contact with know about whatever it was – or is. The Clippings, and Lady Bligh – although we've never met her – and the Dougans. We've never met them, either.'

'They were at Matthew's funeral,' said Peter, 'even if we didn't meet them. Don't forget we're sure it was someone there who then knew who Harry was and left the note at Ship House.'

'I still don't understand,' said Guy, 'why Harry is such a threat.'

'Because obviously someone thinks he knows more than he does,' said Ben.

'Except that I don't know anything at all,' said Harry, thumping the table with a large fist.

'You know the names of your parents,' said Ian, 'and you know that your father was adopted, being the result of a rape.'

'Can you follow that up?' asked Libby hopefully. 'You must have better resources than we have.'

'Only if I'm investigating an actual crime,' said Ian. 'I don't know yet whether I am.'

'What about the Malicious Communications Act?' asked Peter. 'That covers indecent, offensive, and threatening letters, doesn't it?'

'It does. What I meant was, I don't know if I shall be allowed to act. I shall ask the top brass and see what happens. Meanwhile –' he took an evidence bag from his pocket and carefully slid the letter and envelope inside using tweezers. 'We'll get these finger-printed, but I doubt there'll be any. And the envelope, as you saw, was a self-sealer.'

'It's quite mad,' said Harry. 'There I was, leading a perfectly happy and normal life, and suddenly I'm in the centre of some bad third-rate melodrama.'

Ian looked amused. 'You should be used to that. You've known Libby long enough.'

The mood was broken and everyone laughed, including Libby.

'Tell me how you enjoyed the Isle of Wight apart from the melodrama,' said Ian, leaning back in his chair with his mug of coffee. 'I used to go there regularly.'

'Did you?' Libby leant forward eagerly. None of them knew anything about Ian's past, except that he obviously had Scottish ancestry, even Fran, whom he had briefly dated.

'With my parents,' he elaborated, giving her a look that said he knew what she was up to.

They described their impressions of the Island and Harry finished up by surprising everyone and saying, 'Well, if probate comes through and I really do own Ship House, you can go over and stay there, Ian.'

Ian looked as surprised as everyone else felt. 'I'd love that, thank you, Harry.'

Libby opened her mouth and was silenced by Ben's well-aimed foot.

'There's no doubt that you own it, surely?' said Guy.

'No, but Mr Deakin has to wait for probate. It's only a few weeks since Matthew died.'

'And you don't think the bequest is a cause for someone to send anonymous letters?' asked Ian.

'Well, we did sort of wonder ...' said Libby.

'But who would?' asked Ben.

'His cousins are the obvious people,' said Ian. 'They might resent the fact that Harry's walked in and taken over what they've always thought of as theirs.'

'Hang on,' Libby tapped the table with a spoon. 'Ian's just made the same mistake as the writer of that first letter did. He said the Misses DeLaxley.'

They all looked at her, and Harry tipped his chair forward with a bang.

'Of course! They were cousins on his mother's side – they weren't DeLaxleys at all!'

'So, no claim on the estate, then?' said Ian.

'There was something about them all growing up at Overcliffe Castle,' said Fran.

'Probably staying in the holidays, something like that,' said Guy.

Ian sighed. 'It's complex, isn't it? But when wasn't it, when you lot are mixed up in something?'

There was a chorus of indignation, but Libby and Fran both saw the twinkle in Ian's dark eyes. He stood up.

'Now I'm going to go home and get some sleep before I tackle the powers that be about investigating any further. Harry, I'll be in touch.' He laid a hand on Harry's shoulder and was gone.

'He'll do his best, Hal,' Fran said into the silence that followed his departure. 'He always does.'

Harry nodded, and Libby saw Peter grip his hand under the table.

'He didn't say anything about who might have put that letter through the letter box,' said Guy.

'No, but he's having it finger-printed,' said Peter.

'That won't help if the writer's not a criminal,' said Libby. 'No fingerprints or DNA on record.'

'So whoever it is could still be in Steeple Martin – even know we've been visited by the police tonight?' said Harry, eyes widening. 'Reprisals, here we come!'

'That would be a bit too obvious, wouldn't it?' said Fran.

'I won't go an inch from his side,' said Peter. 'I shall be a human – er – bodyguard.'

'But, seriously,' said Libby later, as she and Ben walked home, 'the only way whoever this is could stop Harry inheriting or finding out about this secret, is to … to …'

'To harm him.' Ben gave her arm a squeeze. 'I know. Don't think about it. Peter's right there with him, and, if I know Pete, he'll be a human limpet until this is sorted out.'

To Libby's annoyance, Ian didn't get in touch with Harry over the next few days, and, luckily, neither did anyone else. The weather was getting warmer, and the school holidays were getting nearer. Libby took the chance to spend as much time on the beach at Nethergate as she could before it became overrun with holiday-makers, spending far too much on Lizzie's ice creams and Mavis's lunches. Occasionally she took her materials with her and did a little desultory painting, sometimes borrowing the top room at Peel House, Jane and Terry Baker's home, with its commanding view of the bay. She tried a few new positions, the most ambitious of which was on Dragon Island itself, when George took her out on the *Dolphin* and Bert picked her up an hour later on the *Sparkler*. This gave her a new view of Nethergate Bay, which, although she'd seen it from the boats before, appeared quite different when stationary.

It was on the Monday following Ian's visit that Harry called.

'I've just heard from Alicia,' he said.

'Did she ring you?'

'No, it's a letter. Want to see?'

'Yes. Shall I come round?'

'No, I'll come to you. It's Monday – I'm closed.'

'Where's Peter?'

Harry chuckled. 'I'll unzip him before I come round. He's been stuck like a fly to flypaper since last week.'

Libby put on proper coffee, and went to unearth biscuits. Luckily, Nella from the garden centre made wonderful home-made ginger biscuits, to which Ben was addicted, so there were always plenty of those.

Harry arrived and they took their coffee into the garden to sit under the cherry tree. Harry took a letter from his pocket and handed it over.

'Wouldn't you rather tell me what it says,' said Libby, before opening it.

'Much easier if you read it yourself.' Harry helped himself to a biscuit.

"Dear Harry," the letter began. "We, my sisters and I, have heard from Mr Deakin, the solicitor, that you are now sole owner of Ship House and the Beach House. As we have been keeping the keys here, shall we send them to you? I'm afraid we have let Ship House for a couple of weeks in August, but we will send the rental money on to you, if you tell us where.

"We saw you at Matthew's memorial, and I would like you to apologise to dear Libby. I am so very sorry we caused you all so much trouble when you came to the Island. I can only say we were not thinking very clearly, and were deeply upset by both Celia's and Matthew's deaths. We understand now, of course, that without knowing the background of any event, it is not possible to find out the truth.

"I hope, that now you are the owner of Ship House, we see you on the Island again at some time in the future.

"Very best wishes

"Alicia Hope-Fenwick."

Libby looked up. 'Well, that tells you precisely nothing.'

'Except her surname,' said Harry. 'I called Ian this morning and told him that. Well, left a message, anyway.'

'Apologise to me?' Libby ruminated over the letter. 'What for? Lying? Looking horrified when she saw me at the memorial?'

'That, yes. And just a blanket apology, I think. For messing you about.'

'Well, you did a bit of that, too, remember,' said Libby.

'All right, all right. I've already said I'm sorry.'

Libby shrugged. 'Doesn't matter now. So what do you think Alicia wants you to do? It doesn't sound as though they're bothered about you getting Ship House, or the Beach House.'

'No, but they've got the keys.' Harry looked up. 'Do you think they'll go and strip everything before I get there?'

'Not if they've let it for August.'

'No, but the Beach House. They know we found the address book there. They might think there's something else there to find.'

'They could have done that at any time.'

'Well, they hadn't when we got there, had they?'

'It hadn't occurred to them,' said Libby.

'But it has now,' said Harry. 'I think I'd better get out there, fast.'

Chapter Twenty-two

Libby's mouth dropped open.

'But you said …'

'I know what I said before,' said Harry impatiently. 'I now own property on the Island. I've got a responsibility. And I don't want those women confusing the issue.'

'Confusing …? How do you mean?'

'What I said. They'll go through both properties now like they never have before. They were content to leave you to do it, because they thought you could find something better than they could and they needn't tell you anything they didn't want to. They didn't realise what a serpents' nest they'd stir up, and now they want to protect whatever it is.'

'Yes,' said Libby doubtfully, 'but Alicia appears to be quite honest and up-front in this letter.'

'To lull me,' said Harry triumphantly. 'That's what that is.' He sat forward and peered at Libby. 'Are you coming with me?'

Libby stared nervously at this new fierce Harry. She'd seen him up in arms over the plight of friends in the past, but this was a new side of him.

'I don't know how either of us could,' she said. 'You can't very well close the caff again, not so close to the summer holidays, and I don't like to leave Ben –'

'Oh, come on, Lib! He coped on his own before he moved in with you. And I can leave the caff in the staff's hands for once. Donna will come in and crack the whip if necessary.'

'Donna? What about the baby?'

'She can sort that out.' Harry was impatient again. 'Don't

make difficulties. If you won't come with me, you can run the bloody caff.'

Libby looked horrified. 'If that's a choice – it's Hobson's,' she said. 'And what about Pete?'

'He worries too much. We work well together.'

'*We* do?'

'Course we do.' Harry grinned at her. 'My favourite old trout.'

'We – ell,' said Libby, 'you ask Pete and I'll ask Ben. We owe them both consideration, at least.'

Harry fished his mobile from his pocket. 'Ring them now.'

But Libby was adamant. 'No. I shall talk to Ben in person. And I think you should do the same.'

'Oh, all right.' Harry stood up. 'When will you talk to Ben?'

Libby sighed. 'I'll pop up to the Manor and see him now.'

'Good.' Harry kissed her on the cheek. 'I'll let you know what's been arranged.'

Libby watched him go back down Allhallow's Lane, then turned up it with another sigh, to make her way across the fields to the Manor.

'I can't say I'm surprised,' said Ben, after she'd sat in the estate office and told him about the letter and Harry's determination to drop everything and go back to the Island. 'And I don't blame him. Do you want to go?'

'I don't know. I don't really, but I don't think I can let him down. I wish he'd take Peter.'

At the moment the phone on Ben's desk rang.

'Yes, Pete. Yes, Libby's here, she just told me. What do you think?'

Ben listened, his eyes on Libby. When they widened, she opened her mouth, but he shook his head.

'Why doesn't he want you to go?' he said. 'Nannying? Good God. And Libby wouldn't?'

He listened again, then turned from the handset. 'Pete suggests we all go again. What do you think?'

'Overkill?' said Libby doubtfully. 'What about the caff?

And will your mum take Sidney again?'

'Did you hear that, Pete? Yes, OK. We'll wait to hear from you.'

Ben switched off the phone. 'Let's go and talk to Hetty. Pete's threatening Harry with all sorts of recriminations if he goes without him. I do hope it doesn't upset their relationship permanently.'

Libby trailed behind Ben as he made for the kitchen, wondering exactly the same thing.

Hetty was only too pleased to have Sidney again, and Libby was sure Sidney, too, would be pleased. Peter called while they were still drinking coffee in the Manor kitchen, saying that Harry had been persuaded to let them all go with him, and had called Ronald Deakin, who told him there was no problem with Harry staying at Ship House and asked if he should warn the sisters of his impending arrival. Harry had given a firm no to this, fudging the issue slightly by saying he would be in touch himself. Which he would. In person.

'There are ferry crossings every half an hour up until about ten o'clock, so which should we aim for?' Ben asked.

Peter obviously answered, so Ben ended the call and told Hetty and Libby they were aiming for the five thirty or six o'clock ferry from Portsmouth. Libby sighed and stood up. 'Better get packing, then.'

By two thirty they were on the road, once more in Ben's car.

'What's the plan, then, Hal?' asked Ben, filtering into the A2 traffic.

'I though we could pick up a take-away on the way,' said Harry. 'I don't want to go out again after we've arrived.'

'They aren't likely to creep down after dark, surely,' said Libby. 'They're old ladies.'

'We can eat on the ferry,' said Peter.

'Only sandwiches,' said Libby.

'Let's pre-order an Indian to pick up as we drive through Ventnor,' said Ben.

'How do we do that? We haven't got any menus or

anything,' said Libby.

The three men groaned.

'What?' Libby turned round to look at Peter and Harry in the back. Harry was grinning at her, while Peter tapped away at his phone.

'Oh,' said Libby. 'Is there an app for it?'

Curry duly ordered, they spent the rest of the drive to Portsmouth assiduously avoiding the reason for their journey, but speculating on what they could all do on the Island with the free run of Ship House.

'I shan't let it out,' said Harry. 'I shall keep it just for us. And if any other friends want to use it.'

Libby and Ben exchanged smiles.

'Don't let Fran's girls know. They'll be demanding free holidays all year round,' said Libby. Fran's daughters, Lucy and Chrissie, both felt they had a claim on Fran's life, and, since she had inherited money, that, too. Her son Jeremy lived in America and was no problem at all, but Fran fought a constant battle with guilt over her girls, whom she claimed to have neglected during their formative years while pursuing her career as an actor. Libby understood this, having done the same, but she had given up on the stage a long time before Fran did. Now she helped manage a delightful small theatre and was able to pick and choose parts she'd never have played in the professional world.

'Do you think Hetty would like it?' asked Peter.

'Ship House or the Island?' said Ben. 'I'm not sure. She's hardly been away from Steeple Martin since she first married Greg. London a few times in the early years, because she still had family there.'

Ben's mother had first gone to Steeple Martin as a hop-picker with her mother, Lillian, and younger sister Millie, Peter's mother. Flo Carpenter had also been a regular, and eventually after the war all of them had moved there permanently.

'We can ask her, but I think she'd rather stay at home,' said

Libby. 'I, on the other hand, would have loved to have the run of the place.'

'Would have?' said Harry.

'Well, you said yourself ...'

'So did I,' said Peter, 'but once this is all cleared up, and it will be, everything will be fine.'

A phone call when they arrived at Fishbourne ensured that their curry was ready to be picked up in Ventnor, before driving the short distance to Overcliffe, which was accomplished in silence.

'Now,' said Harry, when Ben had parked the car and switched off the engine. 'It's still daylight, so they can see us coming.'

'Only if they're on this side of the building, and the main rooms are the other side,' said Libby.

'We'll stay here and you go and knock. No need to overwhelm them,' said Ben.

Harry got out of the car, stood with his hand on the door for a moment, then, with a determined look on his face, strode round the corner to the front door of the sisters' house. The other three craned to see.

After a minute, Harry stepped back and they could see Alicia's bewildered face staring at him. She began to shake her head and Libby was out of the car like a shot.

'Hello, Mrs Hope-Fenwick,' she said. 'Aren't we lucky? Harry's brought us over to his new home for a few days.'

Alicia's horrified gaze took in Libby, Ben, and Peter, as they all ranged themselves beside Harry.

'Mr Deakin said it's perfectly all right,' said Harry. 'Just waiting for the final documentation to come to me, now. So perhaps I could have the keys?'

Honoria and Amelia appeared behind Alicia's shoulders.

'No,' growled Honoria.

'I'm afraid,' said Ben pleasantly, 'that it isn't in your power to refuse.' He got out his phone. 'Perhaps I should call Mr Deakin again –'

'No, no,' said Alicia hastily. 'Amelia, dear, get the keys.'

Amelia frowned at her sister. 'Where are they?'

'In – in the usual place,' said Alicia.

'We'll come in while you find them, shall we?' beamed Libby, and virtually pushed her way into the house. Harry attached himself to Amelia and Ben and Peter flanked Honoria, who was looking even more like an enraged bulldog. Chewing on a wasp, thought Libby.

'What do you think you're doing?' snapped Amelia, as they all came to a halt in the kitchen.

'Waiting for the keys to Ship House, and whatever is left of the Beach House,' said Harry.

'*All* the keys,' added Libby.

'Yes,' said Peter. 'We know there are more sets than one, we had three. So all of them, please.'

For a long moment it looked as if there would be a stand-off, until Alicia crumpled into a chair at the kitchen table.

'They're on that hook.' She waved towards a large dresser. Honoria went to grab the large bunch of keys that hung there, but Peter was too quick for her.

'Four sets,' he said, 'and one large brass key.'

'The Beach House,' said Harry, taking it. 'There were two.'

'Celia took the other one, the day she ...' Alicia's voice trailed off.

Libby sat down beside her. 'Now, what was all that about?' she asked. 'Why didn't you want Harry to have what's rightfully his?'

Alicia rallied. Her sisters remained silent.

'I offered to send him the keys. Ask him.'

'I know. And how many sets would you have sent?' Libby looked at all three sisters and saw their faces change according to their personalities. Alicia's became pale, Amelia's red, and Honoria's practically purple.

'Presumably,' said Peter, assuming his most noble and arrogant stance and tone, 'you wished to search the property thoroughly before Harry took possession. And since we found something in the Beach House, you wished to have another look there, in case we missed something. So what is so important?'

The sisters remained silent.

Harry took the keys from Peter and left the room. 'No doubt we'll see you in the morning,' he said over his shoulder.

Peter, Ben and Libby followed him out. They collected their bags from the car and began to make their way down the path, their progress followed by three pairs of eyes behind a window.

'Well,' said Libby, as Harry let them into Ship House. 'That was illuminating.'

'Almost as if they were covering up a murder,' said Peter, taken the curry bags into the kitchen.

'I wonder if that's it,' said Harry, throwing his and Peter's bags into the room they'd occupied so recently. 'Huh – they haven't even changed the beds.'

'If what's it?' asked Ben.

'If they're covering up for a murder. A murder that happened when they were all suddenly away from the Island?'

Chapter Twenty-three

Peter reappeared with plates and they all stood looking at Harry.

'Well, you must admit, it would fit the facts,' he said, taking the plates from Peter and distributing them round the table. 'Whatever this secret is, it's a bad one. And they don't get worse than murder.'

'But murder of who?' said Libby.

Ben went to fetch the foil dishes and Peter put out table mats.

'The man who got Granny in the family way?' suggested Harry. 'That's the most likely, isn't it?'

'Bloody hell,' said Peter. 'It makes sense.'

'It almost does,' said Libby frowning, 'but then we come up against the person who killed Celia and who wrote to the sisters about you, Hal.'

'If they're the same person,' said Ben.

'They must be,' said Libby. 'And that was what they wanted to find out, wasn't it?'

'Who killed Celia?' said Ben.

'And who knew the secret. That's what they were trying to find out, not just Celia's killer.'

Harry was ladling chicken dhansak on top of pilau rice. 'It all makes sense except for my anonymous letters.'

'Yes.' Libby was frowning again. 'I can't see where that fits in.'

'Someone thinks Hal holds the key to the secret?' suggested Peter, fastidiously wiping his fingers after tearing off a piece of puree.

'It was a good job you did insist on coming over.' Peter

patted Hal's arm. 'They could have stripped the place.'

'They certainly weren't going to give up without a fight,' said Libby. 'I wonder what they'll do next.'

'Come down and say some of their stuff is here and could they fetch it, I expect,' said Ben.

'That's easy,' said Libby. 'There's an inventory for renters, so if we go through that we'll soon find out if anything doesn't belong.'

'But that also means that there can't be anything here that Matthew needed to keep secret,' said Peter.

'There are always locked spaces in holiday lets,' said Libby. 'I know, I've been in loads. Whole rooms, sometimes.'

'And that's where the sisters will say their belongings are,' said Peter. 'We'll have to check all the keys, see if there is a locked drawer or cupboard.'

'But,' said Ben, 'Matthew knew the sisters were in and out of here. He couldn't be sure they wouldn't see it.'

'No, but it wouldn't matter. That's why they must be so sure there *is* something. They all knew this secret. It's the possibility of it becoming known that is worrying them so much.' Libby turned her attention to her jalfrezi.

'What I can't make out,' said Harry, 'is when they wanted you to find out who killed Celia, why they thought if you did, the murderer would keep quiet about his reason.'

'And where you come into it,' said Libby. 'Still complicated, isn't it?'

Libby was up early the following morning, and out on the deck with her tea to watch the sun rise over the sea, when she noticed a movement on the path down the cliff. Keeping still, she watched as a figure moved down on to the beach and slowly towards Candle Cove.

Honoria. It had to be. The figure was too tall and bulky to be either of the other sisters, and, besides, Libby could not imagine either of them creeping around a ruined building in the dawn. She wondered whether to wake Harry, and as she did, so Ben appeared by her side.

'What is it?' he whispered. Libby told him.

'I'll wake Harry,' he said and disappeared inside.

'What do you think she's up to?' Harry loomed up before her, struggling into his towelling robe.

'She's going to search the Beach House,' said Libby. 'You were dead right to come out here. Are we going to challenge her?'

'It's a tricky legal problem, isn't it?' said Ben. 'After all, until probate's been granted, whose property is it?'

'Certainly not hers,' said Libby, 'and any minute now it'll be Harry's. Whatever she takes from there, it will be theft.'

'We took the address book,' said Harry. 'But I suppose, technically, that's mine, too.'

'Follow her?' suggested Libby.

'All of us?' Harry looked surprised.

'Just you and me, then. Ben can keep watch here, in case one of the others comes down.'

'Are we being sidelined again?' drawled Peter, joining them.

''Fraid so,' said Ben with a grin. 'Go on, then, you two. Follow the scary monster.'

Libby tucked her feet into her sandals and followed Harry down the steps to the beach. Honoria had disappeared from view by now, so they hurried across the sand and climbed over the rocks into Candle Cove.

'She'll see us!' hissed Libby.

'So?' Harry was now striding purposefully across to the ruins of the Beach House, where Honoria could be made out almost bent double in front of the wall.

'Good morning.' He stopped a yard or so away, and Honoria snapped upright, almost losing her balance. Her hand went to her heart and Libby wondered for the moment if they'd scared her into a heart attack.

'What are you doing here?' she gasped.

Harry glanced at Libby, amused. 'I think I should ask *you* that, don't you?'

Honoria looked confused.

'I must say,' said Libby, stepping forward, 'I would have thought you'd have the sense to look for whatever you wanted to find before Harry took over. You've had plenty of time.'

'We didn't think you'd come over.' Honoria leaned against the crumbling brickwork. 'How could we know?'

'So what is it you're looking for?' said Harry, folding his arms and looking, Libby thought, like an avenging Greek god.

'Nothing.'

'Then why are you here? Come on, Honoria. You must think there's something here, but for the life of me I can't work out why you didn't search here before we came over for Matthew's funeral. You were so convinced Celia was murdered, you must have thought there was a clue here.'

'We –' Honoria glanced at Libby. 'We thought you would solve her murder.'

'Yes, you said.' Libby moved closer. 'But as we've also said, how could we do that when you wouldn't even tell us the truth? So are you going to now?'

Honoria straightened her back. 'I don't know what you're talking about,' she said, and started to walk round Harry, who put out an arm to stop her.

'Honoria, please understand we wouldn't do anything to hurt or upset you, but you can't start poking around here and expect me not to wonder why.'

Honoria gave him a scathing look and shook her arm free, before trudging back to the rocks and clambering awkwardly over them.

'Well,' said Libby. 'What about that then?'

Harry shook his head, watching as the older woman disappeared from view. 'No idea. Come on, I want a cuppa.'

Peter and Ben had made fresh tea and were waiting on the deck.

'We saw her go past,' said Ben. 'She didn't look at us.'

'She wouldn't say anything,' said Harry. 'Except that they didn't realise we would be coming over so soon.'

'This is all so stupid,' said Libby. 'I'd wash my hands of

them, but we can't very well, now Harry's inherited this place.'

'And don't forget someone's after Harry,' reminded Peter. 'It might be all tied together.'

'I know.' Libby sighed. 'What do we do now?'

'Have a thorough search of this place and the Beach House. We can't lock the Beach House, so anything loose we ought to remove,' said Ben. 'After breakfast.'

By the time the four of them made their way back to the Beach House, the day was threatening to turn very hot, and Peter was complaining that his white linen trousers were going to get filthy.

'Should have worn something more practical then,' said Harry, in shorts and a tee shirt. 'We are.'

Peter looked them over and tipped his wide-brimmed hat to a rakish angle. 'But you don't look as good as I do,' he grinned.

The search of the Beach House was less perfunctory than before. The area where Ben had found the address book was pulled apart, planks were torn off the walls and every nook and cranny prodded and poked. After two hours, Libby sat back on her heels and wiped her damp forehead.

'Nothing. I don't think there's anything to find.'

'I think you're right,' said Harry, straightening up from the pile of bricks he'd been sorting through.

'Rotting fabric.' Peter held it up. Libby peered at it.

'Tea towel?' she guessed. 'Not useful, anyway.'

'Let's leave it,' said Harry. 'And I'll ring the old ladies and tell them there's nothing to find here. In fact,' he eyed the ruin thoughtfully, 'I'm inclined to tell them I'm going to have it knocked down.'

'Really? I mean, really? Or just tell them that?' asked Libby.

'Really. It hasn't any sentimental value, has it? I wonder if I could rebuild it?'

Ben straightened up holding a vicious-looking length of barbed wire. 'Ask the planning officer. If Matthew had title to a property here, then you own the land and could probably put up a similar building.' He looked down at the wire. 'I don't suppose this is relevant?'

Harry frowned. 'I never saw any barbed wire here. Where did you find it?'

'Over there.' Ben gestured. 'Near where I found the address book.'

'Must be the architect's eye,' said Peter, going to look over the remains of the wall Ben had indicated.

'By the way, where is the address book now?' asked Libby.

'Guy's still got it,' said Harry. 'I think he was going to have another go at it, or get someone else to look at it.'

'This wire looks like the stuff they put up on beaches during the war,' said Ben. 'They did that here, too, didn't they?'

'I suppose so,' said Libby. 'They would have been on the front line for invasion.'

'As much as we were,' said Peter. 'More so, because I bet if they were invaded, the Germans would have thought they could capture an island easily, as they did with the Channel Islands.'

'Perhaps we ought to try and find out more about it,' said Libby.

'There are some local history books at the house,' said Harry. 'I noticed. I was thinking of trying to see if there was anything in them that could ... well, might ...'

'Be useful.' Peter slipped his arm round Harry's shoulders. 'Come along then. I've had enough grubbing round in the dirt.'

Back at Ship House, Harry called the sisters, not mentioning the barbed wire or suggestions of invasion. He was brief and firm, and when he ended the call, shook his head. 'That was Amelia. I don't think she believed me.'

Peter and Ben were bent over the local history books Harry had pointed out to them while Libby made coffee in the kitchen.

'There's quite a bit here about PLUTO,' said Ben.

'The what?' said Harry.

'Pipeline under the ocean,' said Libby coming in with the coffee. 'It was to take fuel to the troops after the D-Day landings. Very hush-hush. Went from Shanklin, I think, or somewhere nearby. And I've just remembered something else. I don't know why I didn't think of it earlier.'

'What?'

'Operation Sea Lion.'

Three puzzled faces turned towards her.

'It was Hitler's plan to invade Britain. The Battle of Britain was part of it. I read all about it when I was doing some research after we got back last time, Ventnor was to be targeted by the Ninth Army from Le Havre.'

Chapter Twenty-four

'I don't see what that has to do with anything,' said Harry.

'Perhaps the Beach House was used by the military during the war?' suggested Ben. 'That was why I found the wire there?'

'Suppose so,' said Harry, sounding dubious. 'But still ...'

'Suppose ...' said Peter, who had been frowning at his coffee mug, 'just suppose there was something going on here.'

'Spying, do you mean?' asked Libby.

'Possibly. When was PLUTO started? And Sea Lion? Oh – Sea Lion was early if the Battle of Britain was part of it, and PLUTO later.'

'Yes, but suppose people had got wind of this possible invasion,' said Libby. 'Could they have been – I don't know – signalling to the Germans from here somehow?'

'Possible, but only with dedicated radio,' said Ben. 'Let's see if there's anything about Sea Lion in any of these books.'

At the end of an hour of reading through the small collection of books and further internet research – 'Thank goodness for laptops and tablets,' said Libby – they all knew a lot more about the Island's military defences, Operation Sea Lion, and the trial for treachery of a local woman.

'So she was making detailed maps of the defences.' said Libby. 'Could she have been something to do with Matthew's family?'

'Not likely,' said Peter, reading his screen. 'She came from London and was what it says here was a "thoroughly bad lot". And after her imprisonment she said it was all a joke anyway.'

'But there's the book which says she was mentally

disturbed,' said Ben, also still reading.

'And the row about the lost case files,' added Harry.

'But none of it to do with us,' said Libby.

'Suppose,' said Peter, getting up and pacing out on to the deck, 'suppose someone from Matthew's family was also a traitor? They'd want that kept secret, wouldn't they?'

'Doing the same sort of thing as that woman?' said Libby, following him out.

'Makes sense,' said Harry, joining them, 'but only guesswork, and what about my gran?'

'Perhaps it was her?' suggested Libby.

They all looked at her.

'That really does make sense,' said Peter at last.

'But everything says that woman was the first one to be sentenced to death,' said Ben.

'But commuted to – what was it? Fourteen years?' said Libby. 'And if Granny was a bit later than that woman they wouldn't have made much of a fuss about it, would they?'

'Local newspaper archives,' said Peter. 'That's what we want.' He strode back to his tablet and began searching.

'We're going to have to go to the offices, I think,' he said after a moment. 'Not searchable online.'

'Any other sources?' said Ben. 'How about typing in a phrase …'

'Like "woman arrested for spying Isle of Wight"?' said Libby.

'All we'd get then would be more variations on the other woman's story,' said Peter, 'But I'll try something similar.'

They all did. And all came up with nothing.

'Bang goes that theory, then,' said Libby.

'No, just that it was kept quiet. A lot was during the war. And you know how the Bletchley crowd kept quiet – even not telling their husbands and wives sixty years later,' said Ben.

'And those – what were they called? Special operations?' said Harry.

'No – I know what you mean,' said Libby. 'The Auxiliary

Units Patrols. The men who would be the British Resistance if Germany invaded. They didn't tell anyone.'

'Could that have been it, then?' said Ben. 'Not a traitor or a spy, but a secret resistance fighter?'

'But that wouldn't matter if it got out,' said Peter. 'No, I think it's perfectly possible we're dealing with something like spying, but I must say, the war's a bit early. I was thinking more of 1950.'

'So what now?' said Harry. 'Do we go searching for people who were around in the war? What about those old people at the funeral?'

'You know,' said Ben, 'the Auxiliary Units Patrols fit in very neatly with Operation Sea Lion.'

'But relevant?' said Peter. 'How do we find out?'

'You're the journalist, you ought to know,' said Libby.

'Haven't got all my sources to hand, though. But I'll give it a go.' Peter stood up. 'I shall shut myself up in our bedroom and you can all go and cavort around the Island.'

'What shall we do, then?' said Harry.

'I wish we could talk to the old people,' said Libby. 'That Lady Bligh, for instance. I don't even remember her from the funeral.'

'I don't think we could just go up and knock on her door and ask, Lib,' said Ben.

'No, of course not. We need an introduction.'

'Actually, I think we'd be better searching this place,' said Harry. 'That's what we said we'd do. See if there's anywhere locked or whatever.'

'Right,' said Libby. 'And it's practically lunch time. What shall we do about that?'

'Go to the cafe,' said Harry. 'Let's do half an hour here, then break.'

'And we were up so early this morning I could do with a nap after lunch,' said Libby. 'Come on, let's get going.'

Ben and Harry began on the living room, while Libby searched the bedroom she and Ben were using, before moving on to the one Fran and Guy had used.

'I bet I know where it is,' said Peter, emerging from his bedroom. 'There's a secondary loft hatch in the communal bathroom, over the shower.'

Harry was already trying to prise the hatch open by the time the other three got there.

'You were right,' he told Peter. 'This won't open. And I can't see any handle or lock.'

'Pressure point?' suggested Libby. 'You know, like that one on the secret door we found before.'

'My arms are aching,' said Harry. 'Get me something to stand on.'

Ten minutes later and they had all had a go at finding some sort of opening mechanism. The door had shifted a couple of times, but not opened. They stared at it for a silent minute. Then Libby laughed.

'What?' Harry frowned at her.

'Give it a good shove,' she said. 'Push it inwards.'

With a shrug, Harry reached up and pushed. The door swung upwards, revealing a pull down ladder.

'It wasn't even locked!' gasped Peter.

'Probably no need to,' said Libby. 'You expect a loft hatch to open downwards, don't you.'

'No, I don't. Ours has to be pushed upwards and slid aside,' said Peter. 'I don't know why I didn't think of it.'

'Because we were all convinced it would be bolted and barred and we would see a lock or something,' said Libby. 'Who's going up?'

'Lunch, first,' said Ben firmly. 'I'm starving, if no one else is.'

'Without knowing what's up there?' wailed Libby. 'I won't be able to eat a thing!'

'How about if Ben and I go and buy sandwiches from the cafe while you and Harry explore the loft?' suggested Peter.

'Great,' said Libby. 'I'll have crab, please.'

'Me too,' grunted Harry, as he reached up to pull down the

ladder. 'Anyone got a torch?'

Peter and Ben left and Libby found a torch in the kitchen.

'Can you see anything?' she called up, after handing it up to Harry.

'Not a lot. It's not very big. Hang on.'

She heard a creaking and a bang.

'Ow.'

'What's up?'

'That was my head on a beam. There are a couple of boxes here. I'll push them to the hatch.'

'I'll come up the ladder to get them, then.'

'No, they'll be too heavy. Wait a bit.'

She heard a scraping sound and saw the torch beam swinging wildly across the open hatch. Then Harry appeared and climbed carefully back on to the ladder.

'Here.' He handed her the torch. 'Now, put it down and bring me that chair I was standing on.'

Libby brought it. Harry came down two steps, carefully balancing a cardboard box on the steps above him. Two more, and he was able to place the box on the chair, then back up the ladder to repeat the exercise with the second box. Finally, he went back up with the torch to give the now empty space a sweep with the torch, then shot the ladder back up and closed the hatch.

'Made a bit of a mess of the shower,' he said regarding the black marks on the shower tray.

'Doesn't matter,' said Libby. 'Come on, let's take these into the living room. Oof! They *are* heavy.'

'Told you, you silly mare. Come here, I'll do it.'

At last both boxes were on the large dining table and Libby was able to take off the lids, disturbing at least twenty years' worth of dust and cobwebs.

'It's just copies of his articles in this one,' she said a few minutes later.

'Same here,' said Harry, squinting at a yellowing reporter's notebook. 'All old, though.'

'Any of the actual newspapers or magazines they appeared in? There are no dates on these.'

'No, but some of these are dated. Go down a bit further.'

Libby lifted out the top third of the papers and notebook and came to some very old typewritten pages.

'Listen,' she said. 'This must be about you. "Have made arrangements for the baby to go to C." Oh, no – it's dated 1949. Your father, then.'

Harry took the paper from her. 'It doesn't say much else. And it isn't an article. Why did he type this?'

'A note?' said Libby doubtfully.

'But he didn't send it?' Harry frowned.

'Could be it was sent to him from your granny? And typed to provide anonymity?'

'Could be. Is there anything else?'

It wasn't until they reached the bottom of Harry's box that Peter and Ben arrived back with sandwiches.

'There was a queue,' explained Ben. 'Bloody hell, you're dirty.'

Harry looked at his hands in some surprise.

'So what have you found?' asked Peter, trying to find a clear space on the table for the food.

'Nothing except this, so far,' said Libby. 'I'm just going to wash my hands.'

When she returned, she found the three men on the deck, each reading a piece of paper.

'This one's interesting,' said Peter, handing her a plate. 'It's obviously a piece he wrote for a magazine or something about the war on the Island.'

'Ah!' said Libby. 'Success! And what does it say?'

'Not a lot that we don't know – it's mainly about that woman again, but it does include a few details of some of the places she made maps of. Oh, and that there was a radar station at Ventnor. He mentions a few other arrests along the same lines, but no names.'

'But look at this.' Harry had been back to the boxes and

returned waving a plastic folder. 'Newspaper cutting. Dated 1949.'

'That's the same date as that note,' said Libby. 'What's it about?'

'The suicide of a former traitor. Alfred Morton.'

Chapter Twenty-five

'So who's he?' asked Libby.

'Have we come across his name before?' said Peter. 'What was the name in the address book?'

'Andrew something,' said Ben. 'And if this person committed suicide in 1949 his address wouldn't be in the book, would it?'

'No, I suppose not,' said Libby. 'What does the article say?'

'I'll read it out. "The body of Alfred Morton was recovered on Tuesday morning from a beach near Overcliffe. Morton was convicted in 1942 of treachery and released two weeks ago as he was no longer considered a threat to the realm." That's it.'

'Google it,' suggested Ben.

'Already on it,' said Peter, whose trusty tablet was already on the table.

'Which paper is the cutting from?' Libby pulled it towards her.

'It doesn't say, but I would imagine it's the local one, or there would be more explanation of where Overcliffe was,' said Peter. 'Look here – a piece from the *Daily Mirror*.' He stood the tablet up in its case for them all to see.

"An inquest was held on the Isle of Wight on Monday into the death of Alfred Morton, whose body was found at the bottom of cliffs near his home. Morton was convicted of spying on behalf of the enemy in 1942, and released two weeks prior to his death. The verdict of the coroner was suicide while the balance of the mind was disturbed. Morton's family did not attend the inquest."

'So he lived near here,' said Libby.

'That's the *Mirror* reporting,' said Peter. 'It could mean anything.'

'Anyway, it implies that Morton's family are Islanders,' said Harry. 'Are we supposing this bloke is the secret the sisters are trying to hide?'

'If so, was he their brother? Is their maiden name Morton?' said Libby. 'And anyway, that doesn't have anything to do with Hal.'

'Unless he's Grandfather,' said Peter. 'And raped Harry's gran.'

They looked at each other with sober expressions.

'Oh, dear,' said Libby. 'No wonder they're ashamed.'

'If that's the case, yes,' said Ben. 'So what we think is that he was the brother of the sisters, was imprisoned for spying, let out after the war, raped Gran and in a fit of remorse, threw himself off the cliff.'

'It's a nasty enough scenario to want to keep quiet,' said Peter, 'but we may be leaping to conclusions. Do we test it?'

'How?' asked Harry.

'Confront the sisters?' suggested Libby.

'Someone is threatening Harry because they think he knows all, and is going to spread it about. If we tell the sisters, whoever the threatener is will get wind of it. No, I suggest we look up records of Alicia, Amelia, and Honoria Morton. See if that *is* their surname.'

He turned once again to his tablet.

'The only one who's come up is Honoria Morton,' he said 'and she appears to be a sculptress of note associated with "The Geometry of Fear", a movement in British Sculpture in the 1950s. It doesn't say much else. It's a Wiki entry, but one of those that says it needs verification or something. No mention of family, just the association with this movement and other sculptors, like Frink and Chadwick.'

'So that's why she was off the Island in the fifties,' said Libby.

'But we want stories from the late forties,' said Harry.

'1949 is almost 50s,' said Ben. 'Could be the whole family were hustled away to avoid scandal.'

Libby was staring out to sea.

'What's up, Lib?' asked Peter.

'I'm thinking.'

'That's a worry,' said Harry. 'What about?'

'We've leapt to an awful lot of conclusions, haven't we?'

'Well, of course we have,' said Ben. 'This is all guesswork.'

'But if you think about it, all this is just remnants of Matthew's work. There are no birth certificates or mementoes or damning evidence. That cutting is just that – a cutting. Just there because it was a bit of a local scandal. It could have nothing to do with Matthew, the sisters or Harry. And those boxes weren't really hidden, were they? They were in an unlocked attic space. I don't think this is what the sisters are worried about. And another thing,' Libby took a breath, 'why would Matthew have hidden something here? He knew the sisters had access to this place, more than he did, in fact. Surely, if he'd had anything to hide he'd have hidden it in The Shelf.'

'Yes, but we agreed that he wouldn't be hiding it from the sisters – they already know the secret – whatever it is,' said Ben.

'Oh,' said Libby doubtfully.

'Look.' Peter tapped on the table to bring the meeting to order. 'Let's just step back a bit. First, the reason we got involved at all is because the sisters up there think their sister Celia was murdered as a result of something Matthew knew or someone wanted from him. That's the basic scenario.'

'And now, the only reason we want to find out is because someone's after Harry,' said Ben.

'And the link is the letter the sisters sent to Harry,' said Peter. 'The "young friend" letter.'

'So they think there was something this person wanted that gave away their precious secret. That's what it boils down to. In case anyone's forgotten.' Harry stood up. 'So yes, we're jumping to conclusions – which you're used to, you old trout –

but we don't have anywhere else to go. The old witches up top won't tell us, and we don't know anyone else to ask.'

Libby looked chastened. 'Sounds simple put like that.'

'Do we think the Clipping woman and her parents know? And Lady Thing?' asked Ben.

'I think they all know. And this Keith Franklin is around again isn't he?' said Harry, making a face. 'My so-called father.'

'Do you think he's trying to find you?' asked Libby.

'Look – someone *has* found him,' said Peter. 'He got an anonymous letter, didn't he?'

'And the note here,' added Ben.

'So it may be that the original letter to the sisters – the "young friend" one – is from someone different.' Libby looked from one to the other.

'Or,' said Harry, 'the one I got the other day is from someone different.'

'Like the sisters,' said Ben.

'The sisters!' said the other three together.

'Why not? One of them could have come over the day before, popped the letter through the letter box and gone straight back to the Island. Just because they were here when we got back doesn't mean they'd all been here all the time,' said Ben. 'And they're the ones who are trying to stop us finding anything out.'

'It doesn't feel right, somehow,' said Libby, 'although I agree, they'd be the obvious suspects. Ian said so, didn't he?'

'Fingerprints?' suggested Peter.

'Theirs won't be on record,' said Ben.

'But we could get them while we're here,' said Harry. 'You know, the cups, or glasses …'

'I don't think we're on those terms with them any more,' said Libby.

'Oh well, if there's nothing here after all, why are we here?' asked Peter. 'There must be something the sisters think gives away their secret. Something they know about but haven't seen or found.'

'The most probable explanation,' said Libby, the thought popping in to her head suddenly, 'is that whoever killed Celia actually *got* whatever it was.'

'And hasn't let the secret out,' said Peter.

'No. And whoever wrote the letter to Hal doesn't know that.'

'So how many bloody people *are* creeping round behind my back?' Harry kicked a chair. 'Look, we've searched this place and the Beach House. I vote we pack up these boxes, lock up and go home. I can't talk about what I don't know, so unless someone actually comes up with a baseball bat, I reckon we should just forget the whole thing.'

'Again,' said Libby.

'Yes, well …'

'I agree.' Peter stood up. 'Come on, let's pack up.'

'I'm going to strip the beds first,' said Libby. 'And you'd better find out when the booking is for, as we haven't left the sisters any keys.'

It was another hour before they left. Harry refused to go and see the sisters, saying he would write when they got home.

'I'd be interested to see what they do when they see the car's gone,' said Peter, as they drove away.

'Bet they go down and see if they can get in,' said Libby.

'If Matthew had a secret from them, separate from the shared one,' said Ben, 'where would he have hidden that?'

'That's what we were looking for that first evening with the sisters,' said Libby.

'Not quite,' said Peter. 'We were only looking on the computer.'

'But they obviously thought there was a secret,' said Libby.

'No, I think all they were worried about, as we keep saying, was finding out if anyone knew the secret,' said Harry. 'Gawd, it's like a bad Victorian melodrama.'

'You know,' said Libby, as they drove down to the ferry terminal at Fishbourne a little later, 'we've completely forgotten about poor old Lucifer.'

'Oh, I don't think he's got anything to do with it,' said Peter. 'He was just a red herring. And we don't know if he's alive or dead.'

Ben called Hetty to tell her they would be home early, and then reported that she wanted them all to come to dinner.

'I expect she wants all the up-to-date news,' said Peter. 'Not that there's much to tell.'

But when they all got to the Manor later that evening, Hetty surprised them.

'I remember that in the newspapers,' she said, when they showed her the cutting. 'Scandal, it was.'

'But we hardly found any references to it online,' said Libby, surprised.

'Hushed up, I reckon.' Hetty turned to the Aga and lifted a huge enamel pan full of toad in the hole. 'Here you are, gal. You get serving while I get the veg.'

'But they couldn't erase all references to it.' Peter frowned. 'And why hush it up?'

It was Hetty's turn to look surprised. ''Cos 'e was old Reginald Morton's son, wasn't 'e?'

A stunned silence followed this.

'You mean – Reginald Morton the *poet*?' squeaked Libby eventually.

'Yeah, 'im. Had hisself a castle built, or something.'

'Overcliffe Castle!' chorused those round the table.

'Arty set, they were. Some – I dunno – movement, I think they called it.'

'Like St Ives?' suggested Ben.

His mother gave him a look. 'I dunno, do I? Never was arty meself.'

Peter got out his phone and also received a look from Hetty.

'Not now. You're here to eat. It'll wait.'

It was the first time Libby had seen Peter look sheepish. Hetty did, however, allow discussion of the situation over the dinner table. It ranged mostly over the astonishing information

196

that Alfred Morton had been Reginald Morton's son, and therefore, if their assumptions were right, Alicia, Amelia, Honoria, and Celia had been his daughters.

'It sort of explains Honoria going away to be a sculptress, too,' said Libby. 'But why have we never known this?'

'We might be wrong,' warned Ben. 'Just because we found a Honoria Morton it doesn't mean she was the same one as our Honoria.'

'That's true, but it's all fitting together,' said Harry. 'The Castle. They all grew up there, we know that. Perhaps it was a sort of arty commune.'

'I've never heard of one on the Island,' said Peter, frowning. 'And we haven't come across any, have we?'

'There's Dimbola Lodge,' said Libby. 'You know, where Julia Cameron lived. And all the poets and writers.'

'Tennyson,' said Peter.

'Dickens,' added Ben.

'Keats,' said Harry surprisingly. 'Well, there's a Keats Green in Shanklin. It sort of follows.'

'They were all Victorians, though, not 1950s,' said Libby.

'Their parents – Reginald Morton and Matthew's parents would have been born in the late nineteenth or early twentieth century, though,' said Peter. He fidgeted with his phone again. 'Oh, Hetty, please let me look him up!'

'Oh, go on then,' said Hetty grudgingly. 'Impatient bugger.'

The others watched as Peter began the search for Reginald Morton on his phone.

'Ah!' he said triumphantly, looking up. 'There we are. "Reginald Morton, poet and playwright, born 1893, died 1953." There's a proper website, but I won't look at that now.'

'So he's the right sort of era.' Harry was staring into the middle distance. 'And he might be my great-grandfather.'

'Golly, yes!' said Libby.

'And that does make it more likely that someone wants to keep you quiet, doesn't it?' said Ben.

'But I haven't known up until now – don't know for sure

197

anyway. Why would they want to keep me quiet?'

'We've always said, because someone thinks you *do* know,' said Peter. 'And if there's been such trouble taken over keeping the whole Alfred thing quiet for all these years, someone doesn't want it to get out now.'

'Someone thinks Matthew told me.' Harry looked round the table. 'But he didn't.'

'We know,' said Libby. 'And I bet there's only one person he did tell.'

The following morning, Libby was just settling down at her laptop to do more research on Reginald Morton, when her phone rang.

'It's me.'

'Hal? What's up? You haven't had another funny letter, have you?'

'No. What'sisname Deakin just rang me up. He said –' Harry took a deep breath ' – he said Andrew McColl wanted to meet me.'

'Andrew McColl? The actor?'

'Yes.'

'But he's famous! And he was at the memorial service.'

'I know. And you know what this means, don't you?'

'He's Lucifer!'

Chapter Twenty-six

'Well, maybe not,' said Harry. 'That's leaping to conclusions. Let's just say he *might* be.'

'Have you told Pete?'

'Of course, you silly woman. We decided I would meet him. I called Deakin back and asked him to arrange a time and place.'

'Couldn't he come here? I want to see him!'

'Libby, it isn't a show put on for your benefit.' Harry heaved a great sigh. 'I just can't believe this. Bloody melodrama gets more stupid every day.'

Libby was quiet for a moment.

'You still there?' said Harry.

'Yes. I was just thinking. I was starting to research Reginald Morton this morning, so I'll have a go at Andrew McColl, too. And I'll ring Guy and see if he's managed to get any more names from the blue book. Are you working at lunchtime?'

'Course I am.'

'I'll pop in and let you know what I've found out.'

'That's just an excuse for me to give you a glass of wine.'

'And a bowl of soup.'

'All right, and a bowl of soup. Pete was going to look up McColl too, but he's got a deadline. If he's finished, I'll get him to come along too.'

'Ben's over at the timber yard doing something important today, so he won't come,' said Libby. 'I'll see you at – what? When are you likely to be able to talk?

'I've got no bookings, so it'll be foot traffic. No idea. Just text me before you leave.'

It was almost one o'clock when Libby sent Harry a text.

'Empty,' came the reply. 'Come now.'

Peter was already at the big table in the window to the right of the front door. Libby waved through the glass and he got up to open the door for her.

'Got anything?' he asked pulling out a chair.

'Yes,' said Libby, putting her laptop on the table. 'And Fran's joining us with the blue book.'

Peter raised his eyebrows. 'Oh?'

'Yes.' Libby beamed. 'Where's Hal?'

'Here.' Harry appeared carrying the cafetière and a bottle of red wine. 'The Turkish one I told you about.'

'Angora?' read Libby. 'That's rabbits.'

'It's also Turkish wine, dear heart,' said Peter. 'I bet Guy knows all about it.'

'Yes, we must get him to tell us all about that little hideaway,' said Harry. 'I'm going to need it after this.'

As Harry was setting out cutlery and glasses, Fran arrived.

'Now we're all here,' said Harry, 'what have you got?'

'Well,' began Libby, 'I started with Reginald Morton, but broke off after Harry called, so I looked at Andrew McColl first. But let Fran tell you about the book. I called Guy to ask him if he'd been able to get anything more from it, and he said he had. Not a lot, but there were several names that had emerged.'

'And here they are.' Fran took the book from her bag and carefully opened it flat. 'See, there are only a few pages that would open, and Guy thought that was probably the ones Matthew used most regularly.'

'Although he wouldn't have used them so much these days,' said Harry. 'He had a smartphone like everybody else.'

'Except me,' said Libby.

'So where was that?' asked Peter. 'We never heard any mention of a mobile.'

'That is odd,' said Libby. 'The sisters didn't mention it, and as they have phones themselves they would have known how to 'go through it.'

'And probably wouldn't have needed us in the first place,' said Fran.

'So Matthew was as keen as the sisters to keep the secrets, both their shared one and his own personal ones,' said Libby.

'So he chucked it,' said Harry. 'Only thing that makes sense.'

'Perhaps that's what the sisters thought might be at Ship House or the Beach House?' suggested Peter.

'Could be,' Harry nodded, 'but I reckon he got rid of it. It must have had calls on it pointing to someone.'

'Of course! The meeting he couldn't attend and sent Celia to instead,' said Libby.

'Anyway, Fran, go on with the addresses,' said Peter. 'What did you find?'

'I wrote out a list,' said Fran, 'but I'll show you the entries. Here, see? The ones in biro are the ones that have stayed. What could be pencil marks are just faint indentations – not even that.' She carefully turned over pages and then pushed a sheet of paper into the middle of the table. 'And there's the list.'

'There are nineteen names,' said Libby, 'and none of them rung any bells until we looked at the research I was doing.'

'Go on – one of them's a Morton?' said Harry.

'No, but look at the first name we found. That's Andrew Foster McColl, that is.'

Harry and Peter looked stunned. Libby was beaming in triumph.

'Looks as though we're right, then,' said Harry at last. 'McColl is Lucifer.'

'What's even better,' said Fran, 'is that he first made his name in a sixties revival of Marlowe's *Doctor Faustus*, where he played the Devil.'

'And he's married to Fay Scott,' added Libby, 'and has been for donkey's years.'

'So did his and Matthew's relationship pre-date McColl's marriage?' asked Peter.

'We can't tell, nor do we know why there'd been no contact for the last couple of years,' said Fran. 'Harry said he thought Lucifer was dead, didn't you, Hal?'

Harry nodded. 'And he isn't. And I'm going to meet him. Bloody hell.'

'Let's have the soup,' said Peter, 'then we can see what you've got on the Morton story. I've still got my deadline, but I decided I could take a lunch break. As long as it's in by the end of the working day.'

Libby went to help Harry fetch soup plates, bread, and a tureen, and they all helped themselves to Harry's spicy Mexican soup. After his second bowlful, Peter sat back with a replete: 'Ah!'

'You want the rest, now, then?' said Libby, topping up her wine glass.

'Yes,' said Harry. 'Trot it out, then.'

'Reginald Morton, we know, was born in 1893. I couldn't resist looking up a bit about him last night, but Ben got bolshie and said we'd been waiting to watch some programme on television so I had to stop.

'Anyway, his parents were part of a rather arty circle on the Isle of Wight. A lot of artists gathered there, some taking houses on the Island for the whole summer.'

'Like Lamorna Cove,' said Fran. Harry looked confused.

'In Cornwall. Same sort of thing,' said Peter.

'So Reginald was born into this sort of circle, and it continued as he grew up. He began to make a name for himself, and then he fell in love with Tallulah DeLaxley.'

'Matthew's aunt,' said Fran.

'They married in 1918, after he came home from France, where he'd improved his standing in poetry circles by writing war poetry.'

'Oh, of course!' said Peter.

'They had five children. Alicia, Amelia, Honoria, Celia and –' Libby paused for effect.

'Alfred!' chorused the other three.

'So we were right,' said Harry. 'That's the secret the sisters are trying to keep. That their brother Alfred was a traitor – or a spy – during the last war and committed suicide after it. Nothing in that account about Matthew?'

'Not on the website, which seems to be run by a PhD student at Oxford, but on the Wiki entry it does mention that Alfred took his own life in 1949. It doesn't say why.'

'Well, I think we've all been very clever,' said Harry. 'We worked it all out.'

'You did how much?' asked Peter, amused.

'I helped. And I *was* the story to start with, wasn't I?'

'It's all very well,' said Libby, 'but although we've solved both the mysteries – mainly because other people have come forward, like Jeannette and Andrew McColl – and even Hetty – we still don't know why someone's after Harry!'

They all looked at one another.

'That's true.' Peter put an anxious hand on Harry's arm. 'Perhaps I'd better bring the computer in here this afternoon if you've got prepping up to do.'

'Don't fuss.' Harry patted Peter's hand. 'I'm all right here. And who's going to attack me here in broad daylight, especially if I work with the kitchen door open so I can be seen from the street? And lock the back door?'

'Hmm,' said Peter.

'But we don't know who and why,' said Fran. 'The idea that it's the sisters seems a bit farcical.'

'I suppose what we could do is let them know we know all about their brother, then they should stop being silly about everything.'

'You're forgetting something,' said Peter. 'They still think Celia was murdered. And if they're right …'

'You're right, I was forgetting,' said Libby, frowning. 'Now, where does that fit in?'

'Matthew wasn't well enough to meet this person, whoever it was, and Celia said she would go instead.' Harry stated the facts.

'And because she hadn't got, or wouldn't give, whatever it was the person wanted, he knocked her over the head and left her to drown,' continued Peter.

'Then Matthew dies. And the sisters receive the letter about "the young friend". They still think the whole thing is about their traitorous brother, and send the letter on to Harry, whom they assume is the friend in question, but don't believe Matthew would have said anything about Alfred to him,' continued Libby.

'And he didn't,' said Harry.

'No, because it was shameful. And that's the reason,' said Libby, 'that no mention was ever made about the relationship with the illustrious Reginald, because any research on him was likely to throw up Alfred's treachery.'

'But they think whoever killed Celia knows the secret and, desperate to keep it safe, try and find out who killed her by asking us but not telling us the reason,' concluded Fran. 'Neat.'

'Has anyone thought to look up Matthew's Wiki entry?' said Harry suddenly. 'I assume he's got one. He didn't have a website, I know that.'

Libby obediently typed in Matthew's name.

'No.' She shook her head. 'It's one of those "citation needed" pieces. Just says born 1925, worked for the *Daily Sketch* and then as a freelance.'

'Nothing about family then,' said Peter. 'What a nuisance.'

'Let's go back to old Reggie,' said Harry. 'What about this Overcliffe Castle?'

Libby went back to the Reginald Morton website. 'It's not particularly informative about that. It says he lived there with his wife and children, and it became the centre of a group of artists, writers and poets who gathered on the Island every summer.'

'Try searching Overcliffe Castle, then,' said Peter.

'Nothing much more. It was sold in the early fifties –'

'When Reginald died,' put in Fran.

'Probably. The person who bought it tried to turn it into a

hotel, but it wasn't successful. Then the cliff began to crumble and it had to be demolished in the sixties.'

'Which we knew, because it was on that plaque,' said Fran.

'So all along it belonged to the Morton family and not the DeLaxleys,' said Harry. 'So the land probably belongs to the sisters, not Matthew.'

'That's a point,' said Peter. 'You'll have to get your Mr Deakin to look into that for you.'

'Come to think of it, Candle Cove probably belonged to the sisters,' said Libby. 'The steps lead up to the top just below their house.'

'But the Beach House …?' said Harry.

'Oh, I don't know.' Libby sighed. 'Just as we think we've solved it all, up comes something else that needs explaining.'

The bell tinkled over the restaurant door.

'Bugger,' muttered Harry. 'Forgot to lock it.'

'I beg your pardon,' said the elderly gentleman who had come through the door. 'It does say open.'

'Yes, of course.' Harry stood up. 'Please come in.'

'Actually,' said the man, looking up into Harry's face. 'I believe it might be you I've come to see. My name's Andrew McColl.'

Chapter Twenty-seven

In the middle of a sip of wine, Libby choked.

Peter stood up. 'Go up to the flat, Hal.'

Harry, standing fishlike with his mouth open, pulled himself together. 'Er, yes. Pleased to meet you, Mr McColl.'

Andrew McColl, looking amused, shook his hand and looked at the group round the table.

'I don't want to interrupt –'

'No,' said Libby hurriedly, 'we were just –'

'Finishing lunch,' Ben said, and trod on her foot. 'Go on, Hal, you pop upstairs, we'll clear up here.'

Harry led his visitor through the kitchen to the spiral staircase in the back yard and Peter turned the sign to 'Closed'.

'Well.' He turned and looked at Fran, Ben and Libby. 'How unexpected.'

'He had asked to meet Hal,' said Libby.

'But only this morning,' said Fran.

'Mr Deakin must have called him the minute Hal said yes.' Libby began collecting plates.

'And he came straight down? Must be urgent,' said Peter.

'I wonder why he hasn't been in touch before if it is,' said Fran.

'Perhaps he didn't know about Hal the same as Hal didn't know who he was,' suggested Libby.

'That makes sense. Should I take them some coffee?' Peter shook the cafetière dubiously.

'Hal will offer, I expect,' said Fran. 'Come on, let's clear up.'

Ten minutes later, Harry shouted down the outside staircase

for a pot of tea.

'Sorry, Lib, but could you make it? You're best at it. And Earl Grey, if we've got it.'

Libby found the Earl Grey and a china pot.

'Will you take it up?' she asked Peter.

'No. He asked for you, so you do it.'

Libby loaded pot, milk and cups onto a tray and nervously carried it up the spiral staircase. Harry opened the door at the top and grinned at her.

'Come in.'

Libby went past him into the living area of the flat which Fran had rented for a time and Libby's son Adam had occupied until very recently. Andrew McColl was sitting in the middle of the sofa looking tired.

'You're Libby.' He smiled up at her. 'I've been hearing all about you.'

'Not that much,' put in Harry hastily. 'We haven't covered much ground yet.'

'I would like to meet you all properly. Could I take you all out to dinner?' Andrew took a cup from Libby.

'It's very nice of you, but I had a night off from this place yesterday,' said Harry. 'I can't take another. I haven't got the staff.'

'It's Wednesday and we're rehearsing,' said Libby. 'I'm sorry.'

'Rehearsing?' Andrew McColl's eyes lit up, and Libby blushed.

'Oh, only an amateur show for Nethergate's Alexandria.'

'I'd love to hear about that.' McColl looked as though he would quite happily sit in the flat all afternoon.

'I'd better leave you and Harry to finish your conversation. I'm sure you'll sort something out between you.' Libby smiled at both men and went back downstairs, where she reported the conversation. 'And I don't think we'd better still be here when they come down,' she finished, 'or we might look too nosy.'

They duly finished tidying up the kitchen and left. Ben went back to the Manor, Peter to his cottage and Fran accompanied Libby back to Allhallow's Lane.

'You're not going to go back home this afternoon, are you?' asked Libby, as she moved the big kettle onto the Rayburn's hotplate. 'It hardly seems worth it when you're coming up for rehearsal this evening.'

'No, I told Guy I'd eat at the caff. Or the pub.'

'Don't be daft, you can eat here,' said Libby. 'I expect it will be shepherd's pie or something equally boring. So what do we think about what's going on back there now?'

'I was just wondering,' said Fran, frowning, 'if that man found Hal so quickly today, has he been here before?'

'You mean –' Libby paused with mugs in hand.

'Hal's warning letter.'

'I can't see it,' said Libby. 'If he's Lucifer, he's got nothing to do with old secrets on the Island, has he?'

'He *is* an old secret,' said Fran. 'Maybe he doesn't want Hal telling.'

'He was quite happy to see all of us this afternoon and announce his presence. Deakin knows, too, so he can't mean Hal any harm.'

'Oh, well.' Fran perched on the edge of the table. 'We'll hear from Hal soon enough.'

It was another hour before Harry called.

'He's booking in to the pub,' he said. 'And eating here. I shall introduce him to Patti and Anne. Then he wants to go and watch your rehearsal. Can he?'

'Oh, Harry!' wailed Libby. 'He's a professional! He can't come and watch us.'

'Why not? He's not stuck-up or anything. You'd never know he was famous. anyway, he said he'd like to join us for a drink afterwards. Anyway, half of you are ex-pro.'

Libby sighed. 'Just don't tell me if he does come.'

'All right, you silly mare.' Libby could hear the smile in Harry's voice.

'How did it go, anyway? What did he want?'

209

'Fine. He didn't want anything, really, just to know me. Matthew didn't tell him anything about me, just as I didn't know about him. But there's more to tell, so he's going to stay around for a few days. We won't be able to discuss it tonight, but I'll tell you what I can tomorrow.'

'I'll die of curiosity before then,' grumbled Libby.

'Sounds all right, then?' said Fran, chopping onions for the shepherd's pie.

'Yes. Not sure we'll get all of it, though,' said Libby, staring out of the window into the conservatory, where her easel stood, reproaching her.

It was while Libby, Ben and Fran were preparing to leave for the theatre that Harry called again.

'Andrew and I thought we might all have a drink in the theatre bar after rehearsal, then we can talk about everything.'

'Like we did with Ian,' said Libby. 'Poor Anne and Patti. They'll think we don't love them any more.'

'I'm going to explain. They'll be here any minute.'

'Do you think this Andrew will have any light to shed on our mysteries?' asked Ben, as they walked to the theatre.

'No idea. He's known – or rather, he knew – Matthew longer than anyone else except the sisters.'

'And those other old people from the Island,' said Fran.

'Yes. We've still not met Lady Bligh or the elder Clippings, have we?' Libby sighed. 'And Andrew won't have done, either.'

'But Matthew might have told him about them,' said Ben.

'Hmm,' said Libby doubtfully.

Peter was making a lighting plot to take to the technicians at the Alexandria, and causing an interesting effect of colours to play across the cast as they sang their way through Victorian and Edwardian seaside songs.

'Can you stop for the soloists?' Libby shouted up to the box at the end of one chorus set. 'They'll fall off the stage.'

'Remarkable you haven't done so already,' came an amused voice from the back of the auditorium.

Libby shaded her eyes and saw a small figure waving.

'Mr McColl? Is that you?'

'Andrew, please. I hope you don't mind.'

She turned back to the stage to see the entire cast wide-eyed and open-mouthed.

'Andrew McColl?'

'*The* Andrew McColl?'

'The actor?'

'Him that was in that Austen serial?'

'Oh, glory!'

'Look, he's here as an old friend of – of –'

'Matthew DeLaxley's.' Andrew had come up to the stage. 'I've come to see Harry and Peter – and Libby, too, of course. Please don't worry about me. Ignore me. I'll just carry on sitting at the back.' He turned away, then turned back. 'Oh, and Libby, I'm enjoying it!'

The soloists were, quite naturally, nervous about performing in front of so illustrious an actor, so Libby took them through another chorus set to give them confidence. This set concentrated on pub and drinking songs, which allowed everyone to become slightly more rowdy and raucous, so the soloists were suitably warmed up by the time their turn came.

At a quarter to ten Libby called a halt.

'See you all on Friday and we'll run it,' she said. 'Only a week more of rehearsal and then it's for real.'

As the cast drifted out and Libby collected up props and music, Andrew strolled up to the stage again.

'Most impressive,' he said. 'Surely everyone isn't an amateur?'

'Most of them,' smiled Libby. 'Some are ex-pros, some were trained but never broke through. Most of our techies are pros, although Peter isn't. Even my Ben did a stint as a pro stage hand and a tour with a TIE company.'

She called into the backstage area and Ben appeared, turning off lights as he passed them.

'You're pro, though?' said Andrew, as Libby and Ben joined

211

him in the auditorium.

'Ex,' said Libby. 'Now I'm a director of this theatre with Ben, here, and Peter. We don't get paid, but we love it.'

'What about this show you're doing for another theatre?'

'The End Of The Pier Show,' said Ben with a grin. 'We did it for the Alexandria in Nethergate last year when they were let down by another booking, and it went so well we're back again. This time we're doing Fridays and Saturdays for the whole of August, though. It's a big commitment for people with day jobs.'

'And do you get paid for that?'

'Well, yes. It comes to the board, and we elected to distribute among the members who are taking part,' said Libby, as they emerged into the bar area, where Peter was already opening bottles and polishing glasses.

'It's quite handy, too,' said Ben, pulling out chairs round one of the little tables as Fran joined them, 'that soloists can slot in or out, so if someone has a wedding or holiday or something planned they can be out for a week and back in the next.'

'How lovely to own a theatre,' said Andrew a little wistfully as he looked round.

'It is,' said Libby, 'and we're gradually getting round the snooty people who look down on amateur theatre. We have pro companies here, too, and one-nighters. Singers and comedians, usually.'

'I shall have to see what I can do,' said Andrew. 'I should love to put something on here. Your facilities seem excellent.'

'Oh, they are,' said Peter. 'Because we don't pay rent or have the huge running costs of other companies, all our revenue goes back into the building, so we can afford to keep updating lighting and sound and backstage facilities.'

'You don't go on yourself, then?' said Andrew.

'Not me!' Peter grinned. 'I love theatre, but I limit my involvement to fiddling about with the technical stuff, occasional writing, and directing.'

'And Harry?'

'No, he doesn't appear, either, although people have said he should,' said Libby.

'He'll be here as soon as he can shut up the caff,' said Peter. 'What will you have to drink, Andrew?'

After they had all been served with drinks, with coffee as usual for Fran, Harry appeared.

'I've packed Patti and Anne off,' he said. 'They were most intrigued.'

'They were a nice couple of women,' said Andrew. 'I was most surprised to find out that Patti was a priest.'

'The Reverend Patti Pearson, no less,' said Libby. 'We got involved with her through murder, too.'

A tense little silence descended on the company, and Libby felt heat rising up her neck and into her face.

'Sorry,' she said.

'Well, that as good a place to start as any,' said Andrew with a small smile. 'So, as you've all been involved in murder, as Libby says, shall I tell my tale?'

Chapter Twenty-eight

'I met Matthew when we were both at the start of our respective careers,' began Andrew. 'I hadn't yet had my breakthrough with *Doctor Faustus* and he was the lowliest of the low on a Fleet Street paper, which he said was a great step up from the regionals.

'As you all know, being gay was still illegal. In fact, the terrible "cures" were still being used.' His old face looked suddenly harrowed. 'You can't begin to imagine what it felt like, back then. To be attracted to someone of your own sex with the world around you telling you it was wrong, perverted, unnatural, and yet feeling yourself as if it was the most natural thing in life.

'I was doing the time-honoured "resting" occupation of barman in one of the Fleet Street pubs when I met Matthew. He and I recognised each other for what we were straight away, although no one else knew or suspected.' He smiled. 'The universal "gaydar" hadn't developed way back then. If you weren't obviously "camp" – although that was another word we didn't know – there was nothing to tell us from anyone else, although, of course, the theatrical profession was always suspect to a degree.'

'You'd be surprised how little has changed in some areas,' said Harry acidly.

'But in general, Harry, there is acceptance. After all, you and Peter were able to have a civil partnership ceremony and are recognised in law as a couple and each other's next-of-kin. Back then there was nothing.

'But Matthew and I began a relationship. Harry says he

knew of me as Lucifer and Matthew never told him anything about me other than the fact that I had a reputation to keep up. I never knew anything about Harry other than the fact that he was, as Matthew used to put it, his "Hostage to fortune".'

'What did he mean by that?' asked Peter.

'That Harry might cause problems at some time in the future.'

'What?' erupted Harry. 'You didn't –'

Andrew patted his arm. 'Calm down, boy. He didn't mean *you* would cause problems yourself. He meant that your existence would.'

He looked round the table. 'I'm assuming you all know as much as Harry knows now?'

'As much as we've guessed or put together,' said Fran. 'No one's been able to confirm all of it.'

'Especially Matthew's cousins,' said Ben, 'yet they were the ones to call us in in the first place.'

'Ah, yes, the cousins.' Andrew smiled grimly. 'Another responsibility. But one which Matthew didn't like.'

'But – and we've only just found out about this – the land, and Overcliffe Castle was all the property of the cousins' family,' said Libby. 'They weren't DeLaxleys.'

'No,' said Andrew, 'but after the …' he paused, 'the tragedy, when Reginald died, the castle was sold. You knew that?'

'Yes.'

Andrew took a sip of wine. 'By that time, the family had run through most of the money. Matthew bought the land, piece by piece, as he became a voice to be reckoned with in the newspaper world. He wrote some books, too, did you know?'

'No!' They were all surprised.

'Oh, very dated now, but explorations of politicism and what would now be called "Social Mores". At the time, very well regarded.

'Anyway, going back to the beginning of our relationship. At that time, of course, Harry was yet to make his appearance, but his father already had.'

'Keith Franklin,' said Peter. 'And we heard he'd gone back to the Island because Matthew had told him about his real parents.'

'His real mother, certainly. I doubt Matthew said anything about his father.'

Libby looked at Harry, then back at Andrew.

'Would that,' she began nervously, 'have been Alfred Morton?'

Andrew nodded. 'Harry said you'd found a newspaper clipping. The family tried to have the whole thing buried, and Matthew, although fairly new to the newspaper world in those days, did his best to keep it out of the spotlight.'

'Not altogether, though,' said Ben. 'Even though we couldn't find much about it online, my mother remembered it.'

'Because he was Reginald Morton's son, I expect,' said Andrew. 'That's what got most publicity.'

'Yes, that was it,' said Libby. 'So the sisters are all Mortons. Is that why Honoria is a sculptress?'

'Not why, exactly, but Matthew told me they were brought up among artists, poets, writers, and intellectual free-thinkers.'

'Which they aren't now,' said Peter. 'They're bitter.'

Andrew put his head on one side. 'Well, you can't blame them, really, can you? I'm quite sure they expected to be Matthew's heirs, and along comes this interloper Harry taking it all away from them.'

'But they were strange towards us before they knew about the will,' said Libby. 'All friendliness at first, and determined to find out what had happened to their sister Celia.'

'But they were concerned to keep the secret of Alfred's scandal,' said Andrew. 'Oh, yes, I know how they all felt about that. And I'm certain that they think someone had found out about it and that's why Celia was murdered.'

'And what do *you* think?' asked Harry.

'I don't know.' Andrew shrugged. 'Matthew was very worried in those last weeks, that's all I know.'

'You were in touch with him?' said Libby amid the gasps of astonishment.

'Yes. We both had pay-as-you-go mobiles just for communicating with each other. I gather no mobile was found?'

'No.' Harry shook his head. 'But he had another – I had the number. Neither of them were found. But –' he frowned. 'I thought you were dead.'

Andrew's smiled was cynical. 'After what's been going on in the media over the last few years, do you blame us for keeping out of sight? We could have had our personal lives and conversations laid bare for all to read. And it wasn't just for ourselves. I've my poor Fay to consider.'

'Does she know?' asked Fran gently, after a pause.

This time, Andrew's smile was warmer. 'Of course she does. Fay has been my greatest support and my best friend for the last fifty years. We have been the most faithful, the most enduring theatrical couple the world has known. Because we've kept our very private lives out of the spotlight. Not without difficulty, but in the main, the media have only known what we chose to give them.'

'We did wonder if Matthew had thrown his mobile away himself,' said Libby. 'If he had two, would he have thrown them both away?'

'Only if they both contained something he considered damaging. I can understand him throwing mine away, but the other one ...' Andrew frowned. 'If he did, it was because of Celia's death. He must have known who did it.'

'If it was murder, and she didn't just hit her head and drown, as the police thought,' said Peter.

They all thought about this for a minute.

'Andrew,' said Libby, 'do you know who Harry's granny is – or was?'

'Was,' said Andrew. 'She died some time ago.'

'Was it Lady Bligh?' asked Harry.

'No.' Andrew shook his head.

'They all knew her, though, didn't they?' said Fran. 'Lady

Bligh and the Clippings.'

'And the Dougans,' added Libby.

Andrew nodded.

'And you aren't going to tell us, are you?' said Fran.

Andrew smiled. 'I promised Matthew I never would, and I never have. And to be honest, I don't think it has any relevance to the question of murder. There are very few people to whom it would mean that much these days. And why go after Harry?'

'That's more or less the conclusion we came to,' said Peter. 'The sisters are the only ones left who are trying to keep the secret of Alfred Morton. No one else would care.'

'Don't forget Reginald Morton was quite a famous poet in his day. If this was brought up now, it might lead to a resurgence of interest in his work,' said Andrew.

'But that would surely be good for the sisters, if they hold the rights to his works?' said Ben.

'When did he die?' said Harry.

'1953, so he's still in copyright,' said Andrew. 'You're right there.'

'Perhaps they don't realise that,' said Libby.

'No, I think it's more that they are of their generation – and mine, to be fair – and old scandal should not be talked about. They would be ashamed.' Andrew finished his glass of wine. 'Now, anything else you'd like to ask me?'

There were several questions about Matthew's life that Andrew answered genially and without any attempt to gloss over the reality of his relationship with Matthew.

'Fay and I used to stay with him sometimes, and at others, he would come and stay with us. We even stayed with him on the Island.'

'So you knew the sisters?' said Libby.

'Not knew, exactly. We met them. An odd bunch – out of time, almost. Celia was the best of them. She was far more up-to-date in her outlook, and oddly, the only one who didn't marry.'

'The one Matthew was closest to,' said Harry. 'She wasn't

my grandmother, was she?' He shuddered. 'He couldn't have raped his own sister.'

'No, she wasn't,' said Andrew, 'and yes, Matthew was closest to her. She was the only one who didn't expect him to support her. The other three – well.'

'We think Honoria was a sculptor involved in a movement called the Geometry of Fear,' said Fran. 'Are we right?'

'You are. She had always loved making things, and after – well, after the scandal, she went to London and managed to get on to some course or other.' He shook his head. 'I don't remember much about it. Then she married another artist, who eventually died in poverty quite young, so she came back to the Island.'

'What about the others? The only one who said anything was Amelia, and she seems quite proud of the fact that her husband was a diplomat,' said Libby.

'He was a very junior attaché in some very boring places. Amelia rather jumped at the chance of getting away. I don't think it was a love match.'

'And Alicia? She married a Hope-Fenwick, apparently,' said Harry.

Andrew raised his eyebrows. 'That's what she's calling him, is it?'

'Why? Wasn't that his name?' said Libby.

'It certainly wasn't! His name was Helmut Hoffmann. He was German.'

'*German*?' gasped Libby, while the others all muttered in surprise.

'Yes.' Andrew smiled his cynical smile. 'You can see why she disappeared!'

'Was he a prisoner of war?' asked Peter.

'He had been. There were several camps in Hampshire, and when he was released he went to the Island to work on a farm. Alicia met him – don't know how – and they fell in love. She was over twenty-one, so her parents couldn't stop her, and they married in a registry office in Newport. Then Alfred was let out of prison.'

'And they scarpered,' said Harry.

'They scarpered.'

'Leaving poor old Reg to clear up the mess,' said Peter.

'Indeed.'

'So is the assumption that all three of the girls left the Island because of Alfred's suicide?' asked Ben.

'And the rape,' said Harry.

'Oh yes,' said Andrew.

'But what about Celia? What did she do?' asked Libby.

'She was still a minor in the eyes of the law, so she stayed with her parents. And Matthew was there. I think they comforted each other.'

'The sisters said that he was closer to Celia than any of them,' said Libby.

'So poor Celia had to suffer the fallout from the scandal while her sisters escaped.' Peter shook his head. 'What a nightmare.'

'I believe it was. Of course, it had all happened before I met Matthew, and by that time he was living in London. Celia used to go and stay with him, and we used to go out all together.' He smiled. 'She was lovely. If I'd been straight I'd have fallen in love with her.'

'But you *did* get married,' said Libby.

'Ah, yes,' said Andrew, 'but then Fay and I had a mutual secret to keep. You see, Fay's gay, too.'

Chapter Twenty-nine

Harry frowned. 'Why have you kept it a secret?'

'We kept it for so long it didn't seem worth the hassle of making it public now. Think what a field day the press would have! They'd be delving into our past lives and coming up with all sorts of nasty little speculations, even though both Fay and I had long-term – and long-distance – relationships and no grubby little fumblings in the dressing rooms. These days, there would be someone popping up to say I'd assaulted them back in 1965 as soon as the word was out.' Andrew shook his head sadly.

'It's awful, isn't it?' said Libby sympathetically. 'We used to ignore the odd pat on the bottom in the old days, but now … Well, I can think of lots of men I could take to court on that basis.'

'Me, too,' said Fran.

'What did you both do? Were you secretaries?' asked Andrew.

Fran and Libby looked at each other and grinned.

'Actors,' they said together.

'Ah. Of course.' Andrew nodded. 'And now I'd better get back to the pub and bed.' He stood up. 'Just one more thing. You now know what the sisters are so concerned about keeping secret. I think you should leave it at that unless anyone tries anything else on Harry. And your policeman friend is on to that, is he not? I'm sure it isn't connected.'

Harry showed Andrew out and came back to the table.

'What does he know that he's not telling us?' he said as he poured himself more wine.

'The name of your gran for one thing,' said Peter.

'I agree with Harry,' said Ben. 'I think it's more than that. I also think that he's right, the anonymous letter is nothing to do with it.'

'What do we do, then?' said Libby.

'Nothing,' said Peter decisively. 'We know what the secret is, as Andrew said. Ian knows about the possible threat to Harry, we've warned the sisters off and now we even know all about the past lives of the sisters. I suggest we leave it alone.'

Libby nodded gloomily. 'I suppose so. It feels all wrong, though. Just leaving it hanging.'

Thursday was a warm, overcast day. Libby took the laptop into the conservatory and set about looking up Amanda Clipping and Lady Bligh.

Amanda had, as they had been told, spent most of her working life in London. She was currently in PR for a television production company. Her CV was online, together with social media links, but nowhere did it say anything about her personal life or where she came from.

'I suppose that's sensible,' Libby muttered to herself.

Lady Bligh was documented by virtue of her title. Before she had married Henry, Lord Bligh, she was plain Lily Cooper, daughter of Esmond and Alberta Cooper of Newport, Isle of Wight. The Bligh residence was, as Libby already knew, Etherington Manor in Beech. There was nothing more but her birth date, which fitted with the sisters' and Matthew's ages.

'So,' she said to Sidney, 'do we think all this lot gathered up at old Reg's castle being terribly arty? Did they all know Alfred? Did they all dash off after his suicide? And they must all have known the rape victim. I wish someone would talk to us.'

Sidney ignored her and tucked his nose under his tail.

'I suppose you're right. I should leave it alone. But I can't help wondering.'

The housekeeping had been somewhat neglected over the

last few days, as had shopping. Libby aimed a duster at the surfaces she could see in the sitting room, then made a list on the back of an envelope. She decided the eight-til-late, Bob the butcher, and the Cattlegreen Nursery shop would be able to supply everything she needed, collected her faithful basket and set off. The sun was trying to break through the high grey cloud, and it was still very warm. This week the children would break up from school, but today the village was quiet. She was the only customer in both the butcher's and the nursery shop, and only a couple of other people were in the eight-til-late.

She peered into The Pink Geranium as she passed but couldn't see Harry, which was odd as he was usually to be seen in the late mornings, either behind the counter or at the window table. She frowned and walked on. As she did so, a car pulled out in front of her from the car park behind the doctor's surgery and she jumped back as it shot off up the high street.

'You all right, gal?' came a shout from behind her.

She turned to see old Flo Carpenter coming down Maltby Close towards her.

'I saw that. Silly bar steward. What did he think he was doing?'

'Trying to make a quick get-away, it looked like,' said Libby thoughtfully.

Flo peered at her. 'What've you gone and got yourself into now?'

'Nothing. At least I hope not.' Libby looked across at The Pink Geranium again. 'Look, Flo, I must see if Harry's all right.'

Flo's neatly pencilled eyebrows shot up. 'Oh, yus?'

'Just watch me while I try and get into the caff, will you?'

Folding her arms and pursing her lips, Flo nodded. Libby looked both ways and shot across the road.

The Pink Geranium was locked. Libby banged on the door and the window, and even shouted through the letter box in the side door to the flat, but got no reply. She was just beginning to panic when Peter appeared at her side looking astonished.

'Where's Harry?' she panted.

'In the pub talking to Andrew,' said Peter. 'What on earth are you doing?'

Libby let out a long breath. 'I saw – I mean, I thought I saw – oh, look, were you going to join them in the pub? Can I come?'

'Yes, I think you'd better,' said Peter, taking the basket from her. Libby went to the kerb and waved across to Flo, who gave the thumbs-up sign and tottered back towards her own home.

'So what is this all about?' asked Harry when Peter had settled her at the corner table.

'I'll tell you when Pete comes back with the drinks.'

Peter put drinks on the table. 'Now tell us why you were acting like a madwoman.'

'Well,' Libby took a deep breath, 'just as I was going to cross Maltby Close, a car shot out of the doctor's car park and nearly ran me over.' She held up a hand at the three men's shocked comments. 'It wasn't that that upset me. It was the fact that I'm sure I'd seen him before.'

'Oh? Where?' asked Harry warily. 'Not –'

'Yes. On the Island. He was the young man Fran and I saw with Amanda Clipping that time. And he was in a hurry.'

Peter and Harry looked at each other.

'What did you think?' asked Andrew.

'Well, Harry's already had anonymous letters, the last one hand delivered here. I thought – if he knows Harry's here – well, then I couldn't raise Harry, and I thought …'

'Do you think we ought to check the caff?' asked Peter.

'I would,' said Libby. 'He may have tried to get in round the back. He looked young. He could have climbed over the wall.'

'You two wait here,' said Peter. He and Harry got up and left.

'Who do you think he is?' asked Andrew.

'No idea, but he knows Amanda Clipping. It can't be her threatening Harry, she's got no reason.'

'Hmm.' Andrew looked down into his coffee cup. 'He must

be connected to someone else, then?'

'I don't know. I don't know who the other man was either.'

'What other man?'

Libby explained about the older man in the wheelchair. 'We even thought it might be you. Or Lucifer, as we knew him.'

Andrew smiled. 'No, it wasn't me.'

'We know that now. It's just such a puzzle. I thought we were supposed to have left the whole thing alone.'

Peter reappeared in the doorway. 'Attempted break-in. Harry's calling the police.'

Libby stood up. 'Where? At the back?'

'Yes. The kitchen door and the door to the flat. Stay here, I'm going back to Hal.'

Libby had time to drink her lager and Andrew had finished his coffee by the time Harry and Peter rejoined them.

'They've got people dusting everything for fingerprints, or whatever it is,' said Harry. 'I told them we'd been in touch with DCI Connell previously, and I think they were going to let him know. I can't open at lunchtime.'

'Nothing's badly damaged, though,' said Peter, 'and because he couldn't get in, nothing was taken. They want a statement from you, Lib.'

'Now?'

'Someone will get in touch, they said.'

At that moment Libby's mobile began to ring. She looked at the screen.

'Ian,' she said.

'Libby, I need to talk to you. One of the officers at the scene will take a brief statement, then I want to talk to you later. I'm supposed to be off duty, so I could come down this afternoon. I want to look at the restaurant anyway.'

'OK. I'll be in. Do I go and talk to an officer now?'

'You're in the pub, aren't you? They'll come and get you from there.'

Sure enough, an officer arrived five minutes later and took Libby's statement. 'DCI Connell will be in touch, ma'am,' he said.

'He already has,' said Libby. 'Will I have to come into the station to sign that?'

'Not sure, ma'am. DCI Connell will tell you.'

When he'd gone, Andrew stood up. 'You all need to get back to your lives. Are you opening tonight, Harry?'

'I think so. I hope so.'

'Then perhaps Libby and Ben and Peter will dine there with me? I shall go home tomorrow. What about your friend Fran?'

'I'll ask her,' said Libby. 'She'll want to know about this, anyway.'

Considerably shaken, Libby went home to call first Ben, then Fran, who both said they'd be delighted to dine with Andrew at The Pink Geranium.

'If we're allowed of course,' Libby said to Sidney, as she went to open the door to Ian Connell.

'Now, tell me exactly what you saw and how certain you are that you'd seen this man before.' He sat opposite her, his dark eyes intent on her face. Libby thought again how attractive he was, and slapped down a little "What if?" scenario creeping in to her head. She repeated her story, and told Ian about the meeting on the Isle of Wight.

'So he has a connection with the whole business on the Island?'

'We don't know,' said Libby. 'The secret the old ladies seem to be worried about is nothing to do with Harry – well, it is, but not any reason to threaten him. But why would Amanda Clipping want to?' She shook her head. 'I don't get it.'

'Don't worry, we'll get to the bottom of it. He could be someone just employed to spy on Harry, nothing to do with the whole thing personally.'

'But someone employed him,' said Libby.

Ian inclined his head. 'But whatever he was supposed to do this morning, he wasn't equipped to break into the restaurant. The marks on the doors weren't made by anything particularly sharp, and we think a credit card was used to try and open the locks.'

'But they'd be deadlocked,' said Libby.

'Exactly, so whoever he is, he isn't a professional burglar.'

'So what was he supposed to do? Did he expect to find Harry in the restaurant? Did he expect him to be alone?'

'We don't know, but what we do know is that whoever sent that last note knew where Harry was, and it's a workable theory that they've been watching him, and know he's usually alone late morning.'

'Yes,' said Libby. 'That's why I wondered where he was when I went past.' She shivered. 'That's horrible. To think of Harry being spied on like that. It almost looks as if …' she trailed off.

'They were waiting for an opportunity,' Ian finished for her.

Chapter Thirty

'But why? If they've been watching Harry, they'll know we all know whatever it is they're trying to keep secret. There were the other things – the note on the Island. And if the sisters are behind it ...'

'It looks to me as if it isn't anything to do with the sisters,' said Ian. 'We're now instigating a full investigation along with the Island police, who are going to talk to the ladies.'

'Good luck,' said Libby. 'I bet they don't get anything out of them.'

'I don't think they will either, but meanwhile, I shall be interviewing Ms Clipping. Not that I think she'll be forthcoming – all she has to do is deny everything.'

'She will, and look amused while she's doing it,' said Libby. 'I wonder if she'll tell you who the men were with her that day.'

'She might, but then she might say they were completely different people.'

'I've said this before,' said Libby, 'but I wish there were guest lists at funerals. They were both there at Matthew's, although we didn't notice them. The sisters told us, and Amanda confirmed it.'

'What about the memorial service?' said Ian.

'I didn't see them there, but it was so crowded I could have missed them. Amanda was there with the sisters and two older couples, one of whom must have been her parents, and we think the others were some people called Dougan, who were also at the funeral.'

'We can find them and talk to them,' said Ian.

'Which we couldn't,' said Libby. 'Now, I suppose I ought to

tell you all about our discoveries this week.'

'And make me a cup of tea while you're doing it,' said Ian, following her into the kitchen.

Libby related the story of Alfred Morton and included the stories of the sisters' various pasts. She let Andrew stay out of the picture.

'We'll look into it, Lib, don't worry.' Ian took his mug from her. 'And you can stay out of it.'

'I'll be glad to, as long as nothing happens to Harry,' said Libby. 'With some cases, it's quite enjoyable nosing things out.'

'Don't I know it,' said Ian with a smile.

'But this is different. When a friend is threatened ...' Libby shrugged and led the way back to the sitting room.

'It's often personal with you, though, isn't it?' Ian sat down and looked at her over the top of his mug.

'At first it was. Well, I could hardly help but be involved in our first murder, could I?'

'I wasn't around for that one,' said Ian. 'You had to deal with Mr Murray.'

'Oh, yes, our Donnie.' Libby smiled. 'Bless him. You didn't appear until the end of our second – what? Adventure? And we got into that because it was Fran's aunt.'

'I can't say I ever expected to have Harry involved with anything,' said Ian. 'He's always just been there. Being irreverent.'

'Providing the light entertainment,' agreed Libby. 'Although remember that business over in Maidstone, with his friend Cy.'

'I do,' said Ian. 'I remember all your er – adventures. Luckily, I do have other cases to distract me when you aren't in – in –'

'Investigating?' suggested Libby.

'I was going to say "In trouble",' said Ian and drank the rest of his tea. 'I'm going now. I'll call in at the station on the way home and put a few enquiries in train, then I'll see if I can't salvage the rest of my day off.'

'I'm sorry, Ian.' Libby was contrite.

'It was hardly your fault, was it?' Ian bent and dropped a kiss on Libby's cheek. 'Don't get up, I'll see myself out. And,' he paused at the door, 'be careful.'

Libby stared after him. He wasn't *flirting*, was he? She shook her head and stood up. Of course he wasn't. Ian was a friend. A man who had once dated Fran and who had always known her, Libby, as part of a couple with Ben, whom he liked.

'So stop it,' she said aloud. 'I wish people could stop being attractive once you're in a committed relationship.'

With this rather scrambled statement, she took herself out into the garden and took a determined trowel to the weeds.

When Ben and Libby arrived at The Pink Geranium that evening Fran and Guy were already sitting at the big window table with Peter and Andrew. Harry appeared with bottles of wine and demanded to know what Ian had said that afternoon before he went and cooked their dinner. Libby related it all. Except the kiss on the cheek.

'And I didn't mention Andrew at all,' she finished. 'That isn't my story to tell, and anyway, nothing to do with the break-in or any of the rest of it.'

Andrew looked thoughtful. 'You know, I think I ought to see this Inspector and tell him my part of the story.'

Harry looked doubtful, but Fran nodded.

'I think that's a good idea, if you don't mind doing it. Ian's very discreet and understanding.'

'He's had to be, dealing with you two over the years,' said Guy.

'I'd really like to hear some of your adventures,' said Andrew, when the laughter had died down. 'Harry was telling me a little bit about it.'

'I think the boys would be bored,' said Libby.

'They don't really approve,' agreed Fran.

'But you've been in on this one,' said Peter. 'We all have.'

'It all started,' began Ben surprisingly, 'when we were rehearsing for the first production in our theatre.'

Harry rolled his eyes. 'I'll send someone to take your order. Don't leave out my heroic roles, will you?'

By the time they had worked their way through their meals and three bottles of wine, Andrew knew most of what had happened to Libby and Fran over the last few years.

'And this Ian has been involved in all of that?' he said, when they'd finished laughing at a remembered incident.

'Well, mostly. He's our policeman of choice. We're very lucky,' Libby avoided Fran's eyes, 'that he became a proper friend, and he knew he could rely on some of Fran's moments.'

'He came to our wedding.' Guy put his hand over Fran's and they smiled at each other.

'He didn't come to ours,' said Peter, poking the remains of a chocolate empanada. 'We didn't know him well enough then.'

'I must admit to being intrigued about your "moments".' Andrew put his elbows on the table and leant towards Fran, who coloured faintly.

'I don't know much about them myself,' she said. 'They just happen. I don't seem to have any control over them.'

'And not so frequently these days,' said Libby.

'They've come to your rescue several times,' said Ben.

'And Ian trusts them,' said Peter. 'In fact that's why they've got involved sometimes, because Ian asks Fran in. He did that with the Anderson Place business.'

'But Harry asked me to investigate because his friend Danny was a suspect that time,' said Libby.

'I don't think I can sort all these murders out,' laughed Andrew. 'You certainly seem to have a knack of getting involved.'

'It's just that one leads to another, really,' said Libby modestly.

'And the fact that you're incurably nosy,' said Ben.

'It's a thought, though,' said Libby, as she and Ben walked home later. 'I know we've said it before, but Fran does seem to have switched off.'

'She had a couple of thoughts while we were on the Island,

didn't she?'

'Yes, but all very vague. I want her to have a real, concrete vision. Like she did over that witchcraft business at St Aldeberge's.'

'I don't think she can work to order,' said Ben.

'But she did when she was employed by that estate agency. He used to send her into houses and expect her to sense something.'

'I know, and I used her too, as you know, but she was in practice, then. She isn't, now.'

'Oh, well,' sighed Libby, 'we'll just have to rely on dear old Ian, won't we?'

'Did you give him the number plate of the car you saw this morning?'

'I gave the officer at the scene the number,' said Libby. 'What I could remember of it. You always tell yourself that when you see a car doing something dangerous you'll automatically remember the number, but you don't. I'm afraid I didn't even register the make. It was new, longish, and silver, that's all.'

'And,' said Libby the following Sunday morning, 'it was caught on CCTV on the Canterbury Road.' She smiled triumphantly at Ben across the breakfast table as she relayed the news.

'Bloody hell, the poor bloke's been in to work early on a Sunday, hasn't he?' said Ben, forking up bacon.

'They called him yesterday evening, apparently, which didn't please him as he was out.' Libby paused. 'I wonder where? Where does he go on his days and nights off? Do you think he's got a girlfriend?'

'Wouldn't you have winkled that out of him by now?'

'No.' Libby sighed. 'He can be very close when he wants to be.'

'So what else did he tell you?'

'Sadly, the car was stolen. Reported missing on Thursday from somewhere in south London. It was found abandoned in

Surrey somewhere. Actually, parked up quite neatly and completely wiped clean.'

'A professional?' Ben raised an eyebrow.

'If it was someone hired to frighten Harry, I suppose.' Libby shook her head. 'Anyway, that's all at the moment. So what are we doing today?'

Ben looked surprised. 'I don't know, apart from going to lunch with Hetty. Why?'

'Oh, I don't know. I'd just like to get out for a bit. Somewhere we don't normally go, make a proper little trip.'

Ben looked doubtful. 'Do you want me to put Hetty off?'

'No, no, she'll have done all the preparation now, you know what she's like. And she'd be so disappointed. No, I just thought we could go out for the morning and come back for about half past one.'

'We could. What are you up to?' said Ben suspiciously.

'Nothing. I mean it. I just want to get away from the village and Nethergate, if it comes to that, and blow the cobwebs away.'

'Really? Well, in that case, how about a look at Samphire Hoe? We keep saying we'll go.'

'Lovely!' Libby bounced up from her chair. 'I'll go and find my walking boots.'

'Your awful trainers, you mean,' said Ben with a grin. 'Go on, then.'

Samphire Hoe was opened in 1997 as the result of the excavations for the Channel Tunnel. It had been turned into a nature reserve and was now the home to various rare species of plants, animals and insects. Easy to get to, and easy to walk around for lazy walkers like Libby, it had the sea on one side and the cliffs on the other and, on this Sunday morning, a lot of other visitors.

'Lovely, isn't it?' Libby looked down on to the sea and across to the busy port of Dover.

'Yes, but actually, I preferred those cliff tops on the Island,' said Ben. 'Less managed.'

'We weren't going to talk about that,' reproved Libby, 'but yes, I know what you mean.'

'Want a cup of tea here, or shall we head back?'

'It's too crowded,' said Libby, 'and the tea will be awful, anyway. Come on, back to the car.'

On the drive back from Dover, Libby switched on her mobile, which, in the interests of peace, had been off throughout the journey.

'Message from Peter,' she said. 'It says he's been ringing.' She called Peter's number.

'Lib? Thank goodness. Where the hell are you? We've been trying to raise you all morning.'

'Why? What's up?' Libby felt the awful feeling in the solar plexus normally known as heart sinking.

'It's Harry. He's been hurt.'

Chapter Thirty-one

'Hurt? Where? How badly?' Libby turned horrified eyes to Ben.

'I found him in the garden this morning. He must have heard something ...We're at the hospital now.'

'We're on our way back from Dover,' said Libby. 'We'll come straight to the hospital.'

'We're not in Canterbury,' said Peter. 'We're in bloody Ashford.'

'Do you want us to come?' said Libby.

'Yes, please. I came in the ambulance, so I can't get home.'

'All right. We're coming up to the Canterbury slip road now, so we'll be with you in –' She turned to Ben. 'Ashford?'

'Twenty minutes. Are you still in A & E?'

'No. They've whisked him off. Ask at the reception. They'll have the details, because the police have been here all morning. Ian came.'

'OK. We'll be with you as soon as we can.'

Libby switched off the phone and relayed the news to Ben.

'So someone really is out to get him,' he said. 'And the only thing I can think of is Matthew's money.'

'His gran's money,' said Libby. 'I agree. I can't see anyone going after Harry to keep something quiet, as we've already said. It must be someone who expected to get something in Matthew's will who didn't.'

'But did they know about his gran?' said Ben. 'Did they know that Harry was going to get that money as well as whatever he got from Matthew?'

'We don't know if he actually got money from Matthew. We

know he got Ship House and the Beach House.'

'Useless speculating now,' said Ben, as he drove as fast as he could along the A28.

They found Peter sitting miserably in a waiting area with a uniformed officer trying to fade into the background.

'So what exactly happened?' asked Libby as they sat down on either side of him.

'I woke up and found he was already up. That didn't bother me – I thought he'd gone down to make tea and would be back in a moment. After a bit, I thought I'd go down and see what was keeping him.' Peter paused and wiped his hand over his face. 'And then I saw the back door was open. And he was on the floor. On the concrete. I thought ... I thought ...'

'Yes,' said Libby, squeezing his arm. 'So then you called the police?'

'Ambulance, but they said the police would attend as well. Then I rang the doctor over the road, who came dashing over in his dressing gown,' Peter managed a shaky laugh, 'and was brilliant. He couldn't do much, as he said he'd be disturbing the evidence, but he made sure Hal was breathing and – oh, I don't know exactly what he did, but when the paramedics arrived they seemed pleased. The first officers on the scene weren't too pleased, though. I'm afraid I lost my temper with them, and told them I'd sic DCI Connell on to them. Then they got on to him – or the station – pretty quickly, I can tell you.'

'So what had happened to him?' asked Ben.

'The traditional blunt instrument. Removed of course. Luckily, Ian turned up very soon after that. Someone at the station had seen the call come in on the wire and told him, and of course, he came straight away. Good job he did, or I'd still be at home being questioned by those two oafs.'

'Weren't they going to let you go in the ambulance?' said Libby.

'No, of course not! I'd just been found alone with the victim! I was the obvious suspect.'

'Lucky Ian knew all about the case then,' said Ben.

'He called in his forensics people and left the two officers in charge, then followed the ambulance. He certainly gets things done when he's on the case.'

'He was good when you ended up here, too,' Libby said to Ben. 'So does he have any ideas? And what about Harry? How badly hurt is he?'

'They're worried about bleeding on the brain.' Peter shuddered. 'They've got to keep him under until they can assess the damage. Then if it's safe, they'll operate. And I'm afraid Ian's latched on to poor Andrew.'

'*Andrew*? Why?'

'He turned up because he saw the ambulance. He was just about to leave. So of course, Ian wanted to know ...' Peter shrugged. 'Anyway, more-or-less told him to stay put, and now he's gone off to question him.'

'Well, I suppose it might look suspicious. Someone from Matthew's past turns up and the very next day there's an attempt on the caff, and now an attack on Harry. And Andrew due to leave this morning.' Libby frowned. 'You don't believe it, do you?'

'No, I don't,' said Peter, 'but you're right, it does look suspicious. I hope Andrew can convince Ian.'

A doctor appeared through swing doors and approached Peter. Ben and Libby moved away. After a moment, the doctor disappeared and Peter turned to them.

'They're keeping him under for the time being,' he said, 'but all the signs are he'll be fine. I won't be able to see him or talk to him until later, so they've suggested I go home and collect some stuff for him.'

'Good idea.' Ben looked at his watch. 'And just in time for lunch with Hetty.'

Hetty was unfazed by the arrival of an extra guest, probably because she cooked enough to feed the whole village every weekend. As she served slices of perfectly cooked roast lamb, fragrant with garlic and rosemary, Peter told her about Harry..

'I've just thought,' said Libby, helping herself to roast

potatoes, 'what about the caff? Did he have any bookings this lunchtime?'

'I called Donna, and she came down to go through the books, bless her. Brought the baby with her. It's a good job she's used to unsocial hours.'

Donna, who had been Harry's right-hand woman in The Pink Geranium for years, was now married to a registrar at the hospital in Canterbury and worked for Harry doing accounts and occasionally bailing him out (as with the trips to the Isle of Wight) when he needed it.

'Shame her husband's not at Ashford, then we might get inside info on Hal,' said Libby.

'I don't think we'd get it,' said Ben. 'The medical profession is very wary of giving information to anyone.'

'Do you think we should check on Andrew?' Libby asked towards the end of the meal. 'In case Ian's stopped him from leaving?'

'I suppose so,' said Peter, reluctantly, 'although I don't know what I'd say to him.'

'Don't worry, we'll do it,' said Ben. 'You just get off back to the hospital with Hal's best pyjamas.'

'Oh!' Peter put his hand to his mouth. 'We don't wear pyjamas.'

Hetty stood up. 'Bought some new ones for Greg just before – Anyway, still in the packet. Tall bloke, like your Harry. Want them?'

'Hetty, you're a lifesaver.' Peter gave her a kiss. 'Yes, please.'

When Peter left with the blue-striped pyjamas, Ben used the estate office's landline to call the pub and asked for Andrew.

'Yes, I'm still here,' came the weary reply. 'Your tame policeman was very nice, but rather wearing. I don't know if I'm off the suspect list or not.'

'So has he asked you to stay put?'

'For the time being, he said. I guess so that he can check up on the information I've given him.'

242

'Did you tell him about you and Matthew and you and your wife?'

Andrew sighed. 'I felt I should. I'm sure he's far too discreet to let any of the information out unless it's relevant.'

'No, he won't,' said Ben.

'How's Harry? Do you know?'

Ben told him as much as they knew, and that Peter was going back to the hospital.

'They wouldn't let me see him, of course?' Andrew sounded wistful.

'Even Peter couldn't see him this morning, and he's next of kin, so it'll be a while, especially if they keep him in an induced coma.'

'Poor Harry. And poor me. If he could wake up, at least the police would know it wasn't me.'

'We don't know that he saw or recognised his attacker,' said Ben. 'Far more likely that he didn't.'

'Where was the blow? It was a blow to the head, wasn't it?'

'Yes, but I have no idea where it was. We'll keep you posted.'

'Have you eaten today? I was going to book dinner here in the pub.'

'We've just had Sunday lunch with my mother – it's tradition. But Libby and I could perhaps join you for a drink this evening after you've eaten? If you'd like us to.'

'I would, very much. I'm rather bored and lonely, and now very anxious indeed. About eight thirty, then?'

Ben informed Libby when he returned to the kitchen, where she and Hetty were finishing off the last of the claret.

'That's fine,' she said. 'He's a nice old boy, and I really don't think he's got any motive for hurting Hal.'

'Unless he expected something from Matthew's will,' said Ben.

'He's rich enough, so's his wife,' said Libby. 'And he's far too frail to go hitting tall young men over the head.'

When Libby and Ben got home later that afternoon they

found Ian Connell just turning away from the door of number seventeen.

'I was just about to come up to the Manor to see if you were there.'

'We were,' said Libby. 'Is this a formal visit?'

'No, not really.' Ian followed them into the house. 'I could do with tea, though?' He looked hopeful. Libby grinned and went into the kitchen.

'So what do you want to tell me?' he said when Libby had provided mugs all round.

'Tell you?' Libby was surprised.

'Don't you want to tell me about Andrew McColl?'

Ben and Libby looked at each other. Libby sighed.

'What do you want to know?'

'When you met him. What he's told you, his relationship with Harry and with Matthew DeLaxley.'

'I expect he's told you everything already. He said he had,' said Ben.

'Oh, you've been in touch?'

'Yes. We thought you might have put him under curfew, so we thought we ought to check up on him and tell him what we knew about Harry,' said Libby. 'We're having a drink with him this evening.'

'Be careful about what you tell him,' said Ian.

'Oh, you can't seriously think he's got anything to do with all this?' said Libby. 'That old man?'

'That old man, you must remember, is an actor who is still working, and used to be known for his stage fighting skills,' said Ian.

'But not now he's in his eighties,' said Ben. 'And what would his motive be?'

'To keep his relationship with DeLaxley quiet?'

'Rubbish. We didn't even know he had one until he told us – all of us – when he appeared here the other day.'

Ian's face relaxed slightly. 'Yes, that's what he said. So Harry didn't know about him before?'

'Well, strictly speaking, he did. So did we,' said Ben. 'He was the person Matthew referred to as Lucifer. But he can't have been behind the earlier letter. He went to Matthew's solicitor to find Harry, and the solicitor called Harry to ask his permission first. Andrew wouldn't have known who Harry was any more than Hal knew him.'

'That's what he says,' said Ian, 'But he could be lying.'

'Well,' said Libby with a sigh, 'I suppose you have to be suspicious of everybody.'

'Except you, luckily. Oh, and by the way, I heard from the Isle of Wight police. They've traced Keith Franklin.'

'Really?' Libby sat up straight. 'Where?'

'He's living in Amanda Clipping's house.'

Chapter Thirty-two

'He was the man in the wheelchair!' Libby turned to Ben.

'Remind me,' said Ian. 'Man in a wheelchair?'

Libby told him again of the meeting with Amanda in the pub garden. 'And the man I saw in the car was with them.'

'Oh, things are beginning to tie up.' Ian put down his mug. 'I suppose the man you saw couldn't *be* Keith Franklin?'

'Much too young,' said Libby. 'Keith Franklin is Harry's dad. Looks to me as if he's paying the younger man to get rid of Harry.'

'But why? Keith Franklin was adopted and never knew his real mother,' said Ian.

'But Harry was told that Keith Franklin had found out about his mother and come back to the Island. He must have been all muffled up like he was when we saw him to prevent people recognising him,' said Libby.

'But no one on the Island had ever seen him,' objected Ben. 'How would they know who he was?'

'I don't know – perhaps he was the spitting image of his mother, or his father, of course. He might look exactly like Alfred Morton, who people would remember because of what he did.'

'It's possible,' said Ian. 'And it certainly is a link. I'm going over to the Island tomorrow to question him.'

'Have they picked him up?' asked Libby. 'Only if he's pre-warned he'll skip.'

'You've been watching too many TV programmes, Libby,' said Ian, standing up with a grin. 'We do know what we're doing.'

'Well,' said Libby, when Ian had gone. 'That's a turn-up for the books. Do we tell Andrew when we see him?'

'I think it's wiser not to say anything about the business,' said Ben. 'I don't suspect Andrew any more than you do, but we don't want to muddy any waters. We can call Peter though.'

'Won't he have had to turn his phone off?'

'We can try,' said Ben and took out his phone.

Peter answered almost straight away, and was able to tell them that Harry was showing signs of life, and they'd allowed him in to sit beside him for a while. There was a police guard on him, although they didn't expect any trouble. Ben told him what Ian had told them.

'I won't tell Harry anything, even if he does come round,' said Peter. 'But it's good to know things are moving at last.'

Andrew was sitting in the corner of the pub by the empty fireplace when Libby and Ben joined him later. When he came back from fetching drinks he asked after Harry.

'Progressing as far as we know,' said Libby. 'We spoke to Peter this afternoon, but he's had to turn his phone off.' She crossed her fingers under the table.

'You know, I do see why I look suspicious to the police.' Andrew twirled his glass between his fingers. 'I just hope Ronald Deakin can confirm that I knew nothing about Harry before he told me.'

'I was thinking,' said Libby. 'Mr Deakin must be the only person who knew everything about Matthew. He must know who Harry's gran is, because of the money Matthew was administering for her estate.'

'Maybe,' said Ben, 'but it's quite possible that was a private agreement. She just left it to Matthew trusting him to do the right thing.'

'It's worth asking, though, isn't it?'

'I doubt if he'd tell you,' said Andrew. 'Look how careful he was about putting Harry in touch with his natural mother and me. The police might get more from him.'

'I think they've already talked to him,' said Libby.

'Actually, I assume they have, I don't *know*. I expect they'll speak to him tomorrow.'

'To check up on me,' said Andrew. 'And then perhaps they'll let me go home.'

'I can't quite understand why they wanted you to stay here,' said Ben. 'After all, you could just go whenever you wanted. No one's guarding you.'

'It was a request,' said Andrew. 'I thought it best to comply.'

'Well, there's nothing to be done now,' said Libby, 'so we might just as well enjoy your company. And you can tell us some stories from your distinguished career!'

Andrew laughed. 'I've had a very unremarkable career! But thank you for flattering me.'

For the rest of the evening Andrew did indeed tell them anecdotes from his long career, and disposed of a few popular myths. They parted on the best of terms when the landlord called time.

'It's nothing to do with him,' said Libby, as they walked home. 'He's far too nice.'

'I've heard lots of murderers are,' said Ben.

'But we've got to remember whoever is behind this left Celia for dead in that Beach House. And then somehow got out of Candle Cove before the sea came in. Andrew couldn't have done that.'

'But the young bloke you saw could have done.'

'But we decided he had something to do with Keith Franklin.'

'Ian will find out,' said Ben comfortably. 'All we have to worry about now is Harry's recovery.'

The following morning, Peter reported that Harry was awake, and they were allowing Ian to speak to him later.

'That means he won't be able to get to the Island early,' said Ben.

'I expect he thought Harry would find it easier to talk to him than some anonymous officer,' said Libby.

'I expect Pete will tell us later. Do you think we'd be allowed to visit today?'

'I'll ring the hospital and ask,' said Libby. 'You go off to the office now, and I'll let you know if I hear anything.'

Libby worked on the painting still standing in the conservatory until Andrew called later in the morning.

'I've been let off the hook. Although they have asked that I keep them informed of my movements.'

'Did they say why? Who was it told you?'

'Just an officer, and I've no idea why. I assume they'd been in touch with Ronald Deakin and my wife to confirm alibis and so on.'

'Probably,' said Libby, and relayed the information about Harry. 'We'll keep you posted if you like.'

Ian was the next to call.

'Andrew told me you'd let him off the hook,' said Libby. 'I said we'd keep him posted about Harry.'

'Now, Libby, that's exactly what you must *not* do,' said Ian. 'We don't want anyone knowing how Harry is, or even if he's regained consciousness.'

'Oh. In case they try again, you mean?'

'Possibly. I've spoken to Harry, who doesn't remember much about it except hearing something outside. And Ronald Deakin confirms that he knew nothing about Andrew until he sent a letter after Matthew's death.'

'Eh? You mean Matthew left a letter for him?'

'Yes. Apparently there were several things he left, including the letter from Matthew to Harry.'

'The one where we learnt who Hal's mum was.'

'Yes. I shall be talking to her, too.'

'Meanwhile what about Keith Franklin? Are you going over to see him?'

'Yes. You've seen the house, haven't you?'

'Yes, it's called Beech Manor. There's a village shop run by a really nice bloke called Bernie Small. He knows the sisters, including Celia, and grew up with Amanda Clipping.'

'That is actually a help, Libby, believe it or not. If I can, I'll let you know how things go. And don't spread this around. I shouldn't be telling you anything.'

'I know, and I'll only tell Pete and Ben.'

'And Fran. One of her insights would help.'

'I know. Ben and I were only saying how she doesn't seem to get them any more, although she did have a brief one on the Island, but it didn't signify anything.'

'What was it?' Ian was alert. 'Do you remember?'

'First of all, she knew I wanted to talk about Harry as soon as we met her off the ferry. And she wondered if Keith Franklin thought the money should go to him.'

'Based on – what?'

'She wasn't sure herself,' said Libby. 'You could always call her and ask. I'm going to call the hospital and see if Ben and I can visit Harry.'

Permission given, Libby left a message for Fran and one for Peter and went up to the Manor to tell Ben. Hetty gave them lunch and a basket of biscuits and fruit for Harry.

'That hospital food's no good for yer,' she said, as she saw them off.

'That's as good as asking us to give him her love,' said Ben, as he drove down the drive. 'Now, tell me everything that happened this morning.'

Libby repeated the substance of her phone calls.

'Curiouser and curiouser,' said Ben. 'But at least Ian's got things to look at, now.'

'I'd love to know what Keith Franklin has to say for himself. And where La Clipping comes into it.' Libby peered into Hetty's basket. 'Harry won't eat all this.'

'Neither will you,' warned Ben.

Harry was weak, pale and still hooked to various machines, but appeared to be pleased to see them. He was in a room of his own, and the only sign that anything about this particular patient was unusual was the presence of a uniformed officer seated in the corridor outside.

'I feel like a criminal,' he whispered. 'I mean, he can't ask every white coat that comes in here if they're real, can he?'

'I expect it's his presence alone which would stop someone,' said Peter. 'What have you got there?'

'Hetty sent it,' said Libby, tilting it to show Harry. 'She said hospital food was awful.'

'Lovely, but I can't eat much. Grapes would be nice.'

'Bother, there aren't any in here.' Libby poked among the contents of the basket.

'I'll run down to the hospital shop,' said Ben. 'They're bound to have some.'

'What news, then?' asked Peter.

Libby smiled at Harry. 'Andrew's gone home and sent his love and Ian's gone to the Island to talk to Keith Franklin.'

'They've found him?' said Harry.

'Staying in Beech Manor. You know, Amanda Clipping's house.'

'Does that mean anything?' Harry frowned, and Libby explained about the meeting in the pub near Parkhurst Forest.

'And that was the bloke who ran you over?' Harry reached out a hand.

'Nearly. And tried to break into the caff.' Libby took the hand.

'And bashed me on the head, too,' said Harry.

'Have you remembered?' asked Peter.

'No, just guessing.' Harry smiled weakly.

Ben came back with a sanitised plastic bag of grapes which Peter washed at the little sink.

'Have they said any more about when you can come home?' asked Libby.

'Not yet. I've got to be observed. And they might not have to operate after all.' Harry gave a tired smile. 'Thank God.'

'Thank the person who did it not hitting you hard,' said Peter, handing over grapes.

Ben and Libby stayed for another half an hour, but Harry was obviously tired, and they left with instructions to call

Donna and apprise her of the situation, and to go into The Pink Geranium and cancel any bookings made for the foreseeable future.

'They've all got telephone numbers,' said Peter. 'And use the caff phone. You don't want to run up a bill.'

'Awful to see him looking like that,' said Libby, as Ben drove out of the hospital car park.

'Good to see him awake, though. Not as bad as they thought at first,' said Ben.

'No.' Libby frowned. 'But you wonder why not?'

'Eh?' Ben shot her a quick startled look.

'Eyes on the road, Wilde. No, I meant if someone has been after Harry, wouldn't it have made sense to hit him a lot harder when they caught up with him?'

Ben thought for a moment. 'But Harry went out into the garden because he heard a noise. I would have thought that he was hit just so the person could escape.'

'But in that case, what did the person want? Were they looking for something, the same as they were in the caff?'

'They wouldn't expect someone to be in the caff in the morning, and they may have thought they could get in to the cottage while the boys were asleep. Because Peter's so often there during the day.' Ben was frowning at the road ahead. 'So it looks as though they *think* there's something to find, at least. Nothing else explains it.'

'But Harry hasn't got anything.' Libby looked bewildered. 'That can't be it, Ben.'

'Oh, I don't know. Let's just hope Ian has some news from the Island.'

Chapter Thirty-three

Peter came back from hospital and joined Libby and Ben for one of Libby's throw-it-all-together meals on Monday evening. The doctors were cautiously pleased with Harry, and said he could even be released by the end of the week.

'That's excellent,' said Libby. 'I wonder how long before he's fit to work?'

'Too long for Harry, I bet,' said Ben, helping himself to rice. 'He'll want to get back as soon as he gets out.'

'He's already said if he gets out on Friday he'll open on Tuesday,' said Peter. 'At least he'll rest for the weekend. But we'll see. He might feel too crap to bother.'

'Ben's got a theory about the attack,' said Libby. 'Tell him, Ben.'

'I can see the logic,' said Peter, when he'd finished, 'but as Lib says, Harry hasn't got anything.'

'But someone *thinks* he has,' said Libby, 'just like the sisters think he has. Or thinks we've found something.'

'But I thought we agreed we'd uncovered the secret. And found that newspaper clipping. There isn't anything else to find.' Peter pushed his plate away.

'There's only one thing we don't know,' said Ben, 'and that's the name of Hal's gran. That's what must be the last secret.'

'Well, Andrew wouldn't tell us, and he knows,' said Libby, 'but if Ian's questioning Keith Franklin and he'd found out, then he'll have to tell Ian.'

'There's no "have to" about it,' said Peter. 'He can refuse till the cows come home. He hasn't committed a crime.'

'Unless he hit Hal over the head. And we know it wasn't him but the younger one who tried to break into the caff,' said Libby.

'Allegedly,' said Ben.

'Perhaps we'll find out when Ian comes back,' said Peter. 'If he *can* tell us anything.'

'Like who killed Celia,' said Libby. 'We keep forgetting that was the start of all this.'

'I wonder who the sisters really thought had done it?' said Ben.

'My guess would be Keith Franklin. He'd come back to the Island, Matthew said.' Libby shook her head. 'I still can't believe they wanted us to look into it without telling us the background. There was no possibility of solving it.'

'You keep saying that,' said Ben. 'Not your problem any more. Just let Ian and our wonderful police force handle it.'

'I wonder, though,' said Libby, 'if all this will make the police look at Celia's death again?'

'It might, but I don't see how they can investigate it again now. They don't have a body to look at now.' Ben stood up to take plates to the sink. 'Now, let's drop it and go and watch some mindless TV.'

It was almost nine o'clock when Ian rang.

'I just wanted to ask you where exactly these sisters of yours live.'

'Where are you? Did you see Franklin?'

'I'll tell you when I get back tomorrow. Now – I'm on that long road – Military Road, is it? – heading towards Ventnor. Give me directions.'

Ben took the phone and gave concise directions, then rang off.

'What did you do that for? I wanted to ask –'

'I know you did,' said Ben with a grin. 'You already had asked. He was obviously in the car, and presumably wants to go and see the old girls tonight. I'm sure he'll have all the answers when he comes back.'

'I wonder if he'll get anything out of them?'

'Oh, stop it! You'd worry anything to death, wouldn't you?' Ben went into the kitchen and waved two bottles through the doorway. 'Whisky or wine?'

The following morning Libby called Fran.

'I'm dying to know what he found out, and what he made of the sisters. I'm so cross that in the end we were right out of it and have to learn everything second-hand.'

'Safer, though,' said Fran. 'Who knows when Honoria might have lost her temper and shoved you down the steps!'

'I suppose she didn't …' began Libby.

'Kill her sister? Don't be daft! Why?'

'She was the one Hal and I saw trying to search the Beach House that morning.'

'But you worked out why that was. They all wanted to know if there was anything relating to their brother there.'

'That's what we *think*,' said Libby. 'We don't *know* that.'

'So what are you going to do this morning?' asked Fran.

'I don't know. I could get out the vacuum, I suppose.'

'You really are desperate!' laughed Fran. 'How about a shopping trip with me?'

'Oh.' Libby brightened. 'Where? Canterbury?'

'Yes. I need a decent selection of cosmetics. We could have lunch.'

'And go and see Anne in the library.'

'You'll see her tomorrow in the pub,' said Fran, 'and she won't thank us for holding her up at work.'

'That's true. And I really ought to be thinking more about the show. We start next week.'

'Not until the Friday,' said Fran.

'OK, then Canterbury it is. Shall I meet you there?'

'I'll pick you up,' said Fran. 'Half an hour.'

Libby ran upstairs, changed into something slightly more appropriate for shopping in Canterbury and applied some make-up. She was ready when Fran tooted the horn of her little Smart car.

'Be just like Ian to call while we're out,' she said, buckling her seat belt.

'You've got your mobile with you, haven't you?'

'Yes. I remember these days,' said Libby.

But no one called while they sampled the delights of the make-up departments in the Canterbury stores, nor while they ate lunch in a noodle bar.

'Are you coming in for a cuppa?' asked Libby, as Fran drove back towards Steeple Martin.

'Of course. I haven't seen Sidney for days.'

'He's much nicer to you than he is to me,' said Libby.

There was no light flashing on the answerphone, and no missed messages on Libby's mobile when she checked.

'I don't understand it,' she said as she went to fill the kettle, 'He must be back by now.'

'He can't always keep you up to date,' said Fran, accepting Sidney's gracious advances. 'You aren't in the force.'

'No, but he got all the information from me,' complained Libby. 'I need to know.'

'I expect you will, eventually,' Fran put Sidney back on the floor and he stalked off, affronted. 'He may turn up at the pub tomorrow.'

'I suppose so. Then again, we might not hear for days. And I think Harry needs to know.'

'Well, perhaps he'll call Peter first.'

'Pete would phone me.'

'There's no pleasing you, is there?'

Libby poured boiling water into a teapot. 'I'm going to dig a bit further into the sisters' pasts. We know more about them since Andrew's visit. Coming?'

'I was hoping to sit in the garden,' said Fran. 'Don't forget I haven't got one.'

'I can't see the computer screen in the garden,' grumbled Libby.

'Cardboard box,' suggested Fran. 'There's the one in the conservatory you keep old rags in.'

'Eh?'

'Come on, I'll show you.'

Five minutes later they were sitting under the cherry tree, Fran with a mug of tea and Sidney on her lap, Libby with the laptop inside the cardboard box.

'Now, what did Andrew say Alicia's husband's real name was? Helmut Hoffman, wasn't it …' She tapped away for a few minutes, but nothing came up.

'Try Hope-Fenwick,' said Fran.

'Nothing.' Libby scowled at the screen. 'Not even a Facebook page.'

'Try the others then. What about Amelia?'

'We don't know her married name. I'll have another go at Honoria. At least she came up as Honoria Morton.'

'I wonder if there's more about her under her married name?'

'We don't know that, either. Hang on, I'll look into that Geometry of Fear thingy …'

'I'd never heard of that,' said Fran, 'although I had heard of some of the artists.'

Libby shook her head. 'No. There isn't even a proper entry for it in Wiki – just the sculptors, and not all of them. I can't find the article I first read.'

'Just type Honoria Morton,' said Fran. 'That'll find it.'

And of course it did.

'No, it still doesn't say much. No married name or anything.' Libby sat back, frustrated.

'I'll tell you who you haven't looked up,' said Fran. 'Matthew himself.'

'Oh.' Libby looked up in surprise. 'Haven't we? Didn't we do that when we looked up Reginald Morton?'

'Have another look.'

'No, I remember now, it was one of those "citation needed" sites. I'll have another look, though.' She typed Matthew's name into the search engine. 'Oh – look! Obituaries. Why didn't they come up last time?'

'I don't know. Perhaps you just put his name into Wiki and not Google.'

'Oh, look.' Libby turned the box towards Fran. 'This is a report on the memorial service.'

The both read the article on screen, hunched over the cardboard box, tea forgotten. They gasped at the same moment.

'A sister?'

'Who pre-deceased him?'

They sat back and looked at each other.

'Now why didn't we know that?' asked Libby.

'I've no idea, but it does put a new complexion on matters, doesn't it?' Fran picked up her mug. 'Ugh. This is cold.'

'I'll make some more,' said Libby, handing over the laptop-in-a-box. 'You carry on looking.'

By the time Libby got back with two fresh mugs of tea, Fran had found a few more details.

'I don't know why we didn't look further the first time,' she said. 'There are obits from all the broadsheets, and he even gets in to a couple of the redtops, too.'

'So what do they say?'

'Matthew had a brother who died in infancy and an older sister who died two years ago.'

'What was her name?'

'I haven't found it yet. None of them seem to mention it.' Fran looked up. 'That's odd.'

'What is? That they don't mention it?'

'Yes. Usually they do, don't they?'

'Is there anything about him being the nephew of Reginald Morton?'

'No, and no mention of the sculpting Honoria, either.'

'They really were trying to keep the whole relationship quiet, weren't they?' Libby mused. 'The obits would have been prepared in advance, so it looks as though there's been a systematic cover-up of the facts since Alfred died. Everything swept under the carpet, all records destroyed, sort of thing.

'I can't see what concealing the relationship between

Matthew and the Mortons has to do with anything,' said Fran, 'unless the obvious inference has to be drawn.'

'That's horrible,' said Libby.

'But makes even more sense of the sisters' desperation to keep everything quiet. Not only was their brother a convicted traitor and a suicide, but he raped –'

'His cousin,' said Libby.

Chapter Thirty-four

'Are we leaping to conclusions again?' said Fran.

'Possibly, but as you said, it is the obvious inference.' Libby looked up into the cherry tree. 'At least it wasn't one of his sisters, and we did wonder if Celia had been Hal's granny at one point.'

'Nearly as bad, as far as the family were concerned, I expect,' said Fran, 'and after all, they'd all been brought up together.'

'We know where the castle was, but we don't know where the DeLaxleys lived.'

'Must have been where The Shelf is now, don't you think? That's why Matthew owned the land. And Reginald built the castle next door after he married Tallulah. Lovely name, that.'

'So whoever Matthew sent Celia to meet that day was trying to find out about all this,' said Fran, frowning, 'and hit Celia over the head when she wouldn't tell him. Sounds unlikely.'

'That's the scenario we've been envisaging all along,' said Libby, 'and none of our investigations have got any nearer the real reason or the murderer.'

'Perhaps Ian will have some answers when he comes back. I'm getting impatient to hear from him now, too.'

However, all phones remained silent until Guy called Fran to ask what time she would be home and should he start dinner.

'I'd better go,' she said. 'Let me know the minute you hear anything from Ian.'

Libby assured her she would, and went to prepare her own dinner. Ben wandered in and offered a pre-dinner drink.

'Yes, please, G and T. I need it,' said Libby, and filled him in on the details learned from the internet that afternoon. 'I suppose I'd better tell Pete.'

'Leave it until he gets home from the hospital,' said Ben, handing her a gin and tonic. 'You never usually drink this.'

'It's a hot day. Gin and tonic is cooling.'

In fact, before she could call him, Peter called her.

'Just updating on the invalid's condition,' he said. 'He's now fretting about the caff and dying to get up. He's also being very rude to the nurses.'

'Oh, dear. Does this mean he's getting better?'

'Yes, most of the wires and things have been removed, and they're talking about tomorrow or Friday. They need to monitor his temperature, apparently.'

'I'm glad you called,' said Libby. 'Fran and I found something out today.'

'Bloody hell,' said Peter, when she'd finished telling him. 'And has Ian found Franklin?'

'No idea, he hasn't called.'

'Oh, well, I suppose you aren't the police. He doesn't have to. Have you gone through the caff bookings yet?'

'Oh, bugger! I forgot! I'll do it tomorrow.'

'Don't worry too much, Donna did all this week's. But whatever he says, Hal won't be fit enough to open next week.'

Libby had given up hoping to hear from Ian, so when the landline rang at just after ten thirty Ben answered it.

'It's Ian,' he said. 'Will we be in tomorrow morning?'

'We? I will – will you? Is he coming round?'

'Yes, Ian, we'll both be here. Ten? Yes – oh. Really – who? Oh. All right. See you tomorrow.'

'Well?' Libby was practically bouncing with impatience.

'Ian's coming to see us tomorrow and can we ask Peter to be here, too, but ten minutes later.'

'And he wouldn't say why?'

'No.' Ben frowned. 'It doesn't sound like his usual de-brief, does it? More a formal interview.'

'Three of us together? Sounds like bad news to me.'

'Shall I call Peter tonight?'

'No, don't make him worry overnight, too. I'll call him in the morning.'

Peter was as puzzled as Libby and Ben had been when they relayed the message.

'OK – it's got to be something to do with Hal, hasn't it? Do you think they've discovered he isn't entitled to Matthew's money or something?'

'If that's all it is it won't matter too much, will it?' said Libby. 'You're quite comfortable, both of you.'

'You're right,' said Peter with a sigh. 'All right, I'll see you about quarter past ten.'

Libby couldn't settle to anything and eventually took her anxiety out on the kitchen worktops until Ben complained that everything would smell of bleach for weeks. At five to ten the doorbell rang.

Ian came into the front room.

'Libby, Ben.'

Libby gestured him to a chair.

'No, I'll stand for a moment, if you don't mind. I've got something to tell you, and someone I want you to meet.'

Libby's solar plexus did a somersault. Ben took her hand.

'Who is it?' he asked.

Ian stood aside and gestured to the man standing just outside the door.

'This is Keith Franklin.'

Ben recovered himself first, going forward to shake hands while Libby was still gasping like a landed cod. Then he turned to Ian.

'What happened?'

Ian smiled. 'Shall we all sit down, now? When is Peter coming?'

'Quarter past,' said Libby, still staring at the man she now realised she had last seen bundled up in scarves in a wheelchair on the Isle of Wight.

'Then I'll save the long explanation for when he comes. I

265

just wanted you to get over the shock before he arrived. How about some coffee, Libby?'

She turned to the kitchen, then turned back.

'It was you we saw with Amanda Clipping, wasn't it?'

Keith Franklin nodded and looked at the floor. Libby made a sound like steam escaping and continued to the kitchen.

'How about the short explanation, then,' said Ben, when the three men were seated.

'I told you I was going to see Keith Franklin who was staying at Beech Manor, didn't I? Well, that's what I did.'

Libby returned with the cafetière and mugs on a tray.

'And we still don't know how you found out where he was,' she said putting the tray on the table in the window.

'The police do have some resources not open to the public,' said Ian with a grin. 'You've asked me to use them often enough in the past.'

'What were they in this case?' Libby jabbed the plunger down viciously.

'Just checking all ticket sales to the Island,' said Ian.

'For how long? How did you …?'

'You mentioned your mystery man was on the Island for Matthew's funeral, so I started with that.'

'Did you think he was the man I saw?'

'I didn't know,' said Ian. 'There's Peter. Will you let him in?'

Libby opened the door and grabbed Peter's arm. 'This is going to be a shock,' she said, drawing him into the sitting room.

Ian and Keith Franklin had risen.

'Peter, this is Keith Franklin. Mr Franklin, this is Peter Parker, Harry's partner.'

Peter looked as shell-shocked as Libby had been. Franklin looked nervously at Libby and made no move to shake hands.

'Sit down, Pete.' Ben pushed Peter towards the sofa. 'Ian's just going to tell us what's going on.'

Libby distributed coffee and sat next to Peter. 'Go on, Ian.'

'The day before Matthew DeLaxley's funeral Amanda Clipping made a ferry booking for herself, Keith Franklin, and Robert Jones.'

'Who's Robert Jones?' asked Libby.

'My nephew.' Keith Franklin spoke for the first time. His voice was a trifle husky, as though he hadn't tried it out yet.

'How did you know Amanda Clipping? Why were you there?' she asked.

'Libby, if you'll let me go on, I'll tell you the whole story,' said Ian. 'If you keep interrupting we'll never get anywhere, and I want Peter to know it all before he goes to see Harry.'

'All right.' Libby subsided.

'I asked the Island police to see if Mr Franklin was still on the Island, and they went to call on Ms Clipping, who wasn't there, but Mr Franklin was. Sensibly, they didn't say it was him they wanted to speak to, but retreated and called me, as you know.' He paused for a sip of coffee.

'So I went over to the island and went straight to Beech Manor. I did, however, stop at the village shop to speak to your Bernie Small. Most helpful. Mr Franklin opened the door of Beech Manor for me himself and confirmed that he was staying there alone, Ms Clipping being back at work on the mainland.

'Naturally, I asked why he was there, and why he had been at Matthew's funeral. Eventually, when he was convinced of my credentials, and I of his, we arrived at the complete story.'

'May I tell it?' Franklin sounded diffident.

Libby smiled at him for the first time. 'That would be better, wouldn't it?'

He smiled back. 'Well, it all began at a party. My mother – my adoptive mother – is very old now, but had a birthday party a few months ago, arranged by my sister. Robert is her son. My sister had managed to trace many old friends of my mother's, including two couples, the Dougans and the Clippings, and a Lady Bligh.'

Peter, Ben, and Libby exchanged glances.

'I was doing the good son routine, going round with bottles

to refresh glasses and I heard those five, with my mother, talking about the Isle of Wight. It's never been any secret that I was adopted, and during this conversation it became obvious that the Dougans had arranged for me to go to my parents. It was probably crass of me, but I'm afraid I butted in to the conversation and asked if they knew who my parents were.' He looked round at the assembled company. 'They clammed up immediately. My mother said she'd never been told, and they all agreed on that. Eventually, old Lady Bligh said that the person to ask was Matthew DeLaxley and he lived on the Island. They seemed to think everyone knew who he was.'

'He was quite famous, in his way,' said Peter, almost apologetically.

'I realised that at the memorial service,' said Franklin. 'Anyway, after the party I talked to my mother about it, and she genuinely didn't know anything about it. Apparently, she and my father had met the Dougans on holiday on the Island and they'd introduced them to this little crowd of people who belonged to a sort of arty group,' the corners of his mouth turned down, 'and they'd spent several weeks with them that summer. My father was a schoolteacher.'

'The Clippings, the Dougans, and Lady Bligh?' asked Ben.

'Yes, although she was plain Lily Cooper then. They kept in touch until in nineteen forty-nine, the Dougans wrote asking if they still wanted to adopt. They'd discussed this, obviously.' He shrugged. 'And they arrived with me. I knew none of this. I just assumed I'd been adopted the usual way, through whatever Social Services was called in those days.'

He sipped coffee.

'So I got in touch with Amanda Clipping. My mother had all their addresses, but I thought Amanda was a better bet than her parents, and I'd met her once or twice before. She gave me DeLaxley's address and phone number and I called him. He wasn't very forthcoming, but he did eventually confirm that yes, my mother had come from the Island, but she was now dead. I asked about my father, but he merely said that he was dead too. I really couldn't understand his attitude until at last, he let slip that he knew about my son. I argued that my father had also abandoned me, but he brushed that aside. I began to wonder if my father had been killed in the war, but I realised that couldn't be the case as I wasn't born until 1949.'

'When did you write that letter?' demanded Libby.

'Not until later.' Franklin didn't seem put out. 'I spoke to Matthew again, and asked after my son, but he wouldn't say anything. Anyway, I said I was going to come to the Island to see him, and would he tell me anything then. He said he'd think about it.'

'And you went,' said Peter, in a tight voice.

'I went.' Franklin was sounding tired, now. 'And Matthew said he didn't want his cousins who lived next door to see me, so he gave me directions to this Beach House. And then as I was on my way over, he sent me a text to say he wouldn't be able to meet me, he was too ill, but he was sending his youngest cousin instead.' He passed a hand over his face. 'Well, you know what happened next. By the time I got to the Island the storm had broken and I couldn't even get close to – what's it called? Overcliffe?'

'The road was blocked,' said Ian. 'We checked.'

'So you didn't go to the Beach House?' said Libby. 'Not ever?'

Franklin shook his head. 'And I didn't know what had happened to the cousin until later. I couldn't even get off the Island until the following morning, and there was no mobile signal, so I couldn't call Matthew. I know now that would have been useless.'

'So who was at the Beach House?' asked Peter. 'And who killed Celia?'

Chapter Thirty-five

'Don't you think it now looks unlikely that anyone did?' said Ben. 'The police said it was an accident.'

'I want to know about the letter you sent,' said Libby accusingly.

Keith Franklin took a healthy swig of coffee and sighed. 'I made several mistakes, didn't I? I addressed the letter to the DeLaxleys, which was wrong, of course, and I said I knew all about the scandal. I was thinking of the scandal of my birth, of course, even though I didn't know that much about it. I was sure Matthew, or his youngest cousin, was going to tell me more about it. And I wanted to know about Harry.'

'You could have asked Jeanette,' said Libby. From his bewildered expression it seemed certain Franklin was going to ask who Jeanette was, but he surprised her.

'How? I didn't know where she was. Anyway, Matthew had told me Harry was taken into care, so how would she have known?' He shook his head. 'If only Matthew had come to me then …'

'Would he have known where to find you?' put in Peter.

'Apparently he always knew where to find me,' said Franklin bitterly. 'My adoption had been an open secret between him, the Dougans, Lily Cooper, and the Clippings. They kept tabs on my parents and me.'

'Why didn't he tell you, then?' asked Ben.

'I'd abandoned Jeanette. I'd acted badly.' Again, he passed a hand over his face. 'If only he'd told me.'

'So what do you know now?' asked Peter.

'I know who Harry is. My nephew found out where he lived.

I'm not sure how.'

'Ah.' Libby shot a triumphant look at Ian, who smiled. 'So is it your nephew who attacked Harry and tried to break into the ca – restaurant?'

Franklin looked shocked. 'Of course not! He'd never do anything like that.'

'He was here last week,' said Libby. 'I saw him.'

'I asked him to come down. I wanted him to – well, to mediate between us, I suppose.'

Libby looked at Ian. 'Is that true?'

'So he says.' Ian sat forward and put down his mug. 'Robert Jones is living in London and was perfectly happy to talk to us. He says he came down last week and there was no one in the restaurant. He didn't have the home address.'

'Well, that's true. Harry was in the pub with Andrew,' said Peter. 'So Robert Jones wasn't the one who attacked Harry because he didn't know our address.'

'It wouldn't have been difficult to find out,' said Libby. 'He could have asked anyone.'

'He didn't,' said Ian. 'Certainly not in any of the shops.'

'Not the first day he was here, no,' said Libby, 'but Saturday night?'

'He would have had to go into the pub or the restaurant itself,' said Ian, 'which, if he simply wanted to talk to Harry, he would have done. Someone with an attack in mind wouldn't advertise their presence, would they?'

'No,' said Libby reluctantly.

'Do you think Harry will see me?' Franklin asked Peter.

'I'll talk to him this afternoon if he's well enough, but I don't think you ought to meet him until he's out of hospital.'

'Have you met the sisters?' Libby asked.

'No,' said Franklin.

'Yes,' said Ian. 'I'll tell you about that another time. Now I'm going to take Mr Franklin back to his hotel.'

They all stood and bade Keith Franklin goodbye. He went miserably out of the door, and Ian turned back.

'Pub tonight?'

Libby nodded. 'See you then.'

'Well,' said Peter, sitting down again as the door closed. 'There's a bolt from the blue.'

'Somehow, I never imagined that happening,' said Libby. 'Why do you suppose he was still staying at Beech Manor?'

'Hoping Harry would come back to the Island?' suggested Ben.

'Maybe. Where does he live?

'We don't know anything about him. He has a mother, a sister and a nephew who seems to be helping him in whatever his quest is,' said Peter.

'I'm deeply suspicious of that nephew,' said Libby. 'If all he'd been doing was looking for Harry that day, why did he shoot off so quickly? And why didn't he ask around? And why is Ian taking it at face value?'

'Look, Lib,' said Ben, 'Ian brought Franklin here as an act of good faith, partly to tell us the story and partly as an ice-breaker for Harry. I believed Franklin, by the way. I don't think he has anything to with anything, and I don't think he knows who either of his birth parents are.'

'This is ridiculous,' said Libby, collecting the tray. 'There's no one left who could have killed Celia, or had it in for Harry, unless it's someone we haven't heard of. And that goes against the principles of every mystery story there's ever been.'

'I'm sure Ian will have more news for us tonight,' said Peter. 'I'm not needed for rehearsal, am I? I'll go straight to the pub from the hospital.'

Libby fretted over Keith Franklin's story for the rest of the day. When she called Fran, who told her to calm down, it scarcely mattered now, she uncharacteristically snapped at her friend.

'Look, Ben was quite right,' said Fran, without taking offence. 'It looks quite likely that Celia wasn't murdered after all, which means you – and I – got involved for nothing. The rest of the story, about Harry, is almost tied up now. We, and soon, he, know both his mother and father – and grandfather, too. Ian's looking into the attacks and may well come up with something. Anyway, he'll tell us tonight.'

With The Pink Geranium still closed, Patti Pearson and Anne Douglas had eaten in the pub and were waiting for the theatre group when they arrived just after ten o'clock.

'So tell us what's been going on,' said Patti. 'What have you all been up to, and what's happened to Harry?'

Peter arrived in the middle of their explanation of the more public side of the adventure, and one look at his face told Libby he wouldn't relish going through Harry's story with outsiders.

'Anyway,' she said as Peter put his drink on the table, 'that's it, really. We don't know who hit Harry, but it's a good bet that it was a burglar he surprised. How is he, Pete?'

'Becoming a difficult patient,' said Peter with a rueful smile. 'I think they'll let him come home tomorrow.

Libby turned to Patti and Anne. 'I know this sounds rude, but Ian's coming to talk to us about it all – you know how he does – but I think this will be more on the record than off, if you know what I mean.'

'So we'll push off,' said Anne. 'Don't worry, we know the score by now.'

'We don't want to drive you away,' said Fran. 'We'll just move.'

Patti laughed. 'It's fine. We have more wine at Anne's house and we're recording something to watch when we get in, so we're more than happy. In fact,' she put down her empty glass and stood up, 'we might as well go now.'

Anne grinned and let the brake off her wheelchair. 'Fine by me. And do tell us the rest of the story some time.'

With immaculate timing they passed Ian as they left. He stopped and spoke to them, then with a wave saw them off the premises.

'That was tactful of them,' he said as he joined them and Peter went to fetch his customary coffee.

'Well brung up, both of them,' said Libby. 'Pete hasn't been

274

able to tell us yet how Harry took the news.'

Peter returned, put the coffee in front of Ian and sat down.

'Inclined to explode at first, and then, when a nurse came rushing in thinking he'd had some kind of fit, calmed down. We talked about it most of the afternoon, and I think he's decided to see Franklin, but – and this will surprise you – he wants to see him on the Island and wants him to meet the sisters.'

'Oh!' said Libby and Fran in surprise.

Ian frowned. 'Did he say why?'

'He's got some sort of idea that if they both show up together, the sisters will crumble. Especially if we tell them we know that Keith's dad is their brother.'

'Perhaps I'd better tell you what I found out when I saw the ladies,' said Ian.

'Don't tell me they opened up to you?' said Libby.

'Not completely, no,' Ian settled back into his chair. 'At first they definitely didn't want to talk to me. Wouldn't even let me in to the house.'

'I bet,' said Ben. 'Did they flutter?'

Ian grinned. 'They did. It was far too late, ladies on their own – you know the sort of thing. Anyway, eventually, when all three of them were crowded round the doorway, I told them Harry had been attacked hard on the heels of finding out who his grandfather had been.'

'Gawd!' said Libby. 'Bombshell!'

'It certainly was. The first one – Alicia? – looked as if she would faint, the little snappy one went as red as a beetroot, and the third one went as white as a sheet.'

'Really?' Fran was interested. 'Honoria's usually quite threatening.'

'She spent the rest of the meeting glowering at me, certainly,' said Ian.

'So what happened next?' asked Peter.

'The first sister – Mrs Hope-Fenwick, isn't it? – said I'd better come in and we all sat round the kitchen table. She asked after Harry, I reported and they all looked nervously at each other, almost as if they knew who'd attacked him. I don't think they did, though.'

'What *did* you think?' said Libby.

'I think they felt it was their fault for having dragged you all into this business and caused so many problems.'

'So did you tell them we knew who granddad was?' said Peter.

'Yes.'

'I wish I'd been there,' said Libby.

'It wasn't pleasant,' said Ian. 'I should have done it by the book and gone officially with a female officer. Mrs Hope-Fenwick cried, the snappy sister –'

'Amelia,' put in Libby helpfully.

'Amelia, then, erupted. Swore she'd have my badge, my stripes, and sue me for every penny. The biggest one –' he looked at Libby.

'Honoria,' she supplied.

'She just sat there looking as though she would quite cheerfully murder me.'

'All of that sounds in character,' said Fran. 'That's how they were with us. Did you ask them why they asked us to find out who Celia's killer was without telling us why they thought she might have been killed?'

'They were very muddled about it, but it appeared that they all thought Celia had been killed because of the scandal, as they put it, and they were anxious to know who else knew the secret.'

'I still can't see why Celia was killed though, if she was,' said Libby. 'She knew the secret and presumably Matthew had sent her to meet Keith to tell him – or tell him about Harry, perhaps. I still don't get it.'

'I think there's something else, though,' said Ian. 'I think there's still something we don't know, which may well give us all the answers.'

'About Harry's attacker as well?'

'Oh, I think we know who that is, don't you?' Ian grinned round the table.

Chapter Thirty-six

'The obvious suspect?' said Libby.

'Yes, I had to shut you up this morning,' said Ian. 'I'm afraid Mr Robert Jones does *not* have an alibi for the early hours of Sunday morning, and a very strong motive for getting Harry out of the way.'

'Oh, damn, that's a damp squib,' said Libby.

'What did you want – a grand revelation? Or to be held up with a gun again?' said Ben.

'No, it's just that it was obvious. So go on, is he Uncle Keith's heir?'

'He is. And Uncle Keith turns out to be quite wealthy, all from his own industry. His adoptive father left everything to his mother, and on her death it's divided equally between Keith and his sister. But Keith made good, and after the episode with Jeanette Price, devoted himself to work and never married. Robert would have –'

'Copped the lot,' said Libby.

'Exactly.' Ian nodded. 'And Robert, don't forget, was in on the search from the first, helping Uncle Keith, coming over to the Island with him –'

'Did he kill Celia?' asked Peter. 'Was he with him that time?'

'No, apparently not. But he knew that a, Franklin was searching for his own parents who, conceivably had money, especially as he knew by now that the grandson – Harry – had inherited money, and b, Franklin wanted to find Harry, and presumably, make things up to him.'

'By leaving Harry all his money?' said Ben.

'I asked Mr Franklin about that. He said he would naturally make sure Harry was secure. That was how he put it.'

'Unnecessary,' said Peter, with a sniff.

'We know that,' said Libby, patting his arm, 'but Keith Franklin didn't, at the time.'

'Anyway, we're pretty sure that it was Robert Jones who was out to get Harry,' said Ian, 'and as for Celia, the jury's still out.'

'Are the Island police having another look at the case?' asked Libby.

'They let me see everything they'd got,' said Ian, 'but frankly, it wasn't much. The whole beach had been covered in water, the little house, or chalet, whatever it was, was knocked almost flat –'

'Yes, we've seen it,' said Peter.

'And there was no chance of any identifying marks or prints. Celia did have a wound on her head, but she'd been in the water for over twenty-four hours when she was found, and not in one place, either. She was found further up the beach.'

'Horrible,' said Fran.

'So in fact, the sisters already know we know all about the scandal. Harry doesn't need to confront the sisters with Keith after all,' said Libby.

'And I'm not sure Harry will be fit to travel any time soon,' said Peter. 'Can I tell him all this tomorrow?'

'Oh, yes,' said Ian, 'but don't send his temperature and blood pressure up so they don't let him out.'

'Where's Franklin now?' asked Ben.

'Back at home in north London. He said he's quite willing to go anywhere and do anything. He doesn't yet know our suspicions about his nephew.'

'Poor bloke. That's going to come as a shock, on top of everything else,' said Ben.

'What are you going to do about him?' asked Libby.

'Make sure forensics haven't missed anything, for a start, otherwise we haven't got anything concrete,' said Ian.

'Talking of concrete,' said Peter, 'did you find a weapon?'

'No.' Ian shook his head. 'The wound didn't match anything in the garden. I would guess Jones took it away and disposed of it somewhere.'

'As far from Steeple Martin as possible,' said Fran.

'So, that's it,' said Libby. 'All cleared up.'

'Except for Celia, and I think we're just going to have to admit failure on that one,' said Ian, 'although there's something else the sisters are hiding, I'm sure of it.'

'Oh, I know what that is,' said Libby carelessly.

'What?' came the chorus.

'Harry's forebears, obviously. And I think Matthew's sister is in the frame to be his gran.'

'And Franklin's mother,' said Fran, nodding. 'Of course. Do you think if we got the whole crowd together, the Dougans, the Clippings, Lady Bligh and the sisters, they'd break down and tell us?'

'That sounds like a Hercule Poirot moment – gathering the suspects together,' said Ben.

'And Nero Wolfe. He always did it, too,' said Libby.

'Who's Nero Wolfe?' asked Ian.

'American detective. Written by Rex Stout.' Libby looked round at the group. 'What do you think? Could we do that?'

'You could try,' said Ian, 'but not under the aegis of the police. And without us, I doubt you'd get them all to agree. And you haven't met any of them except the sisters.'

'That's true.' Libby sighed. 'Oh, well. Perhaps we'll just have to wait until Harry's well enough to go back to the Island to have his meeting.'

'Although I doubt if they'll tell you anything more, even then,' said Ian, standing up. 'I must be off. I'll keep you informed as and when I can.'

'What a let-down,' said Libby after he'd gone.

'You can't expect every – what? – investigation? – adventure? – to end with a firework display,' said Ben. 'I'm much happier that it hasn't.'

'And none of them are adventures, really,' said Fran gently. 'They are all very sad cases. And look at what's happened to Harry.'

'I know, I know,' said Libby. 'But that's why I want the fireworks in a sense. As revenge. Retribution.'

Ben laughed as he stood up. 'Come on, Nemesis. Let's go home. I've got a timber-yard meeting in the morning.'

Thursday morning Libby decided to make good her promise to go through Harry's bookings for the next couple of weeks, and collected The Pink Geranium keys from Peter before he left for hospital to fetch Harry.

Before settling down with the book, she made herself a cup of coffee and unearthed some of Harry's personal stash of biscuits. Then she pulled the high stool up to the counter, opened the book, reached for the phone, and fell on the floor.

She found herself looking up into a horrified face. Robert Jones's face. Her insides began to go watery, a feeling she was experiencing far too often in life in recent years.

'Get up,' he said, his voice as horrified as his face. Libby struggled to get up and he yanked her roughly to her feet, pushing her in front of him into the kitchen.

'What do you want?' said Libby through a thick throat. 'Harry's not here.'

'No.' Jones, still holding on to her, was looking round the kitchen as if he didn't know what to do next. Libby thought he probably didn't. Which was dangerous.

'Where is he?' he asked suddenly.

'Still in hospital,' said Libby. 'Safe from you.'

Robert Jones shook her. 'Shut up, you cow! It was you who reported me to the police last week, wasn't it? Nosing around like on the Island. Oh, I know, I was there.'

'I know you were,' said Libby, as calmly as she could. 'That's why I recognised you.'

Out on the counter, the landline began to ring. Robert Jones just gripped Libby tighter, his mouth in a thin line. Eventually it stopped, and seconds later, Libby's mobile started warbling, it,

282

too, out of reach.

'Somebody will come looking for me, now,' she said, looking straight into the nervous brown eyes in front of her. 'And then you'll stand no chance.'

'Then they won't find you.' His voice was wavering up and down the scale now. 'Out the back.' He began to push her towards the back yard.

'I know you managed to get over that wall,' said Libby, her heart now threatening to bang right out of her chest, 'but you'll never get me over there. And you'll be seen. It's a Thursday morning, for goodness sake.'

'Shut up!' howled Jones again. '*Shut up*!'

'Mum? What's going on?'

Libby's legs crumpled, and Jones made a panicked sound before gripping her even tighter. She looked up at her son, standing at the back door of the flat, at the top of the spiral staircase. 'Call the police.'

'It's all right, Ma.' Adam smiled. 'They're already on their way. I'm a diversion.'

Robert Jones swung her round to face the kitchen just as Ben, Bob the butcher, and Joe from the Cattlegreen Nursery burst out and grabbed him. Libby sank gracefully to the floor and Adam flew down the stairs and threw his arms around her.

'God, Ma! You do keep doing it, don't you?'

'It wasn't my fault!' wailed Libby, close now to tears. 'I was only doing what Peter asked me to.'

The sirens could be heard now. Bob, Joe, and Ben were still holding a now-limp Robert Jones. Libby stood up and faced him.

'What exactly were you intending to do?' she asked, in a slightly firmer voice. 'How did you plan on getting rid of me, and what did you want with Harry?'

'I don't think there was a plan,' said Ben. 'I think he was just panicking. For all he knew, Harry had seen him.'

'So – what?' said Libby. 'You planned to have another go? Bit stupid, wasn't it? And why here? I'm sure your uncle told you Harry was still in hospital.'

The sound of heavy policemen approaching was now heard, and Robert Jones seemed to shrink, still not having said a word. One of the officers put on the handcuffs while another read him his rights. Then they saluted Libby and told her DCI Connell would be in touch about a statement.

When Bob and Joe had been thanked profusely and given beer, Libby, Ben, and Adam sat round the little table in the courtyard drinking coffee, and Libby had one of her increasingly rare cigarettes.

'Look,' she said, 'that really wasn't my fault. I didn't barge into anything, I was just about to do all Hal's bookings.'

'We know.' Ben had his arm round her shoulders.

'And how did you know? And how did the police get here so quickly?'

'Ian called home and got no answer, then he called me to tell me that Robert Jones, idiot that he is, had been seen in the car park behind the doctor's surgery,' said Ben.

'Seen? Who knew him?'

Adam and Ben laughed.

'Flo!' said Libby. 'Of course! She saw the whole thing last week. Fancy her recognising him.'

'So she called the landline, too, and then with great presence of mind called 999, and then the Canterbury station to speak to Ian. Who called me, and I called Adam. Luckily, he was actually working in Steeple Martin and still has the key to the flat.'

'Amazing,' said Libby, shaking her head. 'Well, we'll have to treat Flo to a bottle of champagne, won't we?'

'She's probably got better than we could buy in her own cellar,' said Adam. Flo Carpenter had been tutored by her late husband, a notable wine buff, and was known locally as a bit of an expert.

Ian sent the red-haired and amiable Sergeant Maiden to take a statement from Libby that afternoon, and said he would call and see her this evening.

'Can you tell Ian – DCI Connell – that we're going to see Harry and Peter this evening, please, Sergeant Maiden? So please could he come there?'

Sergeant Maiden promised to relay the message, and so it was that, at just after eight o'clock, Ian arrived to find Harry ensconced on the sofa and Libby, Ben and Peter just about to pour glasses of champagne.

'Are you allowed any?' Ian asked doubtfully.

Harry grinned. 'Just the one. I've obviously got a very hard head. Now tell us what's been going on.'

'Wait until he's sitting down, Hal,' said Libby. 'Ian, will you have some? One won't hurt, will it?'

Ian accepted a glass and sat down by the table.

'Well, Robert Jones, as you might have gathered, is not the brightest bulb in the bunch. This was one of the reasons he was relying on his uncle's legacy. He's never managed to hold down a job for long, and runs through what money he has got very quickly. He's always done odd jobs for his uncle, and was quite happy to help on this occasion, until he found out what was really going on. Then he decided that it would be totally unfair – his words – if Harry were to inherit after all his hard work. So he decided he would have to put him out of the way. The trouble was, he is not the stuff murderers are made of, and he made a terrible hash of it.'

'I'm glad to say,' said Harry.

'And so say all of us,' said Libby. 'But what about this morning?'

'He'd heard from us, and he'd heard from his uncle. His thinking was that if he could get to Harry again, no one would think anything of it, it would just be counted as some sort of a relapse. He broke into the restaurant thinking there might be keys to the house there. He didn't realise Harry wasn't home yet.'

'How on earth was he going to make it look like a relapse?' said Peter. 'And didn't he realise it would point straight at him?'

285

'I don't think he thought it through at all,' said Ian. 'By today, he was panicking, out of control.'

'That's how he struck me,' said Libby. 'Poor Keith.'

'Yes, he's rather upset about it all,' said Ian. 'But quite happy to fit in with your idea of going to the Island to see the sisters, Harry. When you're quite well. He says he can stay at Beech Manor again.'

'In that case,' said Harry, lifting up his glass, 'here's to our next trip to the Island. And the end of the whole bloody business.'

Chapter Thirty-seven

In fact, Harry felt well enough, endorsed by the doctors, the very next week. Libby took the bookings book home with her and cancelled all bookings for the next three weeks, with the proviso that Harry would ring again if he was open earlier.

The summer holidays had started by now, and so had The End Of The Pier Show. The week after Harry was allowed home, Libby made arrangements for Fran, herself and Ben, all of whom were regular performers, to be out of the cast, and on Thursday they all set off once more for Portsmouth and the ferry to Fishbourne.

Libby and Fran leant over the rail to watch the Island come closer.

'It is a lovely place,' said Libby, 'but I think it is tainted a bit, now.'

Fran nodded. 'I wonder if Harry will keep the houses? With those old biddies as his neighbours it could be very awkward.'

'He might just keep Ship House to let it,' said Libby. 'I'm wondering more what his reaction is going to be to Keith Franklin.'

'Has he said anything?'

'Not a word. Ben had to set up the meeting. He's coming to Ship House this afternoon, then we're all going up to the sisters' house this evening.'

'*All* of us?' said Fran.

'Except Ben and Guy.'

'I don't know what it's going to accomplish,' said Fran, shaking her head.

'I think Harry's hoping to find out about his gran. And

Keith's mother.'

'I can't see them giving that up at this stage,' said Fran. 'And we'll never know about Celia.'

'Do you think they're connected?' asked Libby.

'After all our speculation?' Fran smiled. 'I think Celia was to tell Keith Franklin something about his parentage, yes. And she died before she could do so.'

'And the idea is still that the sisters wanted to find out who killed her because he or she might know the secret. The scandal, as they called it.'

Fran nodded. 'Seems so. Perhaps they'll admit it tonight.'

Harry had decreed that they should not park in the car park behind The Shelf and the sisters' house, as they would be seen, and he was counting on the element of surprise. They parked instead further along the road towards Ventnor and walked down to the path which the men had found previously, leading across Candle Cove and into the bay. Keith Franklin had been given instructions to do the same.

The walk, even though it hadn't been very long, had tired Harry, and when Keith Franklin arrived at Ship House late in the afternoon, he was asleep. 'I'll make some tea,' said Libby, after they had settled an uncomfortable-looking Keith on the deck, and Peter went to wake Harry.

'He says will you go and see him in the bedroom,' said Peter frowning as he came to join the others. 'Is that all right?'

Keith Franklin stood up. 'Quite all right,' he said. 'I'll take in his tea, shall I?'

'Think it'll be OK?' said Libby, watching Keith's retreating back.

'I think it's best they do it privately,' said Peter. 'I don't think Hal's mad any more, except about Robert Jones, but that's hardly Keith Franklin's fault.'

It was half an hour before Keith and Harry emerged, Harry grinning, and Keith looking a little sheepish.

'That's all right, then,' said Harry, sitting down at the table on the deck. 'That's my dad, everyone.'

They all murmured and smiled.

'Not that I'll be calling him Dad, any time soon,' Harry continued, 'any more than I shall be calling Jeanette Mum. But, fancy that, I actually know where I come from after all this time.'

'Nearly,' said Ben. 'And hopefully, you might get the rest of it tonight.'

'Are you sure you want us to come too?' asked Fran.

'Yes. You've been in it from the beginning,' said Harry. 'Let's face it, the old girls wanted you in, didn't they?'

'Right, then,' said Libby. 'Now. Are we going to see if they've got room for us all at the restaurant?'

There wasn't room for them, but the restaurant could, and did, provide a take-away service. Keith joined them for the meal, and after Ben and Guy volunteered to wash up, the other five began the ascent to the top of the cliff.

Libby found that she was incredibly nervous as Harry approached the sisters' front door, although he seemed quite calm. As usual, Alicia opened the door. Her hand flew to her mouth as she saw who stood outside.

'Great-aunt Alicia,' Harry began. Alicia's face bleached of all colour and she hung on to the door frame. 'We're all here to see you and finally clear up any outstanding questions you or we might have. OK?' He took her arm and gently led her inside and to the room at the back which Libby and Fran had only been in once before. Amelia and Honoria both stood as Harry led them all in.

'Sit down, Great-aunts,' he said, obviously relishing the term. 'We'd like to talk to you.'

But he'd lost their attention. Their eyes were fixed on Keith Franklin.

'Oh, yes,' said Harry. 'Sorry. This is my father, Keith Franklin. Son of your brother, Alfred.'

There was a silence so deep Libby felt it as a palpable entity.

'You know,' whispered Alicia.

'Detective Inspector Connell told you we knew,' said Libby.

'No,' said Fran, her eyes on Alicia. 'Not about Keith's father. About his mother. Isn't it, Alicia?'

In the background they were all aware of Amelia and Honoria.

'His mother,' whispered Alicia, and suddenly there was a sharp movement by the window.

'All for nothing,' said Honoria. 'My poor darling Celia. All for nothing.' And she was gone out of the french windows.

Peter started out to follow and then saw a figure darting down the path after her. He stopped and turned round, puzzled.

Alicia and Amelia were staring out of the window, horrified. Harry and Keith exchanged glances and went to put their arms round the old ladies' shoulders, just as Ian Connell walked through the French windows.

'I'm sorry,' he said to the sisters, with a slight bow. 'There was nothing I could do. She went straight over.'

'What? What has she – Honoria?' Alicia tried to get to the French windows. Ian stopped her.

'You're not saying she killed Celia?' said Amelia, tears streaming down her face.

'Of course not! She was here – with you,' said Alicia.

'Well, she was out in the garden, I didn't actually see – oh my God!' Amelia gasped.

'I'm afraid she did,' said Ian, urging both the sisters back into their chairs.

'But why?' said Amelia.

'To protect us all,' sobbed Alicia.

'But what from?' asked a bewildered Libby. 'And how come she was in the Beach House?'

'I think she must have seen Celia heading down the steps, put two and two together, and followed her down,' Ian replied. 'As to why she killed Celia, I suspect that she must have got her to admit she was going to meet Franklin and tell him about his parents. Whether she acted in a blind rage because Celia refused to abandon the meeting, or whether she killed her in order to protect the secret of her brother and cousin, I can't say. I suspect it was a mixture of the two.'

'And that was what they were so ashamed of,' said Libby later. 'Their brother was not only a traitor and a rapist, but he'd raped their own cousin, someone as close as a sister.'

'I don't understand how Honoria could have done it,' said Peter. 'The three of them were all together when Matthew had his heart attack.'

'Don't you remember?' said Fran. 'He was collapsed by the telescope. He'd just seen Honoria kill Celia. That was why he collapsed. Alicia went over, and by the time she called the other two, Honoria was back, having come up that terrible path from Candle Cove.'

'Honoria must have been horrified when the others called us in to investigate,' Harry said. 'It would have been the last thing she wanted.'

'Gosh, yes!' Libby said. 'I remember she looked stunned when Alicia announced Celia had been murdered.'

'What I don't understand, though,' said Peter, 'is why Matthew protected Honoria after, as we think, he saw her kill Celia. He could have told Harry in that letter he wrote.'

'Yes, that's bloody odd,' Harry said. 'Perhaps all he saw was Honoria following Celia and that was enough to cause the heart attack. I suppose he wouldn't have been sure enough to say anything.'

'Perhaps he thought enough trouble had been caused in the family and didn't want to cause any more?' Libby suggested.

'Could be,' Peter said.

'I can't say I'm thrilled at my parentage,' said Keith Franklin, clutching a very large whisky, but I can't see that it was worth killing for.'

Harry nodded. 'Same here. I'm glad you and Jeanette are fairly normal.'

'And what the hell was Ian doing there?' asked Peter.

'He was worried. He had the feeling something might kick off, so he came out, too,' said Ben. 'Although I'm pretty sure he had his suspicions.'

'And he's now quietly covering everything up,' said Fran. 'Good old Ian.'

'So hopefully, the Mortons and DeLaxleys won't have to suffer any more,' said Libby.

'There are only two Mortons left,' said Guy.

'No, there aren't,' said Keith and Harry together. 'There's us.'

First Chapter of *Murder out of Tune*

A breeze rustled through the heavy branches of the old yew tree and moved moon shadows over the body that lay quietly stiffening between the gravestones. Voices drifted back to disturb the silence, gradually petering out to be replaced by the sounds of car engines being started up, until, at last, peace returned to the graveyard and its most recent occupant.

'I don't care,' said Libby Sarjeant mutinously. 'I can't play the bloody things. They hurt my fingers.'

Her friend Peter Parker regarded her with amusement. 'And you don't want to cut your nails.'

'Well, no.' Libby regarded her newly varnished nails with satisfaction. 'I'm so pleased I discovered this stuff.'

Harry Price, Peter's life partner and owner–chef of The Pink Geranium restaurant in Steeple Martin's high street, peered at her hands.

'So what were you talking about anyway?' he asked, sitting down at the pub table.

'The ukulele group,' said Ben Wilde, Libby's significant other, returning from the bar with drinks. 'You know.'

'I don't actually,' said Harry, accepting a pint of lager. 'Oh, I know there is one – isn't Lewis part of it? – but I'm not sure what it's all about.'

'It's a craze,' said Libby. 'These groups have sprung up all over the country and because ukuleles are cheap to buy and fairly easy to play, they've become really popular, especially with the – er – older market.'

'Pensioners,' explained Ben. 'People looking for something to do with their time and who like playing the old songs.'

'Like that cleaning windows bloke?' said Harry.

'Similar,' said Libby. 'Anyway, this chap from Canterbury had a group going and decided to start another one here.'

'Why here?'

'Because it's a fairly large village with a decent village hall,' said Libby.

'Initially, he tried to use the theatre for his rehearsals, until we explained that it was so often in use he couldn't and the hire rate would be the same as for the theatre. That peeved him a bit.' Ben smiled at the memory. 'So he uses the village hall.'

'So why were you going to join?' Harry turned back to Libby.

'I wasn't. Somehow, as you said, he's persuaded Lewis to join to raise the profile, and Edie's joined too. She used to play the banjo in her salad days, apparently, and she's really enjoying it, so she wanted me to join too, to keep her company.'

'And you don't want to.'

'No! I wasn't at all sure about the people – I went once with Edie and Lewis – and the strings hurt my fingers.'

'And now they're going to be part of the big Christmas Concert at the theatre,' said Peter.

'The charity one?' said Harry. 'But haven't you got some famous people in that? Won't they show themselves up?'

'We've got some pro singers and musicians and your Andrew is going to read some Dickens,' said Ben. 'You knew that.'

'Pro musos won't take kindly to a bunch of geriatric strummers,' said Harry.

'Don't be so rude, Harry Price!' Libby bent a baleful eye on her friend. 'It's for a very good cause, and Andrew will keep everyone in line.'

Andrew McColl was a friend met fairly recently, after the death of someone close to both Harry and Andrew. In reality, he was a theatrical Knight, married to a theatrical Dame, but had professed himself delighted with the Oast Theatre, of which Ben was the owner. Peter and Libby were both directors of the company. It was he who had suggested the concert, in aid of a homeless charity.

'How was panto rehearsal tonight?' Harry changed the subject. 'Still having trouble with the chorus?'

'Not my problem any more,' said Libby. 'Susannah's taken them over lock, stock, and barrel. She's making them sound quite good now. And we've got proper dancers again, so they're doing their stuff in Lorraine's studio until we stick them all together.'

'I don't know Lorraine, do I?'

'She's a dancer with her own studio in Canterbury. She takes private pupils, and still appears in TV ads, but says she's too old now for the West End. She's bloody good, and hilarious,' said Peter. 'I'm sure I pointed her out to you the other day. That furniture polish ad.'

'Oh, her,' said Harry. 'You are getting posh. And is Susannah's old man quite happy to be doing all the baby-sitting while she's out gallivanting?'

'He is,' said Libby. 'After all, we're paying her.'

Susannah's brother Terry Baker had introduced her to Libby and the Oast Theatre some years before when they were planning a special birthday party for Ben's mother Hetty. Susannah was a professional singer and pianist, who, since she'd become a mother, was less keen to do the touring that went with the job. She'd happily settled in to the Oast company as almost permanent musical director.

The barman leant across the bar.

'You talking about the ukulele lot? That's some of 'em come in just now.' He jerked his head in the direction of the other half of the bar, where some of the pantomime cast were also drinking.

Peter and Libby craned their necks to try and see round the corner.

'Don't recognise any of them,' said Peter, 'but I can't see properly.'

'Lewis isn't there, then?' said Libby.

'He'd have come looking for us,' said Ben.

Lewis Osbourne-Walker had come to prominence as a handy-man on a television make-over show and now presented a whole variety, from country documentaries to lifestyle programmes. His own series had featured the make-over of his garden by Libby's son Adam and Adam's boss, Mog. He divided his time between London and Creekmarsh, an old house a few miles from Steeple Martin, where his mother Edie had the former housekeeper's flat.

'Well, I'm ready to go home now,' said Libby. 'I've got an appointment with our wardrobe mistress in the morning which I'm not looking forward to.'

'Why?' asked Ben.

'She always wants to make the costumes *she* wants, rather than the ones *I* want,' said Libby. 'I wrote the bloody thing, I know what I want the cast to look like.' She stood up and wandered into the other bar to say goodbye to the rest of the cast.

'And why did you do that?' asked Peter, when she came back to collect her coat. 'Just to have a look at the ukulele people?'

'Of course she did,' said Ben with a grin. 'I wonder she doesn't join them just out of nosiness.'

Libby sniffed. 'I told you, the strings hurt my fingers. Anyway, I've got far too much on with the panto.'

Lewis Osbourne-Walker appeared in the doorway of the pub. He waved distractedly to Libby and her friends but called loudly to the ukulele group in the other bar.

'Old Douglas in here? His car's still in the car park.'

A stillness fell over the bar.

'No,' said one male voice hesitantly. 'He never comes to the pub.'

'That's what I thought,' said Lewis. He turned to Libby.

'Any of you lot seen him? Oldish bloke, white hair, thinning on top, glasses.'

'That could be anybody,' said Peter.

'Nobody's been in this bar but us,' said Ben.

'Where is he, then?' said Lewis. 'His missus just rang me to say his mobile keeps going to voicemail. What's happened to him?'